LOVE
ON
camera

DANA LeCHEMINANT

ONE

MADI MORGAN HAD NEVER BEEN good with decisions, especially when it came to life or death situations. And cake was definitely life or death.

"This again?" Danny's voice bounced with laughter, which didn't help her dilemma as he came up behind her. "You do know it doesn't matter which one you pick, right? Cake is cake, Madi."

"Cake is *not* cake," she countered. "The chocolate is going to be richer and take longer to eat, but I know I'm going to like it better than the lemon and be more satisfied by the end. But I can eat the lemon quickly and without needing something to drink afterward, and I'm less likely to make a mess on myself with that one." She huffed a little. "Why don't people make more red velvet cakes for weddings? They're perfect. Not too much chocolate and just the right amount of sweet with the cream cheese frosting, so it's never a choice."

"Probably because most people don't have such a specific favorite." Bumping his shoulder into hers, he picked up a piece of chocolate cake and took a bite. "Oh, this is amazing," he said with wide eyes. "Maria outdid herself."

"I know," Madi said as she rocked back and forth to the balls of her feet. "She's a miracle worker with chocolate."

"So take a piece of chocolate."

"But I don't have *time* for chocolate."

"You might have if you hadn't stood here for five minutes, freaking out the caterers."

The caterers in question threw grins toward Danny; most of them had witnessed Madi's indecision many times before.

The perk of being one of the best wedding photographers in the state was getting to know a lot of the other vendors and planners, like Maria and Danny. Which meant Madi's choice was going to haunt her until the next time she worked a wedding with the baker extraordinaire.

As both their phones buzzed with a timer, announcing the start of dancing, Madi groaned as Danny snickered. Now Madi wasn't going to get *any* cake.

Rolling his eyes, Danny held out a large forkful of cake. "Don't say I never did anything for you," he muttered as she ate the bite and hurried off.

Oh goodness, Maria really *had* outdone herself this time.

Grabbing her camera out of her bag, Madi checked her settings and battery life before heading out to the dance floor just as the DJ called for the floor to clear so the bride and groom could have their first dance. She jumped right into snapping photos, grinning as the pair of them got lost in each other's eyes. There was nothing like newly wedded couples dancing for the first time, and Madi was so glad she was there to capture the love that shone from their faces.

She didn't often have a long enough break to actually savor a piece of cake, and weddings were one of the most stressful parts of her life. But Madi wouldn't trade these moments for the world.

"I think we got it all." Madi sank into a chair, her feet aching and her hair falling out of its bun and her camera hanging heavy from her neck. But the day had gone more smoothly than most, so she could hardly complain. "Emily, you were spectacular today. Go ahead and go home. I'll finish up here."

Her assistant didn't argue, giving her a smile and rushing out of the venue without a backward glance.

"She's in a hurry." As he settled in the chair next to her, Danny held out a slice of chocolate heaven with a grin.

"Where did you get this?" she asked, snatching the cake out of his hands and shoving a third of it into her mouth, in case he decided to try to take it back. "I thought it was all gone!"

"Please. You know I plan every wedding down to the last detail, including cake for needy photographers. That, or Neil saw you drooling over it and stashed a piece for you. You can thank him at the Hathaway wedding next week."

"I'm not working that one. It's a rare, blessed Friday off for me." Though she knew the caterers had already packed up, she still looked around to see if Neil was anywhere nearby. "Remind me to kiss Neil next time I see him, though."

Danny laughed and leaned forward, resting his elbows on the table as he watched Madi lick her plate clean. "Speaking of kisses…"

Her good mood immediately evaporated. "Danny." He had been doing this for weeks now, and she was really starting to get sick of it. "You don't have to keep trying to set me up with people."

"Oh, come on, Madi. You've got to be tired of being single after all this time." He leaned back in his chair, his gaze locked on hers as if he thought she might run away.

She was tempted. "I'm only twenty-six. It's not like I'm missing out on some big adventure just because I don't go on dates every weekend."

"More like *won't* go on dates. Look, just come to one singles party with me on Friday. I promise you won't regret it."

Madi raised an eyebrow. This was a new tactic. "Singles party? What even is that?"

"It's like a gathering of people who don't trust dating apps. It's better than swiping right, I'll tell you that. At least you've got the real thing right in front of you."

It sounded like a nightmare, no matter what he said. "Yeah, that's going to be a no," she said, hopping up and heading for the exit before he could—

"We could make a bet out of it."

Madi stopped dead. He did *not* just do that. Then again, it had been a few weeks since their last bet, in which Danny had successfully predicted the newly divorced mother of the bride joining in the bouquet toss. Madi hadn't thought she would do it, and Danny had ended up with free dinner from his favorite restaurant courtesy of Madi's bank account.

She was due for a rematch.

Glancing back, Madi tried not to look too eager. She could rarely resist a challenge, especially when she knew Danny always paid up. "What kind of a bet?"

He grinned. "The kind where, if you win, I pay you to redo the photos on my website."

She barely held back a gasp. Danny was one of the best wedding planners in Diamond Springs, and he worked with a lot of photographers who all had impressive resumes. Like she knew other photographers had done, Madi had tried multiple times to convince him to let her redo the photos, which would get her involved with all of his vendors as well as bring in several new clients. But he had remained adamant that his website was fine.

Until now.

She fingered her camera strap, trying to figure out what had changed. Why had he pulled out the big guns? "What's the bet?" she asked warily.

Danny folded his arms, looking a little too smug. "You have to go to a few singles activities with me and actually talk to people. No wait, that's too easy. *Ten* activities." But then he narrowed his eyes. "I know. Ten *double dates* in the next three months."

Though Madi didn't appreciate the fact that he'd apparently come up with this bet on the fly, that didn't sound too bad… Not when the payout could lead to a significant increase in business. "Why double?" she asked.

"Because I'm selfish and want to get something out of this too. If we're both on the date, you can stop me from being a mindless idiot. You know how bad I am on first dates."

Madi *did* know. She'd seen it firsthand on her one and only date with Danny soon after they first met a few years ago. There had been zero chemistry, though Danny misread everything and went for a kiss twenty minutes into their dinner. It might have been salvageable if Madi's reaction during the movie they watched afterward hadn't been to punch Danny every time there was a jump scare.

She didn't usually scare so easily after years of scary movies growing up; she chalked it up to being uncomfortable about the idea of Danny being more than a friend. After that, they'd agreed to never bring up the idea of dating again, and they'd both been much happier.

Folding her arms to match Danny's stance, Madi tried to figure out by looking at him if there was a catch. Ten dates was about ten times more dates than she usually went on in a *year*, but the lure of Danny's website had definitely pulled her in. Finding the time would be difficult, of course—twelve weeks in the summer always went by in a flash—and then there was the issue of actually finding people to date.

That was a pretty big issue.

Why in the world was she considering this?

"You just want me to hire you as my wedding planner when I get married, don't you?" she said with a huff.

Danny snorted a laugh. "Well, obviously. But that's not why I'm trying to get you to go out, and you know it. The longer you spend all your time here at weddings without some love in your life, the more cynical and jaded you're going to get. I know this from experience."

Madi rolled her eyes. "You're, like, three years older than me, Danny. Stop trying to be all wise when we both know I'm the mature one in this friendship. I'm perfectly happy being single."

"Says the woman who cried during the vows today. *Again.* You and I are exactly the same, Madi, but at least I'm trying to do something about it. One of these days, you have to stop lying to yourself about what you really want out of life."

Madi scowled a bit. For a guy who was just as single as her, Danny made a good point, though she would never admit it out loud. With every wedding she worked, a hole in her heart got a little bigger. Like most girls, she'd dreamed about finding the perfect partner and starting a life with him. Outside of her brother's friends, she'd never met anyone who even came close to fitting that description.

Groaning a little, Madi wished she had a better argument than the one she always had waiting. "Dating is awful, Danny. You know that. And you saw how I was when we—"

"You can't compare every future interaction with guys to our first date. So if that's the reason you're so hesitant—"

"It's not." Her one and only date with Danny had been so bad, but not dating had nothing to do with Danny. Putting herself out there really was awful, and she had yet to find anyone who could compare to the guys she'd grown up with. At this point, she was almost afraid to keep trying because she doubted anyone could reach the high bar they set. She might as well just date one of them.

There's an idea... Madi took a deep breath, holding it in her lungs for a second as she considered the ridiculous thought that had popped into her head. Her older brother, Kit, had three perfectly normal friends whom she loved like brothers. Three friends who could easily be her dates to help her win the bet.

Okay, so yes, she didn't want to end up alone for the rest of her life, and one of these days she would need to date for real. But it was *May*, the busiest time of the year for her. She struggled to keep up with demand as it was, and she definitely didn't have the time or the energy to put herself out there like Danny wanted her to. Not while weddings were happening all over the place.

But, like with everything Danny did, this bet would have an expiration date. If Danny was finally looking for new website photos, either Madi could win the bet and do them now, or he would probably give his other vendors a chance and go with a different photographer.

Danny was just as busy as her, if not more so. Why would he choose now of all times to make this particular bet?

"Look," Danny said, shoving his hands into his pockets and taking a step toward the door. "Forget the singles thing. Get yourself a date and come out with me on Friday. You said yourself you're not working"—Madi cursed herself for not seeing the Hathaway comment earlier as a trap—"and you need something to take your mind off work every once in a while. I can prove to you that you'll have a good time away from home and away from editing photos. Besides, dating isn't as bad as you think it is if you've got someone you know to help break the ice. We can help each other. If I'm wrong, then we'll call the bet off and you can keep pretending I didn't see you making a list of baby names last week while you were looking at a guest list."

Wincing, Madi told herself she could say no. She'd shut down plenty of bets in the past, and Danny would probably move on. *Hopefully.* With the way he watched her intently, eyebrows high, it was like he knew he'd given her something she couldn't resist. The prospect of updating his website with her photos was likely the one and only thing that could have gotten her to consider the bet in the first place, and he knew it.

She was probably spending too much time with Danny at these weddings.

"One date," she said, holding up a finger to emphasize. "Then we'll talk about the stupid bet."

She could do that. One measly date? All she had to do was…find a guy. Any guy. As Danny wandered off to the kitchen with a triumphant grin, Madi slowly disassembled her camera and set it in her bag. Unease grew in her stomach the longer she stood there, considering her pathetically limited options. She went out so rarely that she barely knew anyone to begin with, and she'd gone out with most of the guys she had met over the years, with disastrous results. One date…

Maybe this was going to be harder than she thought.

TWO

AT SOME POINT, A GROWN man had to acknowledge that using a secret handshake would never be dignified and just made him look like an idiot. Oliver had been thinking that a lot lately. But convincing the likes of Kit Morgan to do away with tradition was like trying to tell the sun to stay down for another hour every morning so he could get more sleep. It was utterly pointless.

No one hated change as much as Kit.

"No handshake," Kit said with narrowed eyes, "no entry."

Oliver could see Cam and Ben lounging on the two couches that sat at a ninety-degree angle in Kit's living room, and he knew for a fact that neither of them had done a secret handshake in almost a decade. "Come on, man. Is this punishment for being late?"

"Yes," all three of them said at the same time.

Oliver groaned. "It's only twenty minutes."

Kit held out his fist, waiting. "A guy who literally does nothing with his day has no excuse for being late to a club meeting. And don't you dare claim jetlag; you got back from Fiji a week ago."

At this point he was being petty, but Oliver felt like he should hold his ground. "A guy who is twenty-eight years old is probably too old to keep calling his group of friends a 'club,' don't you think?"

"No," all three said at once.

"We're always going to be the Wonder Boys," Ben said with a shrug.

Wow, even Ben was willing to die on that hill? Oliver must have fallen asleep at some point in his life and woken up in an alternate reality where his three best friends in the world had never aged past fifteen. Never would he have called himself the mature one, but there he was.

He tried one more time to level Kit with a look that said he wouldn't do the handshake. When Kit didn't budge an inch, Oliver sighed and bumped his fist against Kit's. From there it moved on to more elaborate movements until the two of them spit into their hands and clasped them together.

"I hate this," Oliver said, making sure Kit understood how deeply he meant that.

It was too bad his best friend didn't care. "I know you do. Now get inside before we end up standing here all night."

"Fellow Wonder Boys." With a salute, Oliver plopped himself down on the giant blue bean bag that had been his spot for longer than he could remember. "Seriously, why do you still call yourselves that?"

"Because Madi called us that," Cam said without hesitation.

Madi Morgan. If that girl knew how much she had controlled the lives of the four of them in this room, she could have been ruling the world at this point. It was a good thing Kit's little sister was the sweetest girl on the planet. Still, being named after a lasso-wielding superheroine wasn't exactly the manliest way to live.

"Alright, men." Kit stood in his spot in front of the TV, his gaze intense as he stared down his three friends from behind his glasses. "You're probably wondering why I called this meeting tonight."

Oliver guessed it had something to do with the comic book-loving little sister who could have at least called them Wonder *Men*.

"We're talking about your dad bod, right?" Cam said. "I didn't want to say it, but if you're pointing it out…"

Kit narrowed his eyes, though his glare was never really all that effective on anyone older than eight. "I do not have a dad bod, Cameron Martinez, and I will go outside right now and whoop your butt in one-on-one if you say another word."

"Ten bucks on Martinez," Oliver said, rolling his eyes.

"I'm not betting against Cam," Ben replied without skipping a beat.

Frowning, Kit must have realized he'd been ganged up on, but he recovered quickly. He always did. "Like I was saying, we're here to talk about Madi and her plan to fake date her way through life and use the three of you as pawns."

Oliver's stomach did a somersault. She was doing *what*?

Sitting up from his spot on the love seat opposite Oliver, Ben glanced between the other three as if hoping to find the answer to his unasked question before he had to say it out loud. "I'm confused," he finally admitted.

At least Cam looked just as lost as Oliver, so all three of them were in the dark.

Kit let out a deep sigh, pulling off his glasses and pinching the bridge of his nose. "Honestly, I don't know the details, and she wouldn't tell me much. I just know she might need some dates and isn't willing to get real ones."

"How did you find out about this?" Oliver asked, still feeling off-kilter from this strange turn of events. Maybe he *was* still jet lagged. Or he had the opposite of seasickness after spending so much time on the ocean while he was in Fiji. Land sickness was a thing, right?

"She asked if any of you guys were free for a double date on Friday, and I wanted to know why."

Oliver glanced at his phone in his pocket. Why hadn't she texted him directly? He'd spent his whole life around Kit's little sister, so it wasn't like they didn't know each other. They used to hang out all the time.

As if reading his mind, Kit shrugged and said, "You weren't here the night she called."

Oliver hadn't even known the guys were hanging out. "I'm free on Friday."

"Big surprise," Cam muttered. "You're always free. But I already told Madi I could—wait, did you say date?" He turned to Kit, his dark eyes wide. "I thought it was just hanging out."

Kit grimaced as he nodded. "And I'm not sure I'm okay with the idea of you guys dating my sister. Even if it's fake."

"That's why we made the pact, isn't it?" Ben said.

The pact. When they "adopted" Kit's sister as one of their own back when they were kids, they all swore they would never try to date her or push things beyond friendship. They were too close a group to risk hurting each other if things went wrong, and Madi was too awesome a girl to have to deal with the pressure of three guys all hoping for her attention, on the off chance they all fell for her if they let themselves. Making that pact had kept them all in a blissful state of friendship that would never change as long as they all kept their words.

"That's why I called this meeting," Kit said. "I don't think Madi's plan is the best course of action. If she's going to be dating, she should date someone she can actually end up with." He glanced at Oliver for a split second. "That isn't going to be any of you guys, clearly."

There was nothing clear about it. "Why does she need us as dates in the first place?" Oliver asked. He still hadn't fully made sense of the situation, and he suspected Cam and Ben were as confused as he was. And why had Kit looked at *him* when talking about people Madi could or couldn't end up with?

This whole thing was all sorts of weird.

Kit shrugged. "You know Madi. Whatever she's doing, she's going to try to fix it on her own. But apparently she needs at least *some* help on this one, and she said there may be more dates in the future."

"So let's help her," Cam said. "Do we really need to know why?"

He made a good point. Despite Kit being the only one actually related to Madi, all four of them had been calling her their sister since they were fourteen. It had started when no one showed up to her birthday party, so Kit decided to step in. The others had followed without question, and that party had beat out anything else they might have done that day. From then on, the five of them were family.

Oliver was pretty sure all of them would go to the ends of the earth for Madi if she asked. He knew *he* would.

"Well," Kit said with a frown. "Let's look at the pros and the cons. Pro—"

"Can we not?" Oliver interrupted. "We're going to be here all night if Mr. Teacher-of-the-Year gets on his soap box."

Kit sent another ineffective glare Oliver's way. "I was not Teacher of the Year, so thanks for reminding me of that. And a pros and cons list does not count as a soap box. I'm trying to be thorough, so even though you don't know what that feels like, bear with me, okay?"

Oliver flinched, surprised by the sharpness in Kit's words when he was usually so civil. They'd known each other since kindergarten, and Oliver had not often been on the receiving end of Kit's rare set downs. They seemed to have gotten more frequent over the last few years, though, and Oliver definitely didn't like that. What had he done wrong this time?

"I'm putting in my vote for it," Cam said before Kit could jump into his rhetoric. "I don't really care what it is; if Madi needs help, I'm going to help her."

"I'm against it," Ben decided, though he sounded less confident. "Not without knowing what she's up to."

"I'm with Cam on this," Oliver put in, though he honestly wasn't sure where he stood on the issue. It was a strange concept, going on dates with little Madi, but he also didn't like the idea of her going out with random men she found on the internet or through blind date setups if they didn't step in. She deserved better than that, and if she wanted to use them as decoy dates, more power to her.

"As weird as it is to think about my sister dating, I would so much rather have Madi date someone for real so she doesn't end up miserable and alone," Kit finished, which meant—as always—their vote was split right down the middle.

Oliver groaned at the same time Ben muttered, "We should have made another friend."

"I think we should count Madi's vote in this one," Oliver said. "She wouldn't go to all this trouble if it wasn't something important." He waited for Kit to immediately dismiss him like he'd been doing lately, but the man actually looked thoughtful.

"You're right," he admitted with reluctance, since that would mean he lost the vote. "But this is going to bring its own set of problems we're going to have to deal with."

"Such as?" Cam asked.

Kit went full into teacher mode, grabbing a notebook and pen and scribbling something down as he resumed his pacing. "Such as the fact that you can't keep your mouth shut to save your life, Martinez," he said first.

That much was true. Cam had never been good at keeping secrets, and he practically imploded if he ever had to tell a lie. Oliver had always thought that would be a terrible trait for a personal trainer to have—they were all about spouting off positive motivation. Apparently, Cam had built himself a reputation for being brutally honest but in the nicest possible way. At least, that's what Oliver had heard. He would have to see it to believe it, knowing how many fights Cam had gotten into in junior high and high school.

"Then there's Ben's schedule," Kit continued, still writing things down. Ben worked at a fun center and had the misfortune of being assistant manager, which meant he usually worked nights and weekends and overtime.

Oliver could sense where this was going, and he wasn't sure how to feel about it. It pushed him up to his feet, but no one seemed to think him standing was strange. They must have seen the ultimate conclusion to this as well.

Only Kit gave Oliver a look of unease, as if hoping for a different solution. He must have come up with nothing, because he folded his arms and shook his head. "Which means most of the dates will be with Oliver, depending on how many she actually needs."

"At least you'll be able to sell the dates," Cam said with a chuckle. "You flirt more than anyone I've ever known."

Oliver pulled his eyebrows low. "I do not."

"No, you do," Ben agreed. "It also means you have to stay in town."

"Oh no," Cam said with sarcasm, "Oliver can't travel the world all summer like he usually does?"

"I've never traveled all summer," Oliver argued, but it was a weak argument. He'd had to keep himself busy somehow over the last few years, so he'd taken quite a few trips to other countries in the hopes of finding something to occupy his time.

"So you'll be around?" Kit pressed.

"For Madi? Of course."

"This means you actually have to try," Cam warned.

What was this, 'Pick on Oliver' night? "What is that supposed to mean?"

Sighing, Kit put a hand on his shoulder and practically shoved him back onto the bean bag. "It means you haven't worked for three years, my man. You've got that whole lazy thing on lockdown. But you'll have to bring your A-game for this."

Oliver resented the fact that his best friend thought he was lazy, but Kit wasn't wrong about not working for the last few years outside of a few freelance programming contracts. One of the benefits of selling his wildly successful software company was suddenly having a lot of free time and plenty of cash to burn.

But being Madi's fake date? That would be easy. He'd known her practically his whole life, and all he would have to do was act excited to see her. He wouldn't even have to act that part! With all her photography gigs and his many trips over the last several years, he'd barely had the chance to spend any time with her, something that badly needed fixing. Fake dates would be perfect for that.

"What's your date on Friday?" Oliver asked Cam, suddenly curious.

"Going out for ice cream with her coworker and his date, apparently."

That didn't seem all that important. What was Madi up to?

"Are these dates work-related then?" Ben asked.

No one had an answer for that one, though it could explain why Madi thought she needed to go through with the dates. Maybe she needed help with networking, though Oliver couldn't see why they had to be specifically dates for something like that.

"We should set some ground rules," Kit said after a long and awkward silence. He looked at Cam first, narrowing his eyes. "First, remember that none of these dates are going to be real."

No one argued against that one.

"Second, don't even think about touching her."

That was also a given.

Or not. "That's not going to work," Ben said, speaking like his thoughts were obvious. When all heads swiveled in his direction, he shrugged. "How is anyone going to believe we're on a date with her if we don't touch her? Especially if we go on more than one."

Grumbling a little, Kit folded his arms and took a deep breath before he spoke again. "Fine. Basic contact. Nothing I haven't seen you do before. Third, all of us should know about the dates before they happen. Just in case you need backup."

"On a date?" Ben asked, raising an eyebrow.

"Maybe Madi should have been a part of this meeting," Cam said with a grin. "She'd probably be a better one to—"

"This is a *Wonder Boy* meeting," Kit argued.

Oliver groaned. "Do you really have to keep calling us that?"

No one replied, which meant Oliver was still alone in thinking it was high time they stopped calling themselves a club and started acting like the nearly thirty-year-olds they were. He'd moved on years ago.

Maybe he'd moved a little too far.

As he sat there, Oliver couldn't remember the last time all four of them had been together like this. It had been several months at least, and while he *had* been traveling a lot lately, there had been plenty of times where he'd sat around his apartment, completely bored. Though Kit's house had always been the gathering place—and Kit's parents' house before this—Oliver hadn't spent much time in his spot since before graduating college six years ago.

These fake dates with Madi would probably be a good way to get them all together more often.

"Moving on," Kit said eventually. "Madi did say something about waiting to see what happened on Friday, whatever that means, so I expect a full report, Cam."

Cam did a lazy salute. "Aye aye, captain. I'll give you all the gory details."

Kit flinched. "Rule number two, Martinez."

Laughing, Cam grabbed a video game controller and tossed one to Oliver, apparently convinced they were at the end of the meeting. He started up a game even though Kit still stood by the TV. "Would you relax, Morgan? We've all known Madi for years. It's not like none of us have spent any time around her before. We know how to behave."

Though Oliver tried to focus on the game, he couldn't help but imagine in more detail what a date with Madi would look like. He'd known her for more than twenty years, and though they'd spent plenty of one-on-one time together, they'd never done anything resembling a date. Maybe it wouldn't be as easy as he'd thought, though he wouldn't know until he got his chance to try it.

He bounced a little in his seat as he considered the prospect. There were few people he liked as much as he liked Madi Morgan, and most of them were in this room. Madi was basically a little sister to all of them, and Kit had no reason to be worried when none of them would do anything to hurt her.

"We'll let her take the lead on this," he muttered, looking up at Kit until his friend got the message.

"Okay," Kit finally said, shuffling over to Cam's couch to take his usual spot. It made everything feel a bit more normal, something Oliver hadn't realized he was craving until his shoulders relaxed. He definitely needed to make more of an effort to be a part of the gang again.

"I'll set up a calendar just in case," Ben said. "That way she'll know when all of us are free if she needs someone."

They fell into a familiar silence as the game continued on for several minutes until Kit snapped, "Cam, will you just beat him already?"

Cam growled. "Believe me, I'm trying."

Honestly, Oliver had barely been paying attention, but when he realized he was only a few moves away from winning the round, he turned his focus back to the TV and beat Cam in only a few seconds.

"No fair," Cam complained with a groan. "How did you even do that?"

"It was that summer he and Madi played every day," Kit replied for Oliver.

That had been Oliver's favorite summer, by far. He'd been eight at the time—Madi had been six—and they'd both gotten the chickenpox, so they'd had to stay inside for almost a full month. Oliver had looked it up years later and realized chickenpox definitely didn't last a month, and he had profusely thanked Kit and Madi's mom for pretending it did. That month away from his own house had been the best of his life.

While they were stuck inside, they'd only had the one game, so they'd played it for hours on end. And instead of getting sick of the game, both he and Madi had ended up loving it more than ever and still played it all the time.

Or they had, before adulthood got in the way.

Oliver tried not to dwell on his childhood very often, but he thought about that summer more often than he should. It was one of his few truly happy memories, and he wondered if Madi thought about it as much as he did.

Maybe, thanks to these dates, he would actually get a chance to ask her.

THREE

Kit: Are you sure you don't want a real date tonight?
I've got a couple friends from the school I could set
you up with.

Kit: I take that back. They're not worth your time. But I
could still find you a real date.

Madi: In the next five minutes? I thought you were fine
with me using the Boys as fake dates.

Kit: Why do you even need fake dates?

Madi: It's hard to explain.

Kit: That doesn't sound sketchy at all.

Madi: Let's just say it's to help out a friend and call it
good.

Kit: That does not sound good. How does lying help
anyone?

Madi: It's not lying. Technically, tonight's date with
Cam is real. You and I both know it won't go anywhere, so it's fine.

Kit: I have something at the school tonight, but I can
send Oliver as backup if you need it.

Madi: I'm fine. Calm down. This is hopefully a one-time
thing.

Madi: DO NOT send Oliver.

Madi had known her brother's friend, Cam Martinez, since she was eleven years old. He was like another brother, and she had been around him so often over the years that she considered him one of her best friends. The idea of going on a date with him was almost laughable at this point, and she did *not* need Oliver there to make things even weirder.

Thank goodness her brother was busy that night, or he and Oliver might have shown up in trenchcoats and hidden in the corner of the ice cream shop for the entirety of the date. Madi could only imagine trying to concentrate on pretending to be on a date with Cam with Oliver Hamilton watching her from across the room. Oliver may have been one of her closest friends, but that meant he knew her too well—and could read her body language better than anyone. He would look for any excuse to step in and fix things.

She didn't need that.

Unless she decided to take the bet, of course.

The more she considered the stupid bet, the more tempting it sounded. If she thought about it hard enough, she could close her eyes and see Danny's website with its shiny new photos, and the extra money would put her one step closer to…something.

As she waited outside the ice cream parlor, she gripped her phone and pretended it didn't bother her to not have a goal in mind. She had plenty of smaller options—the usual new car/vacation/updated wardrobe kinds of things—but her life was pretty great as it was. Outside of a house or something, the next big thing wasn't exactly in her control.

"Danny," she growled, though she wasn't really angry. She just didn't like when he was right.

The next big thing was finding someone to share her life with. Why did the next thing have to be so terrifying? Even the thought of going out with a stranger made her heart race, and she hadn't been on a date in over two years. For good reason.

Compared to some of her other past dates, her date with Danny had been one of the good ones.

"Madi!" a deep voice called.

"Hey, Cam!" She was so used to seeing Cam in workout clothes that she hadn't recognized him until he was right in front of her. That was ridiculous, considering the man was huge, with bronze muscles for days. Grinning, Madi threw her arms around his shoulders and laughed when he picked her up in his usual bear hug.

"What's up, little sister?" he said.

As soon as she was safely back on her feet, Madi smacked his arm, regretting it when his giant bicep felt like a rock beneath her fingers. "You'd better not say anything like that tonight or Danny will get really creeped out."

"Right." He coughed, shaking out his arms as if getting ready for a deadlift.

Madi stuffed her hands into her back pockets and searched the area to make sure Danny hadn't shown up yet. "Are you sure Halley is okay with this?"

Cam flinched. "No idea. She broke up with me two weeks ago."

"Oh. Sorry. What happened?" But Madi was pretty sure she already knew the answer to that. Cam had had more relationships than the rest of the Wonder Boys combined, but they always fell flat before getting very serious. Madi had never even met any of his girlfriends over the years.

Grunting, Cam suddenly became very interested in his sneakers. "She wanted more, and I didn't," he said with a shrug.

Madi didn't push the issue. Whatever Cam's reasons for avoiding deeper connections with the girls he dated, she hoped he got over it soon. Like the rest of the Wonder Boys, he was a total catch and would make someone ridiculously happy someday.

"So, you're going to have to tell me what the plan is tonight or I'll ruin everything," Cam said, changing the subject. "Remember that surprise party we threw for Kit?"

Madi made a face. "You mean the surprise party that got ruined when you blabbed about it two weeks before it happened? Yeah, I remember." And now she was realizing how terrible an idea this was. Cam could turn literally anyone into a prime athlete, but he couldn't tell a lie to save his life. "This is going to be a disaster, isn't it?"

"Nah. As long as we stick to the truth, we'll be fine."

"So this is our second date?"

Cam grinned, his smile a little lopsided. "You're calling my graduation dinner a date?"

"Aren't you? I took you out to dinner, didn't I?"

Laughing, Cam shook his head. "My aunt took me out to dinner once too. If that's your idea of a date, we've got bigger problems than whatever this is." He waved a hand between them. "A good date has chemistry, and you and I don't."

Madi probably should have been offended by that assessment, but she wasn't. It only made her wonder if she'd ever had chemistry with anyone before. With how poorly most of her dates had gone in the past, she doubted it.

Maybe Cam would be willing to offer up advice while they waited for Danny. "What else makes a good date?"

He raised an eyebrow. "You don't know? And here I was thinking you had all the guys wrapped around your finger."

Madi snorted a laugh, gladder than ever that Cam had been free tonight. His open and honest personality was perfect for breaking the tension before Danny arrived. "Um, you do remember that this is me we're talking about, right?"

Cam shrugged. "You do remember you got all four of us to wear tiaras when we were teenagers, right?"

Warmth spread through her at the memory of her twelfth birthday party. The day she gained three more brothers. "Be honest with me, Cam," she said.

He barked out a laugh. "You know you'll never get anything else." That was true. The man was a compulsive truth-teller.

"How much does Kit hate this idea?"

Wincing, Cam tucked his hands into his pockets. "He doesn't love it. But he was outvoted."

Madi groaned. "He called a meeting for this? Really? It's probably not even going to happen after tonight." Unless she gave in to Danny's challenge, of course.

"Are you allowed to tell me why it's happening?"

If she told Cam about the bet, he would inevitably tell the others, and she knew Kit wouldn't be okay with the idea of lying to get something. It wasn't lying. Not *technically*. But she also didn't feel great about the plan to date guys she would never actually end up with. As much as she loved Cam, he was right about them having no chemistry. He was fun and flirty, but he'd never given Madi the feeling of being home.

That was how her mom had always described love, while her dad said it was like knowing the world could never touch him when his wife was in his arms. Madi just wanted what her parents had.

Maybe, after summer was over, she would have some time to throw some real dates in there. She just needed the Wonder Boys to get her through the next three months.

"My friend Danny thinks I'm lonely," she told Cam, which was true. "And he's also pretty lonely himself. So he thought it would be a good idea to double date to help us both out, but I'm not looking to date right now." That last part was mostly a lie.

Cam studied her for a moment before grinning again. "Fine by me. As long as this Danny guy isn't pressuring you into anything."

"No, he's a really great friend. He's just bad at dating, like I am. And really bad at setups."

Cam chuckled, watching as people wandered the popular street around them. "I feel that. There's a trainer at the gym who thinks she should set me up with every girl who comes in, and my clients are eighty percent female now because she's the one who sets up the schedule."

"Lucky you."

"It's a nightmare. You try telling a stick-thin wannabe Instagram model to lift more than three pounds when all she wants to do is bat her eyes at you and stroke your arm." He shuddered as if reliving a recent memory. "I don't even think half of them actually want to get strong. They spend the whole time sneaking pictures and pretending they don't know what I'm talking about when I call them out on it. I'm pretty sure there's a hashtag for me now, something my coworker finds hilarious. I think half the pictures are from her, trying to drum up more business."

Madi sighed, though she made a note to look up that hashtag. "They have our best interests at heart, right? That's what I keep telling myself. Oh, here comes Danny. Act natural." She waved at Danny, who had just rounded the corner with a blonde girl next to him.

Danny immediately perked up when he saw Madi, his shoulders dropping in relief, while his date looked around like she was tempted to jump ship before they even reached the ice cream parlor. "Madi! You made it!" Then he caught sight of Cam and froze.

Madi nearly laughed. *Natural* for Cam was apparently to hunch into a ball so he wouldn't look so huge. It only made his shoulders more enormous, and while he wasn't quite as tall as Kit, he still cleared six feet and had a few inches on Danny.

"Hey," Danny said, eyeing Cam out of the corner of his eye as he gave Madi a hug. "This is Vanessa."

"Hi." Madi shook Vanessa's hand, then introduced Cam, who opted to keep his hands in his pockets, probably in case he broke fingers with his grip. He'd done it before, and now he was incredibly selective with his handshakes.

"Should we go in?" Danny said, and he led the way inside.

With it being Friday night, the ice cream shop was especially crowded, and Madi instinctively drew a little closer to Cam as people bumped into her on their way out the door. He immediately put his arm around her shoulders in a protective way, and though she loved how safe she felt with her pseudo brother, she didn't miss the lift of Danny's eyebrow when he glanced back and saw.

Her face burning, she considered moving out of Cam's hold but knew that would only make Danny more curious. "Cheese sticks," she muttered under her breath. This was going to be harder than she thought.

Cam snorted a small laugh. "Did I just hear what I think I heard?"

"Shut up."

"She works with kids a lot," Danny offered, which meant he was intently listening despite the rumble of conversations around them. Madi had told him once about accidentally swearing in front of a bunch of kids in her studio, so she'd adopted some less colorful language by necessity. "Vanessa, did I tell you Madi is a photographer?"

Vanessa glanced back, and though her smile was friendly, she didn't seem to appreciate her date talking about another girl. Still, she was nice enough to say, "That's cool. What kind of photography?"

This whole date was because Danny was trying to help Madi stop living her life alone, and she was supposed to be doing the same for him. Standing up straighter, Madi did her best to sound confident and casual. "I mostly do weddings. That's how I met Danny. Did he tell you he's a wedding planner? Like, a really good one. Danny, you should tell her about that giant wedding you planned in December."

Vanessa seemed intrigued and turned back to Danny, who jumped right into a detailed description of the venue, complete with wild hand gestures.

When they reached the front of the line and Danny and his date got properly distracted by sampling flavors, Cam leaned down and muttered, "You're a good friend. I hope he knows that."

Heat spread through Madi's cheeks. "Yeah, well, he saved me a piece of cake last week, so I owe him."

"How's that going, by the way? The wedding stuff and all that?"

Madi and Cam didn't often get a chance to really talk about life since they most often saw each other when they were all in a group. And when they were in a group, it was usually Kit dominating the conversation with Oliver or Cam, leaving Madi and Ben to sit back as observers. It was nice to have some one-on-one time now and then.

"Things are going really well," Madi said. "I'm busier than ever, and I have weddings scheduled all year." She had to pause her explanation when they reached the counter, where she was suddenly faced with a decision. As always, she froze.

Thank goodness for Cam, who knew her well enough to know the problem. "What are you torn between?" he asked with a grin.

Madi bit her lip. "Double fudge and mint."

"One of each in sugar cones," Cam told the teenage server.

Though the kid nodded, he hesitated a moment, then pointed to their different cup sizes. "You could get both scoops in one if you did a cup," he suggested helpfully.

Madi smiled at him. "But I really want the cone," she admitted. "It's my favorite part. Cam, you're sure you want to share?"

"With you? Of course."

Madi paid for the ice cream before Cam could offer, as she knew he would, and then the pair of them joined Danny and Vanessa at the table they'd managed to snag despite the shop being so busy. Danny was still talking about decorations—Vanessa looked like she was being a good sport and pretending to be interested—so Madi focused on the ice cream.

She'd been handed the mint, and while it looked delicious, she could smell the fudge in Cam's hand. It was the same problem as the wedding last week. The double fudge would be tastier but definitely messier, and it would take her longer to eat because it was so rich. The mint would be good, of course, and it wouldn't stick to her mouth as easily so she could eat it before it melted. But it wasn't chocolate.

Should she play it safe and stick with sensible, or go for the longtime favorite?

Fighting a laugh, Cam held his cone toward her. "Taste them both," he suggested.

Madi licked the mint first, then the chocolate, then went back to the mint, forcing herself to just make a decision and choose one. "Mint," she said and practically took a bite out of it to prove she was confident in her decision.

"Good choice." Cam literally did take a bite out of his scoop.

"Wow," Vanessa exclaimed. "My teeth would hurt so bad if I did that!" She'd opted for a cup and was still using a tiny sample spoon instead of one of the big ones they gave out at the counter.

Cam shrugged and took another bite. His scoop was already halfway gone. "It's a superpower, I guess."

Madi took another lick of her mint, and though it was good, she was not enjoying it nearly as much as Cam was enjoying his. Grimacing, she took a deep breath and was about to ask if he wanted to switch when he held out his cone to her and smiled knowingly. Face burning, she accepted his offering and gave him the rest of her mint.

Chocolate was definitely the better choice.

"So… How long have you two known each other?" Danny asked, his eyes jumping between them.

"We grew up together," Cam said without hesitation.

Madi almost dropped her cone. They hadn't talked about their backstory beyond going on that date (or not-a-date, according to Cam). She probably should have told Cam to pretend like they'd met only recently so Danny wouldn't wonder why Madi hadn't been on a date with him before now. That was assuming Cam could have pretended in the first place.

She scrambled for a save. "Uh, Cam and I have some mutual friends, but he was a couple grades above me."

"So this is our second date," Cam finished, which didn't make sense at all. He grimaced, apology in his eyes.

"Our first date was years ago," Madi said. "Now we're, uh, reconnecting." She chanced a glance at Danny, who for some reason was looking at her like she'd found her soulmate in Cam Martinez, as if sharing ice cream was the epitome of intimacy.

"At least he knows how much you like chocolate," Danny said with an awkward laugh, and then he put his arm around Vanessa.

She stiffened, shifting forward from his touch. "I don't like chocolate," she mumbled, her eyes on the door.

Poor Danny. Something told Madi this was not going to lead to a second date for him.

The rest of their conversation hovered around small talk until Vanessa announced she had an early appointment in the morning and needed to head out. Danny offered to walk her to her car, which she declined, so he was left standing on the sidewalk with Madi and Cam behind him trying not to look like they pitied him.

Before Madi could come up with something positive to say about the evening, Danny turned to her and said, "Can I talk to you for a quick second? Cam, I promise I won't keep her long."

"No worries," he said, which wasn't exactly a date thing to say.

Madi counted herself lucky when Danny pulled her off to the side and said, "I'll be the first to admit tonight didn't go exactly how I'd hoped. Sorry my date was a bust."

"You'll find someone better," Madi replied, tucking her hands into her back pockets. "And I'm not sure my date was all that much better. I'm clearly way too awkward for dating. It was nice to get out and do something, though."

Danny immediately grinned, making Madi realize her misstep. "Told you!"

She resisted the urge to groan, knowing she'd been telling the truth when she said it was nice to get out. "You really want to make this bet?"

He nodded.

"Why?"

"Because I watch you at these weddings, and I see the way you look at the bride and groom. I know how badly you want that, but you're never going to find that kind of happiness if you never go out."

Sighing, Madi wished he wasn't so observant. But she *did* want that. She wanted a reason to say no to clients because she wanted to spend time with someone more than she wanted a paycheck. The last ten years had kept her busy—too busy—and she felt like something was missing from her life.

The Wonder Boys could be her dating gurus until she was ready to venture out on her own, and she could help Danny at the same time. He may have struck out with Vanessa, but she'd seen much worse. He'd told her plenty of first date stories where he panicked on his own and took things too far. He needed someone to keep him grounded.

"Okay," she said, flinching.

Danny's eyes went wide. "Really? You don't have to—"

"I'll do it. Nine more double dates in the next three months." Oh, Madi was most definitely going to regret this, but now that she'd made the decision, she couldn't back down. Whether she had the time or not, she was about to go on a whole lot of dates this summer.

Grinning, Danny held out his hand so they could shake on it, sealing the bet. "By the way," he said, his hand still around hers, "if you lose, you owe me new website photos for free. They'll still be watermarked, of course, so you get the credit, but I wouldn't mind keeping that chunk of change for myself. You're not cheap."

Madi sighed, blowing a bit of hair out of her face. *Of course* he would tell her that *after* she'd agreed. And of course he would let her do the photos regardless. "You're too good for your own good, Danny Camper."

"I know. And I'm about to be even better. How about I help you out on the next date? There's this singles barbecue next week."

"A singles barbecue?"

"Yeah. You know, for young singles in the area."

"Has anyone ever told you that you sound like a dating website? You can't just put the word singles in front of something and expect that to be a normal thing."

Wrinkling his nose at her, Danny tried to look angry but couldn't pull it off well. He was too nice for that. "Okay, so it's a little unorthodox. But these things are actually pretty fun. I thought maybe we could be each other's wingmen. Wingwomen. Wingpeople?" He shrugged. "Make it easier to meet people—I need to find dates for the bet too. And I'll even let you count it as your next date, even if you don't pair off with anyone because I'm nice like that."

Despite hating the fact that Danny thought she needed help, Madi wanted to say yes to the barbecue and see if she really had been missing out on something. But even just thinking of having to socialize with a bunch of strangers was exhausting, and she wasn't sure she had the energy for something like that. Or if she ever would. She had always been shy, which was part of the reason she spent most of her childhood with the Wonder Boys; she didn't have anything to fear from them.

Between weddings, engagement shoots, and appointments at her studio, Madi's summer was already full of an introvert's nightmares.

"What day is the barbecue?" she asked warily, hoping Danny didn't take her question as an immediate agreement.

"Tuesday."

Grabbing her phone, she pulled out the calendar Ben had made and prayed at least one of the guys was free that night. Otherwise, she would have to lie and say she was busy, and that would definitely backfire. Danny had a copy of her schedule so he could tell his clients if she was free for their weddings, and he knew better than anyone that she didn't have a social life. To her relief, both Cam and Oliver were free. Going out with Cam again so soon would be dangerous, though, since Danny would take that as a sign that things were progressing toward something, so she decided to pick Oliver for this one.

With him being the most charming of the Boys, he would probably make the whole thing nice and easy.

"I can make that work," she said, hoping that was accurate. "Just send me the address, and I'll be there."

Danny did a subdued fist pump, apparently pleased by her response. "You're the best. I promise this will be good for you."

Madi wasn't so sure, but she smiled at Danny anyway as he gave her a wave and headed for his car. Either this summer would lead to something incredible, or she was going to start questioning her friendship with the guy.

"So…" Cam came up beside her as soon as Danny disappeared around the corner, a question in his raised eyebrow.

Madi sighed. "Sounds like I'm going to need some more dates."

"And that's a bad thing? It means you get to hang out with us more."

Pulling out her phone, she typed out a text to Oliver to ask him to be available on Tuesday to "meet" her at a singles barbecue. "That's true," she muttered to Cam as she sent the text. That was a definite plus.

Oliver texted back almost immediately.

> Oliver: What in the world is a singles barbecue? Is this
> a date, or what?

Madi's stomach twisted at the thought of being on a date with Oliver Hamilton. She'd known him the longest—since she was four—and he was probably the one who knew her best. But going on an actual date? They'd never done anything like that, and it almost felt wrong. It had been several months since she last saw Oliver, though, and despite her apprehension of the situation, she really was excited to see him.

But was it a date? It had been easy to call tonight a date with Cam, but her pounding heart didn't seem to like the idea of being on a date with Oliver. Or it *really* liked the idea. She wasn't sure which, and she opted for a vague response.

> Madi: That depends on who's there. Let's head over
> together and get there early. You'll be my backup if
> I don't meet anyone good.
> Oliver: Cool, I guess?
> Oliver: So you're going to need more dates?

Madi: Sounds like it.

Oliver: Just let me know what you need. I'll be there.

So that was that. Madi had accepted the terms of the bet, which meant she was about to go on a whole lot of dates she didn't have time for. At least she would get to see more of the Wonder Boys, but as her ice cream churned in her stomach, she cursed under her breath.

This was going to get complicated. Quickly.

"I'm going to tell the guys about your new brand of curse words," Cam said with a lopsided grin.

Madi's eyes went wide. "Don't you dare. Do you know how hard I fought to kill phrases like 'cheese sticks'? They're so stupid, and the only reason Oliver even used them was because his parents are so strict."

"I do know how hard you fought," Cam said, laughter making his words bounce. "I also know that Oliver is going to—"

"If you tell him, I swear I'll…" But Madi couldn't think of a valid threat. Cam was way bigger than her, and it wasn't like he had any secrets she could expose when he was honest to a fault. So she sighed and shook her head. "I've got to get home and do some editing. Thanks for tonight, Cam. And *don't* tell Oliver."

The last thing she needed was a reason to bring out Oliver's way too attractive smile when she saw him at the barbecue.

She was nervous enough as it was.

FOUR

Oliver was excited to go to a singles barbecue.

That was weird.

What was weirder was how *nervous* he was to go to a singles barbecue. He didn't even know what a singles barbecue entailed, but he had a feeling it was a lot different from the way he usually dated. It had been a while, but back when he was actively dating, he would walk up to pretty women on the street and ask them out to dinner. It only worked about fifteen percent of the time, but he had actually gotten a few good dates out of it; those women had seemed to like the confidence.

A barbecue specifically designed for matching people up? That was throwing a whole lot of desperation into one place, and while the pool of candidates would be greater—theoretically all of them would be unattached—there was a much higher chance of some of the ladies being marriage-hungry. He was in no way ready for that kind of commitment. He just hoped he could find a normal girl who was looking for something casual, like he was.

At some point, he was going to have to move beyond casual dating, but he had never been able to see himself as something more with any of the women he dated. He figured he just had to find the right person. Someone who could live up to the standard he'd set years ago.

That person would unlikely be at a singles barbecue, but miracles had been known to happen.

"Don't forget you already have a date tonight," he reminded himself as he walked up the stairs to Madi's apartment and knocked on her door. That didn't mean he couldn't do a little recon for the future. Surely at least one woman there might be worth some interest, and it wasn't like he was being unrealistic.

If Madi Morgan could possess all the qualities he hoped for in a partner, so could someone else. Even if Madi set the bar pretty high.

Madi gave him her signature grin when she opened the door, and his breath caught like it usually did when he saw that brilliant smile. For being his best friend's sister, he had never understood how she always managed to look incredible no matter what she was wearing. Maybe it hit harder today because it had been a while since he'd last seen her.

Too long.

Her smile, however, slowly faded as she looked him over. "That's what you're wearing?" she asked.

Oliver glanced down. Because this wasn't an actual date, he hadn't put much thought into his appearance, but a t-shirt and jeans seemed entirely appropriate for a barbecue in May. "Uh, yeah?"

Though she smiled again, it was the kind of smile that said she was disappointed. The kind that made him squirm. "Well, maybe next time you can try a little harder, and then it'll look like you're wanting to impress me. Danny would love that."

It had been a few days since Cam's comment about Oliver needing to try, but it still stung to know that even Madi—who was almost incapable of insulting anyone—thought Oliver was lazy, just like his friends did. Maybe a life of luxury the last three years hadn't been good for him and he had lost all sense of self-worth.

Once upon a time, he had been so confident in who he was. Had he really fallen so far that one look from his friend's little sister could make him question everything?

The answer to that was a definite *yes*, but he'd known that already. It wasn't like he'd been feeling all that great about himself for the last few years, so it didn't take much to knock him down.

"I'll do better next time," he assured her as his stomach twisted with the familiar feeling of failure. "I thought maybe this way you could catch the eye of someone else since I won't be competition." *Self-insult?* Oliver shook that one off and plastered on a smile. This singles event was for him too, and he would never spark anyone's interest if he moped the whole time.

He opened her door when they reached his car, not missing her high eyebrows as she looked around while he slid into his own seat.

"This is your car?" she asked when it purred to life.

Oliver was rather proud of his Mercedes-Benz, though he could admit it was a bit gaudy if he thought too hard. He'd bought the little red sportscar before he sold his company, and it was the last piece he had of that life. Apparently, she had never made the connection that it was his whenever she saw it outside Kit's house. "It's a little much," he said with a shrug. "But it drives like a dream. You look amazing, by the way."

That last bit should have come much sooner, when she had done her appraisal of *him*, and he was starting to wonder just how out of practice he was with this whole dating thing. Was he going to end up making a fool of himself? Poor Madi needed someone who could hold his own, and all she had were the Wonder Boy extraordinaires who hardly ever lived up to that never-ending nickname.

"Thank you," she said without looking at him.

She did look good, though. He usually saw her when they were in a group, hanging out as friends, so she didn't put much effort into her appearance. Not that she ever needed to. She'd tried a little harder today, which begged the question: Was she more eager to attend this event than she let on? Was she actually hoping to meet someone? If that was the case, what was the point of dragging Oliver along with her?

She'd said he was backup in case she didn't meet someone, but what was he supposed to do if she *did*?

He grunted a little, reminding himself that this pretend date was not about him. This was about helping Madi, and there was no better reason to show up than that.

In the twenty-two years he had known Madi, he had never felt this out of place and awkward, and he didn't like the silence in the car. He considered turning on some music, but he had no idea which preset the radio was set to and worried what would start playing—probably something embarrassing, because luck had never been on his side. He could play music from his phone, but he didn't want Madi to think he was an unsafe driver as he pulled it up. Besides, they only had a few more minutes before they got to the address she'd given him, so maybe it would be best to start up conversation and hope he wasn't a total weirdo.

He had never been weird with Madi, and he wanted to keep it that way. The fact that she was his best friend's little sister made him want to keep himself in her good favor. His life had always had Madi in it, and he refused to let that change.

He cleared his throat, trying to relax a little. "So…"

"We should probably set some ground rules for this thing so Danny doesn't get suspicious," she replied. She didn't hesitate in the slightest, so she must have been thinking about this the whole time.

"Rules," he repeated. "Right. That's a good idea."

There were Kit's rules, and then he had his own rules for when he went on dates, but his rules wouldn't exactly apply when his date was Madison Morgan. He couldn't very well stick to "Kiss on the fourth date. Not before. Not after." Something buzzed to life inside his chest, like a little swarm of bees, and he cleared his throat as subtly as he could. Kissing Madi? No point in entertaining that thought.

"I think you and I can easily make this seem like a first date," Madi said. "It was harder with Cam, with him being so affectionate."

Oliver's hands tightened around the leather of the steering wheel. Since when had Cam been affectionate? Had he followed the rules? He made a mental note to confront Cam about that one, though he dearly hoped that conversation wouldn't turn into a reason to fight the man. Martinez was huge, and Oliver was…not. A personal trainer with a penchant for getting into fist matches versus a professional coder who'd never fought anyone at all wasn't much of a fair fight.

"So you probably shouldn't hold my hand," Madi continued. "Not on this date, anyway."

"Can I touch you at all?" It was more a question to get permission, less for clarification of boundaries. Never let it be said that he disrespected a lady.

Thankfully, Madi threw him a grin as he pulled into the park. "I'll let you decide that one. From what I remember, you're quite the flirt, and I'm curious to see if that's still true."

Oliver would never call himself a flirt. He was friendly. But if that was how Madi saw him, he supposed he could lay into the stereotype a bit. It would be a lot easier with Madi than it was with strangers on the street since he didn't worry too much about crossing a line with her. After a person plays so many rounds of chicken in the pool, he stops worrying about what a little touch of the hand might do to a girl. They had wrestled and fought and had tickle fights the way siblings often do, so he had considerably more freedom when it came to Madi.

Except when it came to holding her hand, apparently.

At least that also fell within Kit's rules; Oliver had never held Madi's hand before. *Huh.* That surprised him. Never held her hand in twenty-two years of knowing her? That couldn't be right.

As he slipped out of the car, he idly wondered what she would do if he skipped that step and moved into deeper intimacy. She outlawed hand holding, but would she condemn him for stealing a kiss?

That made him laugh internally as the bees buzzed a little stronger in his chest. He had no intentions of doing anything like that and never had. Besides, if he kissed Madi, Kit would most certainly kill him. And the other two would cheer Kit on, if not join in. If nothing else, Madi had a pretty mean right hook when she was angry.

The Boys had taught her well.

Madi was saying something as they climbed out of the car, but Oliver was distracted by the sheer number of people in attendance, all of them milling around the large park pavilion and in clumps on the grass.

Apparently, the single scene was hopping in Diamond Springs.

"Does that work?"

Oliver blinked. "Sorry, I missed that."

"I said we could stand here and pretend we just met so we're in the middle of a conversation when Danny gets here."

Oliver glanced at his car. "What happens when it's time to leave and it looks like you're going home with me?"

Wincing, Madi bit her lip and folded her arms around her middle. "I didn't think about that. I guess we just tell Danny we hit it off and want to go get ice cream or something?"

"Madi!"

Both of them turned as a man hurried up the sidewalk toward them. With the way Madi immediately took a step away from Oliver, he guessed this was Danny and their charade had just begun. So much for making a game plan.

"Hey, Danny," Madi said, suddenly bright and cheerful.

Danny matched her energy, giving her a wide smile as he came to a stop right in front of her and scanned the people milling around. "I'm glad you actually showed up. How are the prospects?"

Oliver tensed at the same time Madi did, though he was pretty sure he was the only one who noticed. Danny's smile hadn't changed. Oliver honestly had no idea why *he'd* tensed, but Madi had never been very social. Looking at a crowd of people as "prospects" probably freaked her out.

"Oh," Madi said, trying and failing to look excited about the crowd, "I hadn't really looked around. I've been talking to…Oliver."

Danny *did* notice that hesitation, looking back and forth between the two of them. "Did you guys just meet?"

"Yes," Oliver said at the same time Madi said, "No."

Their gazes met, and Oliver spent a whole lot longer than he probably should have staring at her, trying to figure out what her wide-eyed expression was supposed to mean. He was usually so good at reading her, but the weirdness of this whole thing had thrown him off balance and left him feeling useless. Which was great, since he was pretty sure she was asking him to help her. *What do I do?*

"Um." She tucked some hair behind her ear. "Oliver and I met at a…at a shoot a little while ago."

Did they now? Oliver raised an eyebrow at her until he realized Danny was looking at him again. "Yup," he grunted. "At a shoot. And we…"

"We just ran into each other again," Madi finished for him, sounding way too breathless for someone just standing there. Had she been this unconvincing on her date with Cam? "Crazy, right?"

"Crazy," Danny repeated, though he seemed more confused than anything.

Oliver didn't blame him. Madi had just flipped their flimsy narrative on its head, and there was no way it would hold up. "Should we get some food?" he suggested, hoping to change the subject before Danny wised up.

Danny and Madi both agreed, and Danny immediately started talking to a girl as she passed on her way to the food.

Oliver used the opportunity to grab Madi's arm and hold her back a second. "Uh, what was that?" he whispered.

She shrugged, looking anywhere but at him. "I don't know. I guess I didn't think I could pretend like I didn't already know you."

"But neither did you want him to think we were friends," he guessed. "Okay. So, what are we?"

As they got in line behind a guy wearing a Yankees hat, Madi bit her lip and seemed to think really hard about that question. "Casual acquaintances with the possibility of being more?"

The guy in front of Madi turned. "I'd love to be. Hi, I'm Terry."

Oliver immediately went tense again, the bees in his chest humming angrily. Though Terry looked relatively harmless in his baseball hat and shirt that looked a size too small, something about him rubbed Oliver the wrong way. He couldn't quite place the reason for it, but he strongly disliked him.

Madi, on the other hand, jumped right into conversation with the guy and gave him a smile almost as bright as the one she'd given Oliver.

Yeah, Oliver *really* didn't like him. Especially when Mr. Too-tight Shirt reached for the same dressing scoop as Madi so their hands brushed. He laughed and apologized, letting her go first, then went for the other dressing. Which meant he had absolutely touched her hand on purpose, and Madi hadn't even noticed. It was so obvious! But Madi probably liked the attention; she kept smiling and talking to the guy until he invited her to share a table with him.

A table that only had two seats left.

Oliver froze as soon as Madi sat down. He still didn't know what he was supposed to do if she found herself an actual date, but if she really thought Yankees Cap was her best option…

Either Madi saw something in Terry that Oliver couldn't, or she had terrible taste in men.

It was the way Terry had no concept of Madi's personal space that bugged Oliver. The longer he stood watching, the more he knew that was where the problem lay. There was a fine line between flirting and invading, and this guy was seriously toeing that line. Did Terry not see the way Madi sat stick straight, the way she did whenever she was uncomfortable? He probably hadn't given her a choice of seat, and she was too nice to be rude and say no.

And Oliver had been too busy watching Tight-Shirt Terry to notice her discomfort until now. Some friend he was...

"Hey, wanna come sit with us?"

Oliver glanced at the girl who nudged him with her elbow. She was cute, and if he weren't preoccupied with Yankees Cap sitting hip to hip with Madi despite having a few inches to spare on the bench, he might have even been interested in getting to know her better. The girl and her small group of friends all looked like they were here for a good time rather than to hunt down a husband.

But Oliver was here on a mission, and the guys would kill him if he failed. Besides, it didn't look like Madi could save herself this time. Hopefully she didn't hate him for making a rescue.

Giving the girl a smile, he moved over to where Madi was sitting, then put his hand on her shoulder. "Hey, Mads," he said. "What if we turn this into more of a picnic on the grass?" He jerked his head toward the lawn, where a bunch of others were already sitting, and did his best to ignore the glare Terry was giving him.

"I think she's good," Terry said gruffly.

"We can all sit in a circle and get to know each other!" the girl behind Oliver said, bumping him with her elbow again.

He was sorely tempted to turn around and raise his eyebrow in the way that had withered some of his past employees, but he refrained. He was here to keep an eye on Madi, and that meant keeping his focus on getting her away from Terry. They didn't agree on everything, but the Wonder Boys would definitely hate this guy and the way he was already possessive over Madi.

Oliver really needed to stop calling them the Wonder Boys in his head; no wonder the name still stuck around.

"Okay," Madi said after a painfully long pause, as if she'd already forgotten that this fake date was her idea. Oliver was fine if she wanted to get to know some of the guys here, as long as none of those guys were the pretend baseball fan who had probably never been to a game in his life. "Do you guys want to come sit on the grass with us?"

Most of those at the table agreed. Most of them were men and seemed to have picked up on the gaggle of ladies standing behind Oliver. As the group rose and headed out of the pavilion, Oliver reached for Madi's plate at the same time Tight Shirt Terry did. Oliver strengthened his hold on it as he made eye contact with his contender.

"I got it," Terry said.

"No need," Oliver replied.

Madi rolled her eyes in between them but was probably smart enough to know that offering to carry her own food would only make things worse. She had spent plenty of time around the Wonder Boys and their collective need to be the best at something; she likely knew the two of them would be standing there all day if she didn't say something.

"Thank you, Terry," she said at the same time she slipped her arm into Oliver's.

Oliver had to resist the urge to smirk triumphantly as he relinquished the plate. He'd gotten the better end of the deal.

Terry—Oliver felt bad for all the other male Terrys out there who were being poorly represented right now—wasn't happy, but he still carried Madi's plate over to the circle that had formed in the grass and took his seat on Madi's other side, way too close for someone who had given up the fight. He was still hoping to score. It was too bad it wasn't Cam on this date, because Terry definitely wouldn't have been so bold with the likes of Cam Martinez on Madi's arm.

Oliver liked to think he was in decent shape, but his daily runs and occasional climbs up the rock wall with Ben at the local rec center didn't exactly compare to Cam's beefy workout routine. The man was the poster child for great deltoids. Cam had stopped begging Oliver to sign up for training at his gym, but maybe if Oliver showed up and did a few sessions, he would stop thinking Oliver never tried.

To Oliver's relief, Madi stayed close to his side for the next hour and spent most of her time talking to other people in the circle and ignoring Terry. She was a lot more social than he remembered her being, and he wondered when that had changed. It had probably been a gradual thing, and it wasn't like he had been around her all that much since graduating high school.

The more he thought about that, the more he hated it. They'd lived in the same town for all but four years of their lives, and yet they only ever saw each other when they were both at Kit's house.

Oliver really should have made an effort instead of expecting introverted Madi to do that.

She had always been shy. She had few friends in elementary school and was always begging Kit and Oliver to let her tag along whenever they did anything at the house. Junior high was even worse, and not a single person had shown up to her twelfth birthday party. While Oliver hated all the kids who had ignored her invitation, he couldn't resent the fact that that birthday party was the reason the five of them had become the five of them.

"What about you, Oliver?" a girl asked him from across the circle, interrupting his thoughts. Apparently she had learned his name, though he didn't remember hearing hers. He'd been too focused on Madi.

"Sorry, what?"

She blushed. "What do you do for work?"

Oliver glanced around the group, trying to gauge their own levels of education and career paths. Some of them looked young enough to be in college and home for the semester, while others had more mature vibes, watching him with mild disinterest as if they didn't see him as either a potential date or a threat.

Then there was Madi, who watched him with furrowed brows and curiosity in her honey-colored eyes.

Oliver cleared his throat, suddenly worried what she might think of him even though she already knew he had sold his company. "I don't work," he muttered.

Terry scoffed, most of the girls in the circle got looks of disappointment, and conversation moved forward.

Not super great for the ego, but Oliver would survive. He always did.

With Madi distracted by some girl talking about her new job, Oliver hopped up to grab a bottle of water and went right back to trying to figure out what had changed Madi. What had made her so much more social than she used to be?

When the Boys went off to college, Oliver had worried about her. Her four best friends had left her behind, and sometimes he'd been tempted on the long weekends to drive back home and check on her. He might have, if it hadn't meant being in the same city as his parents. Even the proximity was too much back then. But he had called her a few times a semester, making sure she wasn't lonely. Not that she would have told him if she was, but those conversations had always been good ones.

College had been hard on all of them. Oliver had been lucky and had Ben attending a school only half an hour away from him, but Kit and Cam went clear across the country for school, states apart. The four of them only saw each other in the summers—interrupted by summer jobs and internships—and long holiday breaks. Madi had cried every time they had to leave, and honestly, Oliver hadn't coped super well either. After so many years of having his core group of people always around, it hadn't been easy to learn to be without them. He and Madi had that in common.

Now, Madi was all smiles and easy conversation, and he was proud of her for making strides in her life when it came to friendships. Standing at the edge of the pavilion with his water, Oliver watched her with a sense of contentment because this meant one of his biggest fears was gone. Whether or not she chose to start dating for real, at least she would never have to be alone. He hoped she would start dating, though. Based on the number of smiles she was getting from the guys in the circle, she could have her pick of them all, and lucky would be the man who got her attention.

As long as it wasn't bubble-bursting Terry, who had ignored all of Madi's attempts to put some space between them. She was several feet from where she'd started, but Terry was right by her side.

Oliver shuddered. Whoever Madi dated, he would have to be cream of the crop or the Wonder Boys would never allow it. Not that they had any say in the matter... But Madi deserved so much, and Oliver wanted her to be happier than she'd ever been. Maybe they would have to help her find the right guy, someone who understood her and saw beneath the surface.

Ben would probably be really helpful on one of these dates. Though quiet, Ben was the most personable out of all of them and had a way of making anyone feel comfortable around him. He would be the ultimate wingman at one of these and know exactly how to talk Madi up. Besides, he was the best looking one out of all of them, and that was sure to dredge up some jealousy for anyone who saw the girl he had on his arm.

Grabbing his phone, Oliver sent out a text to the group chat he had with the guys.

> Oliver: Anyone want to make bets on how soon Madi will be engaged?
>
> Kit: Excuse me?
>
> Cam: Yeah, what is that supposed to mean? I thought she was on a date with you today.
>
> Oliver: *picture of the people surrounding Madi*
>
> Oliver: She's having a grand time without me.
>
> Ben: Which one is Danny?

Oliver looked around, surprised to see Danny had disappeared. He'd been at the other side of the pavilion twenty minutes ago, still talking to that same girl he'd met at the beginning. He must have slipped away with his new lady friend.

> Oliver: Looks like he skipped out. Mission accomplished?

As his phone lit up with a call from one of his college buddies, Oliver checked to make sure Terry hadn't crossed any lines. Madi seemed to be doing just fine, her smile firmly in place, so he answered the call.

It wasn't like she needed him.

FIVE

HALFWAY THROUGH A GAME OF partner tag, Madi realized she was actually having fun. At a singles barbecue. The game involved everyone standing in pairs and one person chasing another until they linked up with a pair and forced the person on the other side to start running. It had given her a chance to get to know a lot of people of both genders, many of whom came to these things often. She had actually considered going to the karaoke night someone was throwing in a couple of weeks before she realized she had a reception to shoot that night.

The consideration alone surprised her, and it gave her a strange thrill she couldn't describe. Maybe she was even more interested in dating than she'd thought? It was too bad she didn't have the time.

The current person being chased latched onto Madi's arm, leaving her partner to hurry off before she got tagged. "Looks like it's my lucky day," he said, and Madi tensed.

It wasn't that she didn't like Terry, but ever since Oliver suggested they go sit on the grass, he had been too much in her bubble for her to be comfortable. That, and his cologne was way too strong. He might have smelled nice if it didn't smell like he'd dumped half a bottle over his head.

"You're very fast," she said and tried to pull her arm a little out of his grip so they weren't so close.

He held her a little tighter, giving her a grin as he watched the two runners skirt around groups of people and switch pairs. "I was always pretty good at sports," he said. From the looks of him—his clothes left little to the imagination—he hadn't played one in a while. "So, what do you do, Mandy?"

She silently willed the person being chased to come join her pair so she could be free of Terry and the spot of ketchup on his shirt. He must have been too busy staring at Madi to notice when it fell from his hot dog. The man liked to stare, and her skin itched just thinking about it.

"I'm a photographer," she said through a grimace she couldn't hold back.

Where had Oliver gone? He'd been on a phone call before the game started up, and she hadn't seen him since. He was supposed to be her date, and the only reason she'd been comfortable at all when she got here was because she had someone extra familiar at her side. Someone who would have her back no matter what. Danny had abandoned her the moment he saw that cute girl on the way to the food line.

Terry managed to pull her even closer. "A photographer? No way! You know, I actually did some modeling back in the day. Maybe you've seen some of my stuff."

Madi glanced at him, trying to picture him being a model for anything but adult Lego sets. She couldn't see it. "Oh, I'm not that kind of photographer, so I doubt it. Could you loosen your grip a bit? I need to be able to run if someone—"

"Do you wanna get out of here?"

Madi's eyes went wide, the hair rising on the back of her neck. "What?"

Terry leaned in close enough that the brim of his hat bumped her forehead. "There's this cozy little chocolate shop down on Fourth Street, and one of the booths has a light out, so it's extra dark."

And this was why Madi had refused every time Danny tried to get her to come to one of these. There was always that one guy who thought everyone was there to get some easy action. Tugging her arm free, she considered how blunt she wanted to be, and then someone suddenly appeared on her other side, which meant it was Terry's turn to run. He was so caught off guard, however, that the person who was "it" tagged him before he'd even taken a step. The whole group laughed as he fumbled to get his bearings and chase after the new person.

"What on earth did you say to him?"

Madi jumped when she realized it was Oliver on her other side, and the relief that washed over her burned in her face as she met his eyes. "Where have you been?" she breathed.

His eyes followed Terry with suspicion as Terry tried unsuccessfully to catch three different people in the span of ten seconds. Madi had always loved Oliver's eyes, a hazel mix of brown and green that seemed to change color with his mood. Most of the time they leaned toward green—most of the time he was in a good mood—and they were always bright. Like they danced with excitement no matter what he was doing.

Today, in the evening sun, they were practically gold beneath his sandy brown hair.

"Sorry my call took so long," he said and leaned in, as if they were having a private conversation. He actually smelled a good deal like Terry, only Oliver had mastered the art of subtlety. It was just enough that she wanted to move in closer to breathe in the clean scent and better iden-tify it. "By the way, Danny is gone."

Madi's heart stumbled a bit as she looked toward the pavilion. "Cheese sticks," she cursed. She was supposed to be his wingwoman, and she had done nothing to help him avoid blowing things with the girl he met. "When did he leave?"

"Not sure," Oliver replied, and his voice wobbled, like he was trying not to laugh. "I'm sure he's fine, though. Did you just say what I think you said?"

A girl suddenly latched onto Oliver's other arm, but Madi didn't move, even though she knew it was ruining the game. She was too worried about Danny and was busy grabbing her phone so she could text him.

"Sorry," Oliver told the girl, sounding very charming and sincere. "We have to take off, so you won't find any rescue here."

As Madi's thumbs flew across her screen, Oliver led her off the field and toward his ridiculously nice car. The car that everyone had been talking about all night, though he didn't seem to have noticed. Nor did he notice the dozen disappointed girls behind them. Madi glanced back once she sent her text, and it seemed the two of them were quite the interesting topic, because the game had stopped entirely as soon as they left.

"I hope you're okay with leaving," Oliver said. "I've ac-tually got some work to do, but I don't really want to leave you here on your own with Tight Shirt Terry on the loose."

Madi couldn't tell if he had joined in the game to get her attention or to rescue her, but she was glad he did. So much socializing had left her exhausted, and it felt like she'd just shot an entire wedding without the satisfaction of a fat paycheck to go with it. Though she should have thanked him and told him she was perfectly fine to head out, she latched on to a different topic.

"Work?" she asked. "I thought you said you didn't work anymore."

"I work."

"On what? Kit says you haven't done anything since you sold your company. Aren't you, like, crazy rich now?" That was a stupid question. The answer was right in front of her as he opened the car door for her. But as he walked around the front to get to his own door, he put his hands into his pockets and let his shoulders droop a little, which was a strange way for Oliver to be when he was always so tall and confident.

Maybe her comment had been a little harsh. If Oliver didn't have to work to live, then more power to him. She was pretty sure her brother was just jealous; a teacher's salary didn't exactly bring in the big bucks. Things had always come easier for Oliver than they did for Kit, and Kit had always been a little envious of Oliver's cushy life. Not that he'd ever admitted that out loud.

Mr. and Mrs. Hamilton were rich. Super rich. Though Madi hadn't been to Oliver's childhood home, she knew from Kit that it was the kind of house that had a gated driveway and extra security and a personal chef on staff. Oliver had always had the latest gadgets and fanciest toys and didn't have to worry about student loans.

He had never flaunted his parents' money, though. In fact, if Kit had never said anything, Madi wouldn't have guessed he had such a different childhood from hers.

Once Oliver had settled into his seat, he sat there for a moment instead of pushing the button to turn the car on. "I'm not actually that rich," he said after a moment. "I mean, I'm alright, but it's not like I'm my parents or anything.

They sort of cut me off when I didn't pick the school they wanted for me. Not that I wanted their money in the first place."

Madi might have commented on that if he hadn't kept talking, speaking a little faster as if to cover up that last bit about being cut off.

"And I don't have anything to spend my money on, so it's not doing me much good."

It had been so long since Madi really had a one-on-one conversation with Oliver that it felt like she didn't know him all that well. It was a strange feeling, and she really didn't like the way her heart ached. They used to be so close. They used to tell each other everything.

Though she wanted to ask him about the thing with his parents, she could tell he didn't want to talk about that. "Is that why you've been traveling so much?"

He shrugged, though he seemed to breathe easier with the subject change. "It passed the time, but it's starting to lose its appeal. Not as much fun when there's no one else there to see it all with you."

Madi hadn't been anywhere. She'd always had another wedding to shoot and editing to do, but she'd dreamed of the places she would go once she'd "made it."

"So, what's next?" she asked, trying to keep her disappointment in herself out of her voice. "Now that you've sold your company, what's your plan?" She was curious to know what someone as smart as Oliver would want to do with his life.

Shrugging again, he reached forward and started the car without answering.

Madi wondered what that would feel like. She basically had her life mapped out for the next decade, and she had always had a plan for herself. It made her feel steady, even if it didn't leave much room for being spontaneous. Or vacations. She would have to work on the spontaneous part, considering coming to the barbecue had actually been a lot of fun—outside of dealing with Terry.

He had caught her attention at first—he was a decently good-looking guy—but the closer he'd gotten, the more uncomfortable she'd become. Madi liked her personal space, which was probably one of the reasons she liked being behind the camera. It made for a great buffer. It wasn't like Madi had met a ton of guys over the years, but she was pretty sure they tended to act more like Terry than not, and she shuddered at the thought of having to deal with more overeager guys if she decided to try dating for real once summer was over.

If only there were more guys like the Wonder Boys. They'd always recognized when she was uncomfortable.

Her phone chimed with a text as Oliver pulled out of the park and onto the street, and she breathed a sigh of relief when she saw it was from Danny. "You were right about Danny."

"I'm guessing he didn't get kidnapped?"

"He went out for ice cream with that girl he met at the barbecue." Madi was happy for him, though she wished he would have told her sooner. Then she could have avoided the terrible tag time with Terry and all the alliteration that came with it. What had happened to double dating?

Another text came in right as she asked herself that question.

> Danny: I was so nervous that I dumped my ice cream into her lap. She's cleaning up in the bathroom right now, and I'll be lucky if this goes anywhere.

"You know," Oliver said, "that's not a bad idea. Want to?"

Madi frowned, trying to remember what she'd said. "Go on a date with someone from the barbecue?" If he was talking about Terry, he was completely crazy.

Chuckling, he pulled the car over in front of a little ice cream shack in a grocery store parking lot. "Get ice cream," he said, though he hardly needed to clarify at this point. "That was our cover story anyway, wasn't it?"

Madi was torn. She wanted to spend some more time with Oliver, especially because she'd had to pretend to enjoy talking to strangers instead of him, but going to the barbecue had meant she couldn't spend all that time working on some much-needed edits of last weekend's wedding. But when Oliver gave her a crooked grin—she'd never been able to resist that smile of his—time with him won out.

"Okay," she said and slipped out of the car, telling herself that she would only stay for fifteen minutes before she had him bring her home.

Thankfully, the need to be quick helped with her decision-making this time around, and she chose cookies n' cream because it gave her a taste of chocolate without being too rich to eat with gusto.

"I got it," Oliver said as she reached into her pocket for her card. He handed his card over before Madi could argue, though she still tried.

"Because you're filthy rich?"

He rolled his eyes. "Because that's what a good date should do. I haven't forgotten my duty."

"You know, technically I was the one who asked you out, so I should be paying. I make pretty decent money, you know."

"I know."

"You do?" Madi followed Oliver over to the grass on the nearby parking strip since all the picnic tables outside the shack were full, and she waited for him to explain. When he kept his focus on his ice cream cone, she smacked his arm.

Chuckling, he shook his head. "If you knew how often Kit still talks about you, you'd be embarrassed. It's like he thinks we'll forget who you are if he doesn't bring you up at least twice a meeting."

Heat flooded her cheeks at that, but it was a nice reminder of how much she loved her brother. He was such a stickler for rules and stability that he could be difficult to deal with at times—Kit and change did not mix well. The man held to things like super glue, like the little leather bracelet he'd worn without fail since junior high. But he really was the most fiercely loyal person she'd ever known. Without him, she never would have met the other Wonder Boys, and her life would have been a whole lot darker without them in it.

Kit had basically collected the boys. Oliver was first. He and Kit had been in the same kindergarten class, and Kit had stepped in when Oliver was teased by everyone else for wearing a suit and tie the first day. Apparently, his parents had thought he needed to make a good first impression, not understanding that a five-year-old should have been wearing Power Ranger t-shirts and pants with holes in the knees from too much time on the playground.

Ben was next. They were eleven at the time, and Ben's massive family of seven kids meant he was often forgotten in the chaos. Kit had seen him sitting alone at recess and invited him over to play video games after school, and Ben spent practically every afternoon at the Morgan house after that.

Then there was Cam. Cam and Kit got into a fight at school one day when they were thirteen. Madi wasn't sure why since no one would tell her, but they'd been sent to detention together for three weeks and had come out of it as best friends, practically inseparable.

And when they were fourteen, and Madi was twelve, the boys threw her the best birthday party she'd ever had.

Kit had found her in her closet, where she'd been crying because no one had showed up to her party, even though she invited everyone from every single one of her classes in the hopes that at least a few of them would show up. But they hadn't, and Kit had sat just outside the closet while Madi sobbed for a full twenty minutes. He didn't say anything, but him being there had brought a calmness to her heart until she felt she could move forward and pretend none of it had happened.

But then she'd gone downstairs and found Ben, Cam, and Oliver waiting for her with huge smiles and a promise to be the best birthday party guests in the world. They all donned tiaras, decorated cupcakes with pink frosting, and played all the stupid games Madi had hoped would make her classmates like her. They sang a terrible rendition of "Happy Birthday" and cheered when she blew out the candles, and then Ben had handed her a poorly wrapped box.

Inside that box had been a camera.

Everything about that day had changed Madi's life. It had started her on the path to her career, and it had given her three honorary brothers to add to the one she already had, making her sure that she had the best family in the world.

Madi sighed with happiness as she thought about that day. "Thanks for the ice cream," she said quietly. "And for coming with me to help Danny. It really means a lot."

"Anytime," he replied, and she knew he meant that. Like the others, Oliver had never lied to her, and he would always be there whenever she needed him. Just like he'd been their entire lives.

SIX

OLIVER WAS PACING. HE HADN'T paced in years, and he didn't like what this restless energy could mean for his future sanity. When he paced, it meant he didn't have a solution to a problem, and right now Oliver's life was pretty much perfect. AKA he didn't have a problem needing a solution. AKA he had no idea why he was pacing. And that only made him feel the need to pace more.

He had dropped Madi off last night with a wave and a promise to be available the next time she needed someone, and after knocking out a simple coding project, he had played some video games before going to bed, imagining that every alien he killed was a certain guy in a Yankees cap. Maybe not the best way to get some catharsis, but it did the trick. Oliver had been prepared to send the guy packing if he got too close to Madi, but that phone call from an old college buddy had thoroughly distracted him, leaving Madi to defend herself. She'd done pretty well on her own, but Tight Shirt Terry deserved a good punch in the nose from someone.

Oliver paused in his pacing. Maybe that phone call was the reason he was worked up. His buddy had mentioned something about getting in on the ground floor of an up-and-coming tech company, and he wanted Oliver to buy in.

It wasn't that Oliver didn't have the funds, and he liked the idea of helping a budding business in such a competitive market. He'd picked up a bunch of freelance coding work over the last few years for that reason. But he didn't have the motivation to dedicate his time to something like that, and therein was the real issue. That, combined with Madi's question about what was next for him, and now he was pacing.

Maybe the guys were right. Maybe Oliver didn't try because he didn't *want* to try. Not until he found something worth doing. Unless he was passionate about something, it was so hard to find a balance between putting enough energy in it to avoid disappointing anyone, and losing himself in it.

Finding a solution to this problem wasn't going to be an easy one, and Oliver had been trying for three years to come up with what to do next. A few hundred laps around his living room weren't going to help anything, especially since his run that morning hadn't done him any good. He liked to run most mornings to clear his head and get his thoughts pumping, but this problem seemed to have a stronger hold over him than most.

He needed something deeper, something to really get him moving and take his mind off the uncertain future. He needed a way to work out his frustration over not having an answer for Madi.

"Cheese sticks," he cursed and grabbed his keys. This was a terrible idea, but it was the only one he had.

A few minutes later, he was pulling into the parking lot of the gym where Cam worked, hoping he wasn't about to make a huge mistake. Cam would absolutely not go easy on him, even if he was a beginner. Though it took him ten minutes of pacing the parking lot before he worked up the courage to go inside, he put on a calm and confident expression—the kind he had used in board rooms when dealing with companies ten times the size of his own—and marched up to the counter.

It wasn't hard to spot Cam. He was deep in a training session with a woman who had to be seventy years old, but she was squatting with a good deal of weight on her shoulders and making Oliver sweat prematurely. Was that what he would be up against?

When Cam looked up a moment later and saw Oliver standing there, his confusion pulled his eyebrows together. He grabbed another trainer, likely to get her to take over with the old lady, and then he crossed the gym to the front desk and folded his massive arms across his ridiculous chest. There was nothing small about this man. "You lost, Hamilton?" he asked in his deep voice.

Oliver swallowed. He wouldn't let Cam intimidate him. He couldn't. Recalling childhood memories—like the time they went camping and Cam was so convinced he heard a bear that he slept in a tree all night—was the only way he would make it through this. "I was thinking it was time I start doing a little more with my workouts," he said. His voice cracked, and he mentally slapped himself for choosing *this* gym and *this* trainer when he could have gone literally anywhere else.

He cursed his endless need to prove himself.

Cam narrowed his eyes. "You gotta sign up for a membership if you want my help."

Oliver was prepared for that. "Okay."

"You have to pay for the whole year."

He was less prepared for that part. Though he saw the girl at the desk open her mouth to say something—probably to tell him that they actually only charged month-to-month—

Cam shot her a glare that kept her mouth shut. He was trying to call Oliver's bluff and get him to admit that he was only here because of what Cam had said at their last Wonder Boy meeting.

Oliver really needed to kill that whole Wonder Boy thing.

Keeping his gaze locked on Cam's and doing his very best to stay strong, he tried to silently tell his friend that he was willing to try in his life. He had to prove to Cam—to himself—that he wasn't just a lazy washout with no ambition. That he was willing to put in the effort when it mattered.

Then, when something worth pursuing came along, he could jump right in and hit the ground running.

"Fine," Oliver said and slapped his card down on the counter. He almost flinched when the girl told him the total for a year of personal training, but he managed to stay impassive. Mostly. It was a good thing Oliver was decently wealthy, because Cam was apparently making an obscene amount of money with each training session. Until this moment, Oliver hadn't realized how lucrative Cam's profession could be, and he wondered if Cam had ever considered opening his own gym so he didn't have to share those profits.

"Are you sure you're ready for this?" Cam asked, definitely too excited for Oliver's liking.

But Oliver stood tall. He was willing to do what it took, and he would prove that, even if it killed him. "Bring it, Martinez," he said, desperately praying this wouldn't actually kill him.

Sometimes, after a good rock climbing session, Oliver walked out of the climbing gym with a stiffness in his shoulders and his muscles tired and sore. He often got back from his runs with very little energy, and he was proud of himself for pushing beyond his comfort zone and getting himself to a new level of fitness. The pain was a good indicator of hard work.

Oliver had never known pain until this moment.

He was honestly amazed he made it back to his car after Cam finished with him, and he collapsed into the seat and considered taking a nap right there in the parking lot because he wasn't sure he would be able to turn the steering wheel and drive himself home. Though he was pretty sure Cam had pushed Oliver harder than he would have a regular client, it was no wonder the man was as huge as he was.

Oliver would need to sleep for three days before he would be able to do anything that required movement.

Just as he was about to turn his car on and attempt the drive home, his phone lit up with a call. Oliver smiled when he saw it was Madi, but he was not eager to lift the phone to his ear. Honestly, he wasn't sure if he could. Tapping the button to turn the car on, he waited for the bluetooth to connect, then answered the call. "Hey, Madi."

"Oliver? Are you okay? You sound breathless."

Oliver sent a silent curse to the heavens and hoped it would reach Cam quickly. "No, I'm fine. What's up?"

"Um."

Immediately on high alert at the edge in her voice, Oliver sat up a little. Then regretted the movement. "What's wrong?"

She took a long time to answer, during which Oliver peeled out of the parking lot and onto the street, even though he had no idea where she was. And then she let out a shaky laugh.

"I need your help," she said finally. "If you're not busy."

"Help? Madi, where are you?"

Why was there so much traffic? Oliver weaved between drivers who clearly didn't understand the urgency of an emergency.

"At my studio."

Her studio? "What's going on?"

"My assistant is out sick, and…"

Oliver eased his foot off the gas a little. Getting a speeding ticket wouldn't get him to Madi any faster, and she sounded a little calmer now than she had a moment ago.

"I have a huge family coming in for a session," she continued, "and usually my mom comes in to help if I need it, but she's in the middle of a rotary club meeting that'll last for hours. You're the only person I could think of who has the afternoon free. I'm desperate, Ollie."

He should have been angry that she got him all worked up for something that wasn't an emergency at all, but he wasn't. Besides, this was Madi Morgan. She only asked for help if she really needed it, so maybe it was an emergency. "What can I do?" he asked, altering his course a little to bring himself back to his apartment. He was not about to show up to Madi's studio covered in sticky sweat and smelling like someone had pushed him to every limit he had.

"I promise it's nothing complicated. I just need someone to help calm the chaos while I try to get everyone into place. And it's totally fine if you can't help. I can make it work. I just thought…"

"I'll be there." Oliver slid into his space in the parking garage and started working up the courage to move. Thank goodness his building had an elevator, or he would never make it up to the fourth floor. "Give me half an hour, okay?"

"Thanks, Ollie. I knew I could count on you."

Her praise gave him the push he needed to get himself to the elevator and up to his apartment. Though he struggled to get his arms to rise high enough for him to wash his hair, he pushed through the pain and exhaustion and forced himself to get as clean as he possibly could. He even attempted to shave, cursing himself for not doing that this morning, then slipped into some dark jeans and a green short-sleeved button up.

He doubted she would care what he was wearing, and it wasn't like this was another date, but he didn't want Madi to think he didn't sometimes try with his appearance. Once upon a time he had always put in the effort, and it felt good to do a little more than the bare minimum. It made him feel like he was working toward something instead of going nowhere.

He chugged a protein shake as he drove across town to her studio, questioned why he had never been there before now, then hurried up to the door and pulled the door open (with a good deal more strain than his ego would have liked).

Madi looked up from her camera when the door chimed, and her huge smile made the anxious pounding in his heart worth it. "You came."

He crossed over to her, doing his best not to look like his knees were about to give out from under him. "Of course I came," he said. Then he looked around, taking in the large prints that hung on the walls. She had everything from individual portraits to full wedding party shots, and she even had some pet portraits and landscapes thrown in. "Mads, these are amazing." He'd always known she was a good photographer, but these were next level.

"Thanks. I've had a lot of practice."

"You have a lot of *talent*," he countered. It was no wonder she was doing well for herself. "So, how can I help?"

She walked him through the studio, showing him props and backdrops, as well as a mini fridge with waters for her clients while they waited. She mostly needed him to help coordinate the placement of the family members since she wanted to be behind her camera and directing things rather than moving back and forth trying to get a sense of balance.

Oliver was grateful that was something he could do without a lot of movement.

The family arrived a couple of minutes after Madi finished her explanation, and she wasn't kidding when she said it was a big family. Oliver, who was an only child, had thought Ben's family with the nine of them was overwhelming, but these people kept coming, filling the small space of Madi's studio until there was barely room for anyone to move around.

Oliver tried to count them and figure out who was related to whom, but he stopped counting after twenty and gave up on the relation thing when he realized seventy-five percent of them were redheads. They were clearly all related to the same person, probably the older woman whose steely gray hair still had traces of the red she once had.

"Is this everyone?" Madi asked the family matron, who glanced around and shrugged.

Oliver couldn't imagine having so big a family that he couldn't keep track of them all. But that didn't mean he didn't love the idea. Someday he hoped to have several kids who could call Madi's parents Grandma and Grandpa because he couldn't picture his own parents wanting anything to do with their disappointing son's children. Who could have three fantastic uncles who spoiled them rotten and tried to turn them against him. Who could make him feel like he'd done some good in the world and wasn't doomed to follow the trend history had set with his awful parents.

Okay, so maybe he was more ready to let go of casual dating than he'd thought. That future sounded amazing.

"If everyone could go stand over there..." Madi stood on her toes, trying to catch the attention of screaming children and the grown adults who ignored them. "I'd like to... Ollie, can you whistle or something?"

Oliver scrunched his nose up. "You know I can't whistle," he said with mock offense. "I can't believe you would bring something like that up."

Sighing, Madi tried shuffling the closest people in the right direction, but the chaos of the family only seemed to be growing. "Excuse me!"

Oliver dearly wished he could whistle, but try as he might, that was one talent he had never been able to acquire. He did, however, have a childhood full of shouting matches to see who could be louder between him and Kit, and Oliver had most often been the champion.

"Hey!" he shouted as loudly as he could.

The chaos immediately stopped, and though Madi jumped, she sent him a grateful smile and climbed onto a chair. "If I could have all of you go stand at the backdrop, then we can get started. Oliver, let's put Mrs. White in the middle there."

For the next ten minutes, Madi rearranged the massive family by telling Oliver who to move as she looked from the vantage point of her camera. Though he was glad he didn't have to use his arms much, his legs had started to wobble, and a stiffness had settled into his shoulders that wasn't going to go away anytime soon. Each step was harder than the last, but he gritted his teeth and did his very best to pretend he was perfectly fine, even though his limbs burned with the effort of propelling him around the group.

Madi was amazing. She took so many pictures that Oliver wondered how she ever had time to go through them all, but he imagined she got some really great ones by snapping photos in between the staged moments. She knew exactly what she was looking for as she placed each person in the perfect spot so everyone could be seen, and she had a confidence he had rarely seen in her. This was her calling, and he couldn't help but beam at her, proud of her for being brave enough to go for it.

He was so glad he could be of use to her, even if it was just shuffling people around, and he praised his body for holding out and pushing through the pain.

Until Madi asked him to hold the reflective circle thing.

He swallowed, looking at the size of the fabric-stretched hoop. It didn't look all that heavy, but... "You want me to hold it where?"

"Over your head. I just need to get some better lighting on that left side."

Oliver bit his lip. He could do this. It wasn't that big a deal, and he could lock his elbows overhead and hope for the best. As soon as he lifted the reflector, he knew he was in trouble. His shoulders complained, his biceps burned, and he cursed Cam again because it was like his friend had known that he would need to do something like this today.

"A little higher," Madi said.

Oliver clenched his jaw and closed his eyes tight. He could do this.

"A few more minutes, and we'll be done!" Madi sounded so happy.

Oliver thought his arms were about to fall off.

"One more big smile!" Madi's camera clicked away until she finally said, "And that's it!"

And Oliver collapsed.

He was probably being dramatic, but at this point he didn't care. The ginger family gasped as he went down and sprawled across the floor, and he might have been embarrassed if Madi hadn't appeared overhead with wild concern in her dark eyes.

"Ollie!" She put her hands on his face, practically leaning on his chest as she got close enough to make sure he was okay. Had she always smelled so good? She smelled like vanilla cupcakes and sprinkles. Did sprinkles even have a scent? "What happened?"

He grinned. She had always had a kind heart, and her stuffed animals had had plenty of doctoring over the years. "I'm fine," he said with a chuckle.

"You just fainted."

"Technically I collapsed. There's a difference." He would know. "I promise, just give me twenty minutes down here, and I'll be good to go." Assuming he was ever able to move again… With the current situation, he was perfectly content to stay where he was. Oliver's personal bubble was a good deal smaller than Madi's, but he would let her invade it any day.

Lifting his head just enough to get a good look at all the people peering down at him, he smiled at them as well. "Just step over me," he told them. "Thanks for coming in."

Though Madi didn't seem to believe him as she forced a tight smile, she at least waited until the family had cleared out and left them alone before she went back to freaking out. "Ollie, talk to me. Are you okay? What happened?"

He closed his eyes, tempted to take a nap right there on the floor. There was something utterly calming about the way Madi pressed her warm hand against his chest. Part of him wanted to pull her closer just to get more of that feeling. "Cam happened."

He expected confusion, but instead she laughed and sat on her heels next to him when he looked at her again. "You did a training session with him." It was not a question. "Was this the first one? That one is the hardest; I couldn't walk normal for a week."

Oliver let her grab hold of his hands and pull him into a sitting position, though his abs were as sore as the rest of him and would probably make even breathing difficult for the next couple of days. "You've trained with him too?" he guessed.

"A few years ago. Before my business really took off and took all my time with it." She grinned, though Oliver wondered if a part of her missed those early days, before she was so busy. He hoped she wasn't taking on too much, but he didn't know how to tell her that without sounding like he was telling her how to live her life.

He would hate that as much as she would.

These dates, whatever their reason, were probably stretching her limited free time to the max.

"I don't remember the last time I actually worked out," she said with a sigh. "Unless wrangling toddlers counts. And I guess I usually get, like, twenty thousand steps when I do a wedding without an assistant, so there's that."

Talking about working out was making his body hurt worse, so Oliver changed the subject. "I can't believe you're doing well enough to have an assistant on your payroll," he said. "That's amazing, Mads."

She turned red as she glanced at him. "I have three, actually. But one just went on maternity leave, and the other has classes on Monday, Wednesday, and Friday. Emily was my only option today, until she got sick. Thanks again for coming to help. I get really stressed with these big ones, and you know how I am with strangers."

Madi's whole job was dealing with strangers, and from the looks of things she was doing just fine. Oliver grinned at her and looked around the studio again, taking it all in. "You're doing great," he told her. "And if you ever need another assistant, I'm there. Just maybe not on training days."

"Deal. Can I buy you lunch? As a thank you."

Oliver was about to say he needed to get home to his very soft and comfortable bed where he would stay until morning, but Madi spoke again before he could even open his mouth.

"Actually, that wasn't a question. I'm taking you to lunch. Come on, you big weakling." She grabbed his hands again and used her own weight to pull him up. He nearly fell over again—thankfully she caught him—and they stood there a moment in each other's arms, smiling at each other.

This was what Oliver had been missing over the last several years. Being around Madi was making everything feel normal again, and he badly needed that. He badly needed a reason to try again.

SEVEN

RUNNING INTO DANNY WHILE ON her lunch date with Oliver was not part of the plan, and Madi cursed her bad luck when she realized Danny had spotted the pair of them as they waited for a table at the pizza parlor. Now it looked like she and Oliver were on another date, and Danny would definitely read too much into that. Two dates was big on its own; two dates in two days was monumental. At least she could count this toward the bet now that Danny had seen her.

"Act casual," she hissed at Oliver as Danny hurried over to them.

Oliver immediately sank onto the vinyl waiting bench, probably too tired to hold himself up anymore. At least he looked casual…

"Madi, what are you doing here?" Danny gave Oliver a glance but tried to keep his focus on her, which she appreciated. He was letting her explain the situation rather than speaking his assumptions out loud.

She decided the truth would probably be best in this case. "Oliver was helping me at the studio today because my assistant called in sick and he had the afternoon free. What are you doing here?"

Danny turned bright red and glanced back at the booth where he'd been sitting. "Hannah and I are on another date, actually."

"Hannah?"

"We met at the barbecue last night."

"So she agreed to a second date?"

He shrugged, turning a little red. "Today was her idea—a way to get past first impressions—but I'm pretty terrified I'm going to mess things up again. I've been on edge since we started talking last night, and my palms are sweating like crazy. See?" He held his hands up, then cringed and tucked them into his pockets. "You showing up is kind of perfect. Hey, are you okay, Oliver? You look a little tired."

Oliver huffed a laugh, his eyes closed as he rested his head against the wall. "Never better," he said.

Though he frowned at Oliver, apparently still concerned, he generally wasn't the sort to get into other people's business if he didn't know them well. It was great for weddings, but not so great for Madi because he did know her well, which meant he saw no problem with saying, "Do you guys want to join us? We have a booth, and it could be fun to get to know each other a little better." Based on his pleading expression, he really didn't want Madi to say no.

Madi couldn't tell if Danny's date heard his offer, but she definitely didn't look all that thrilled about him talking to other people instead of sitting with her. Maybe, in this case, it would be better to leave Danny on his own and hope he didn't follow past trends.

"Oh, we don't want to intrude," Madi said. "We can wait for a table."

The hostess cleared her throat just then, her expression apologetic. "You're probably looking at an hour wait," she said with a wince.

"I think sharing a table is a great idea," Oliver said and forced himself up to his feet with a grunt. Cam must have really done a number on him with the way he could barely move. "Dan, good to see you again."

Danny frowned a little and glanced at Madi as if asking her if Oliver was always this standoffish or if it was just today.

Honestly, Madi didn't have much of an answer to his unasked question. She knew full well that Oliver knew Danny's name—she had never once called him Dan—but she wasn't sure what calling him by the shortened nickname was supposed to accomplish. In fact, she wasn't sure if Oliver knew either since he seemed to be trying to figure Danny out as they stood there awkwardly.

Wanting this moment to end, Madi agreed to share, then followed Danny back to his table. "Hi," she said when Danny introduced her to Hannah, and then she frowned a little because Hannah was definitely eyeing Oliver with interest as they slid into the booth.

And Oliver, being as friendly as he was, gave Hannah a smile right back that made her blush.

Oliver had always been able to get girls to swoon with his perfect smile, and Madi didn't like the way Danny frowned at Hannah. Nor the way Hannah examined Oliver more closely. Hoping it would help keep Hannah's interest off of Oliver and get her focus back on Danny, Madi took hold of Oliver's hand and twisted their fingers together.

Oliver immediately froze, staring down at their hands on the table.

And to Madi's dismay, so did Danny. This whole afternoon was getting out of hand. Or *in* hand, technically. Madi was just as distracted by Oliver's hand as he seemed to be by hers, and the whole table was sinking into deep awkward. She'd never held his hand like this, with their fingers intertwined, and there was something… right…about how they fit together. How some sort of electricity hummed between their palms.

Suddenly she was wondering why she'd never been worried about personal space with Oliver. Things were so easy with him, but that was probably because of how long they'd known each other. Twenty-two years was nothing to laugh at.

How had it taken this long to hold his hand?

Thank goodness for the waiter showing up to take their orders and diffuse the awkwardness.

While Danny and Hannah waffled over whether they should get a pizza to share or get their own, Madi breathed a sigh of relief over having chosen this particular restaurant. She had lost track of how many times she and the Wonder Boys had come here, which meant she knew all their favorites. And Oliver was the easiest out of all of them; he always got the same thing she did.

"We'll share a Hawaiian pizza," she said. It was the only decision she never floundered on.

Danny suggested he and his date also share a pizza, though they had to split the toppings down the middle because they couldn't agree.

When the waiter left, Hannah giggled a little and turned her attention to Oliver again, leaning forward. "Ew, you like pineapple on your pizza?"

Oliver tried to match her, though his body didn't let him move as easily. Madi made a mental note to reprimand

Cam for pushing Oliver too hard. Oliver was trying, at least, and that was a big deal. He'd been coasting for a while.

Still, he would probably do better to sit still instead of trying to get closer to someone else's date.

"I love pineapple on my pizza," Oliver said with a wide grin. "Don't you?"

"No, thank you. Fruit should never be on something like pizza!"

"I agree," Danny said quietly. He was squished into the corner of the booth, and he looked miserable as Oliver and Hannah continued their conversation, his lips pulled downward and his eyes locked onto the table. This probably wasn't what he'd had in mind when he suggested double dates.

"What about French fries dipped in your milkshake?" Hannah said.

Oliver grimaced. "Gross. String cheese dunked in applesauce?"

Hannah couldn't have laughed more obviously if she tried. She was really pushing this interest in Oliver. "People do that? That's disgusting."

"Hey, Danny," Madi said at the same time she squeezed Oliver's hand as hard as she could. "Remember that wedding where they served chicken with chocolate pudding?"

Danny perked up a little when Hannah turned to him. "How could I forget that?" he said. "I had a bite, and it actually wasn't too bad."

For the next twenty minutes, Madi did her very best to keep Danny talking, which forced Hannah to be nice and keep her attention on her date. She wished she had a way to tell Oliver he needed to stop being a distraction—Danny seemed to really like Hannah—but their booth was too small to do it subtly, and she didn't want to add to his pain by kicking him under the table. Not that she wasn't tempted.

So, when their pizza arrived, Madi said she had a lot of work to do at her studio and asked if they could take their pizza to go. Oliver was clearly confused based on the way he stared at her, but he was smart enough to keep his questions to himself, especially when Madi still kept their hands tightly wound together and even leaned into him a little as they walked out. Danny would question the depth of their relationship and probably lead to a headache the next time they talked, but she hoped Hannah would realize Oliver was off the market and she should keep her focus on Danny.

When they reached her car, Oliver set the pizza on the hood and said, "What was that about?"

"What?"

He wiggled his fingers, which she'd freed once they got outside. "I thought you said hand holding was off-limits."

"I thought you were smart enough not to flirt with another girl while on a date," Madi grumbled back.

To her surprise, Oliver's eyes went wide with genuine shock. "I wasn't flirting."

Madi rolled her eyes, deciding she needed pizza to fuel her annoyance. Grabbing a slice, she slid all the pineapple onto his slice, then stole half his ham to replace the fruit on her piece. "Of course you were. It's, like, your default setting whenever there's a pretty girl around."

Oliver picked off a piece of pineapple and chewed it slowly, as if truly thinking over what she'd said. "I promise I wasn't flirting," he said eventually. "You would know if I was. And I'm not stupid enough to do that to the girl I'm dating. Even if this was only our second fake date. I'm not that kind of guy."

Madi sighed. Though she wanted to keep being annoyed with him, she knew she had to believe him. Oliver had never lied to her before, and she couldn't imagine him doing it now. "Okay. But maybe stop being so cute."

He grinned. "You think I'm cute?"

Groaning, she shoved him hard enough that he lost several chunks of pineapple from his pizza.

"Hey! That's the good stuff!"

Madi rolled her eyes. "I have no idea how you like pineapple on pizza. It's so sweet and chewy and gross."

He took a massive bite of his pineapple-laden pizza and grinned. "It's so good."

"I'll stick to my ham, thank you very much. You could just start asking for double pineapple, you know."

"Why do that when I have people like you to double it for me? It's a win-win situation in my opinion. In case you haven't noticed, ham pizza isn't a thing. You're missing out on one of the joys of life, Mads."

"I am perfectly happy with my life how it is."

"Are you?"

Well, that was a loaded question, and Madi watched Oliver finish off his slice, as if hoping to figure out by looking at him if he really wanted an answer to that question. He watched her right back, and his expression didn't give much away. She was happy, and she wanted to tell him so, but something held her back. She wasn't sure what it was, exactly, but something felt a little off. Like a crucial component of her life was missing, so everything was out of balance.

"Thanks again for your help today," she said instead of answering his question. Hopefully he wouldn't read into that. "I'll take you back to your car so you can...do whatever it is you do with your day."

They were both quiet as she drove back to the studio, and Madi wondered if Oliver had an answer to his own question. Was he happy? And if he wasn't, how could she help him get there?

EIGHT

FOR A GUY WHO HAD managed to build up an extremely successful company while still in college, Oliver had no good ideas. He'd been thinking the last few days about starting something up. Something small, so it didn't get out of hand like the last one. But apparently his brain had turned to mush over the last three years and was completely empty.

He'd been lying on his couch for two hours now, failing to come up with a direction to go as he repeatedly tossed his TV remote in the air.

It didn't help that he had Madi's face in his head. She kept looking at him with disappointment, the way she did when she expected better but knew she wouldn't get it. She had only ever looked at him that way once before, and it had been enough to push him to fix the thing he'd done wrong.

And now Oliver was thinking about junior year of high school, and he didn't like it.

He had gotten into a disagreement with Kit. It happened fairly often since both of them were pretty strong headed, but that time had been different. Kit had liked a girl, and Oliver had gone on a date with her to try to talk Kit up. Kit hadn't believed him when he told him the reason, and he'd accused Oliver of trying to steal her out from under him.

Oliver had hated how quickly Kit lost his trust, and he'd accused Kit of being small-minded.

They didn't talk for two weeks.

It had taken Madi stepping in and forcing the two of them together to talk things out, and she'd given them both the stare of disappointment, the one that dug down deep beyond his defenses and unlocked a humility he hadn't realized he had until that day. Oliver had apologized first for not telling Kit his plan, and Kit had been soon to follow with his own apology for being so suspicious.

They'd been closer than ever after that, true brothers, until they parted ways for college after graduation.

Madi had given him that same look yesterday at the restaurant, and it was eating Oliver from the inside out. He hadn't been flirting with Hannah. He barely remembered what she looked like, and if he was going to flirt with anyone, it would be Madi.

The remote slipped through his hand, whacking him in the face.

The thought of flirting with Madi brought back that strange buzzing sensation in his chest, and Oliver frowned at the vaulted ceiling, grabbing the remote again and gripping it tight. Why in the world would he flirt with Madi? Beyond these fake dates, he had no reason to see her any differently than he had his entire life. He had never flirted with Kit's sister because he'd never been allowed to.

Wait, did that mean he had *wanted* to flirt with Madi?

Oliver groaned. This whole thing was getting confusing and messing with his head, and they'd only been on two fake dates.

When a text came in, Oliver eagerly abandoned his strange thoughts about the girl he'd known his whole life and opened up the group chat he shared with the guys.

Ben: I'm a little confused about this pretend date thing. Cam, Oliver, can you weigh in?

Cam: Confused how? She needs dates. I think it has something to do with her coworker being lonely, but she made it sound important.

Kit: As far as I know, she needs you guys to step in because she doesn't have a choice on whether the dates are happening.

Kit: I don't like the sound of this Danny guy.

Cam: He seems fine to me. He just wants Madi to be his wingman, I think.

Ben: So why is she the one setting up double dates?

Oliver sat up straight. Madi had willingly set up a date with Danny? What was she playing at? There had to be more to this than what she'd told any of them since she had seemed pretty reluctant about all of this.

Oliver: She's what?

Cam: She's probably just choosing something better than whatever Danny comes up with. He's harmless, but he's a weird dude.

Ben: She picked bowling tonight. SHE picked it.

Oliver: *GIF of a confused little girl*

Oliver: Doesn't she hate bowling after that one time we went after graduation?

Kit: You mean when she got her finger stuck in a ball and the fire department had to come cut her out? Yeah. I don't think she's been since.

Kit: Oliver, you and I need to do a little recon.

Cam: What about me?

Oliver: And when Danny asks how you know us?

Kit: It's a miracle you got through your date without having to lie. We can't have you blowing this for her, whatever it is.

Cam: Fair point.

Ben: You guys will have to pretend not to know me, or
    this is going to get really weird.
Oliver: Duh.
Cam: Oliver has no muscle in his arms, so he'll need
    one of those kiddie ramps.
Oliver: I've always wanted to use one of those. Can I
    get the bumpers too?
Kit: Please don't embarrass me. This is a stealth oper-
    ation, and a 28 yr old using the bumpers is just
    sad.
Oliver: You're only saying that because you're afraid I'll
    beat you.
Ben: You guys are idiots. Madi is doomed.
Cam: You said it, Ben.

Oliver waited for the conversation to continue, but apparently that was the end of it. Ben was right to be confused, especially if Madi really had been the one to pick bowling. And why would she take Ben with her when he had the most difficult schedule to work around? Why wouldn't she take Oliver?

"Cheese sticks," he muttered. It was the whole flirting thing. Oliver's friendliness must have made Madi think she needed someone else to be the buffer so Danny could try to woo his lady without someone else distracting her.

But Ben?

That was going to be a disaster. The man was handsome, charming, and so nice that he made the rest of the world's male population look bad. Every girl in high school had been in love with him, and he had nearly failed one of his classes in college because the girls kept asking him out on dates and he was too kind to say no for the sake of studying. He was also way too shy to ever start dating someone, but that was beside the point. All he had to do was smile to get someone to fall for him.

Oliver grabbed his phone and typed out a text to just Ben. He had to make sure that the quiet man didn't make things even worse like he had with his roommate's girlfriend senior year of college. Oliver had been over at Ben's apartment when she broke up with her longtime boyfriend and confessed her love for Ben, claiming she had caught on to his hints.

Really, he had just been nice and said hi to her whenever she came over.

> Oliver: Whatever you do, do NOT smile at or talk to Danny's date.
>
> Ben: That is a very specific warning. What's wrong with her?
>
> Oliver: She's not the problem. You are.
>
> Ben: Is that supposed to make sense to me?
>
> Oliver: Remember Scott's girlfriend?
>
> Ben: …
>
> Ben: Oh no.
>
> Oliver: Oh yes.
>
> Ben: What do I do?
>
> Oliver: Be the best date Madi has ever had. And don't even LOOK at Danny's date.

NINE

MADI WAS NERVOUS. IT WAS stupid to be nervous about a double date with people she already knew, but she was so nervous she had had to use the bathroom twice already while waiting for Ben to show up because her anxiety apparently resided in her bladder. It didn't help that she'd picked bowling as their activity. Though the odds of her getting her finger stuck in one of the balls were slim, the chances were never zero.

At least she would have Ben here tonight, and that kept her from calling Danny up and bailing on him.

She still wasn't sure why she'd been so eager to set this up in the first place. Danny had said something about a lucky streak with Hannah and wanting to see her again before his good luck ended, and Madi had had a relatively open evening…

She told herself it was to help Danny endear himself to Hannah. Danny wasn't the smoothest guy out there, but he had a whole lot to offer, and Madi knew that if he got a proper chance to show Hannah what he was really like, she would never look at another guy like she had yesterday.

But really, Madi wanted to win the bet sooner than later. Did that make her a bad friend? It wasn't like she was lying. Ish. These *had* been dates, even if they were never going to go anywhere, and Danny's only real rule was he had to be there too so he could get some good dates in as well. The sooner she got in her ten dates, the sooner she could stop stressing about all of this.

If Danny managed to start dating someone, all the better. If he had a person, he might forget Madi didn't have one and let her live her life in peace.

Even if that sounded nice, knowing someone would be there through the good and bad.

Besides, spending the last couple of days with Oliver had reminded her how much she missed the way things had been when they were growing up. She missed the guys, and though she was slowly falling further behind on editing, she'd liked getting to spend more time with the Wonder Boys.

When Ben finally showed up in the same beat-up car he'd been driving since high school, Madi breathed a sigh of relief. If anyone could show Danny how to be on a date, Ben could. He had a way of making everyone comfortable.

"Sorry I'm late," Ben said as he jogged up to where she waited by the front doors. He wrapped her in a quick hug and glanced around. "So, where's this Danny guy?"

"He's running late too. I guess he and Hannah went out to dinner first." Madi smiled at the thought, though she hoped Danny hadn't done anything crazy at dinner. This was three dates in a row, though, so that had to be a good sign.

"Should we reserve a lane?" Ben suggested. He must have seen how full the parking lot was already, even though it was a Thursday.

"Good idea."

Apparently, bowling was more popular than it had been when Madi was younger; she'd expected the alley to be pretty much empty. She had hoped for it, actually, in case she managed to trap her finger again. She would prefer to not have a big audience for that.

Madi paid for two games up front, so they wouldn't lose their lane before they were ready to be done, and then the pair of them grabbed some shoes and headed to their spot at Lane 12. Ben went to grab some balls as Madi laced up her shoes, and when he returned, she eyed the neon green ball he held out for her. It was pretty light, but not so light that she thought she should be insulted. But she still bit her lip as she stared at the thing.

It's not going to eat you, she told herself, but past experience made that hard to believe.

Grinning, Ben set the balls in the return rack and sat to change out his own shoes. "Don't worry," he said. "The holes are huge. Even Cam would be able to fit his fingers in there."

Madi nearly threw her arms around him but restrained herself. She couldn't let Danny see something like that on a "first date" with Ben. "I can't believe you remember that," she breathed.

The bowling incident had been a decade ago, and the boys had been pretty concerned about the fact that they'd just graduated high school and only had a summer left together before they all moved away. And sixteen-year-old Madi had gone and ruined their fun by getting her finger stuck so bad that it swelled up and got stuck even worse. She'd felt awful, but the Wonder Boys had stayed with her and distracted her until she could be cut loose.

Ben bumped his shoulder into hers. "Of course I remember that. Besides, that was the same night Oliver broke his hand playing Whack-a-Mole, so it was a pretty memorable evening. Injuries all around."

Madi had practically forgotten about that part. She and Oliver had stayed up most of the night commiserating over their shared pain while the other boys passed out in front of the TV during their Star Wars movie marathon. They had talked about all of their favorite Wonder Boy memories that night too, and Madi was pretty sure Oliver was as ready to leave them behind as she was. As in not at all.

So why was he so often missing now?

Shaking away the worried fluttering that settled in her stomach at the thought of Oliver being lonely, Madi tried to keep her focus on the present moment. She needed her full focus to keep up the pretense. "Thanks for coming tonight, Ben. It really means a lot that you guys are all willing to do this."

"Anything for my favorite adopted sister."

Madi laughed. "I'm really glad you specified, because I'm pretty sure your four actual sisters would have gotten really mad at me if you called me your favorite sister."

Ben's family was huge, which was why he'd spent most days at Madi's house. While Oliver and Kit would get into trouble and play stupid games like seeing who could be the loudest, Ben would hang out in the corner and do his homework. Sometimes he helped Madi with hers, and he was the only reason she passed sophomore English.

He loved his family, but when he was right in the middle of seven kids, he too often got lost and forgotten. Thanks to Kit, he actually had a place at the Morgan house whenever he was there.

Danny and Hannah finally appeared, apologizing for being so late, then hurried off to grab some shoes and balls so they could get started. After Madi made introductions, Hannah offered to put in their names on the board.

Madi pulled Danny aside and raised her eyebrows at him. "Three days in a row? This is looking promising."

Danny shrugged, though he turned somewhat red when he glanced over at Hannah as she typed. "I hope so. She's seriously cool, and she keeps saying yes to meeting up again despite my blunders. I'm taking that as a good sign."

"It's totally a good sign!"

Before she could head back to her seat, Danny grabbed her arm and gave her a small smile. "Seriously, thanks for being such a good friend, Madi. I know you're crazy busy. But these double dates make it so much easier to be myself because there's less pressure, so thanks."

Madi grinned, giving Danny a quick hug. "You've been such a good friend at all these weddings; it's the least I could do. Without you, I would be so nervous around all the other vendors."

"Not to mention you've been on more dates in the last week than you've been on in the last year," he said with a wink.

More than in the last four years, Madi corrected silently. Maybe Danny was right, and maybe it was time she really put herself out there. But that wasn't something she could think about until summer was over.

"I'm really here so you have to pay for my photos," she joked, hoping he didn't think that was the only reason. "Let's go bowl."

"I gave us all nicknames," Hannah said when they returned.

Madi glanced up at the screen, frowning a little as she tried to figure out who was who. "I'm guessing Danny is The Godfather."

"And Hannah is Baby Spice," Danny guessed. "She's in culinary school."

That meant Madi had to be Top Gun.

"You know, because you shoot pictures?" Hannah said with a shrug. "I dunno, it sounded cool."

Ben scrunched up his face as he looked at the final name. "Why am I Pretty Boy?" For how smart he was, he never really understood how handsome a man he was. Which was nice, because he never had an ego, but Madi was pretty sure it left him feeling embarrassed in moments like this.

Like when Hannah said, "Yours is obvious," and giggled a little.

Madi felt terrible. Turning to Danny, she tried to tell him with a look that she hadn't intended for this to happen. In fact, she had brought Ben because he wouldn't be as flirty as Oliver, but she'd forgotten how women tended to gravitate toward him.

She'd never understood that, actually. All of her brothers were good-looking guys, but in different ways. Cam was so strong and steady, and his darker skin always made Madi a little jealous because her skin refused to tan. Aside from his glasses, Kit was like Madi when it came to appearance, but he was the tallest of the bunch and always dressed well. His confident smile had gotten him plenty of attention over the years. And yes, Ben was handsome as well. His Japanese family had given him bold features that combined well with his natural softness, giving him an approachable look.

It was Oliver who was the best-looking one out of them, Madi had always thought. With those bright hazel eyes of his beneath sandy brown hair, his easy, ever-present smile—and ridiculously defined jawline—should have been pulling all the girls his way. The problem was he knew he was attractive, and most girls must have picked up on that big ego, choosing instead to go after the much humbler Ben.

Now that Oliver spent more time away from the Wonder Boys, Madi didn't understand why his schedule was the most open. Surely he went on plenty of dates.

For some reason, she didn't like that thought.

"Should we get started?" Danny suggested. He ignored Madi's silent apology, and she hoped he wasn't mad at her for bringing along dates who set a high bar for him to meet.

It wasn't like Danny was below their level in any way. He just had to believe he could compare, and he'd be fine.

By the eighth frame of their first game, Madi was starting to feel a little better. Ben pretty much only talked to her, ignoring Hannah entirely unless she spoke directly to him, and he kept throwing out casual compliments to Danny. He must have picked up on Hannah's interest in him and was doing what he could to fix the situation, for which Madi was extremely grateful.

"You're a wedding planner, right? You must be pretty good if you're working the same weddings as Madi."

Madi heard Ben ask Danny that question as she was setting up her next throw, and she smiled. She missed Danny's response, but she returned to her seat just as Ben remarked on how impressive it was that Danny had the rest of the year booked out already.

"You must do a good job," Ben said, then hopped up to take his turn.

"You didn't tell me that," Hannah said, her eyebrows high. Then she turned back to Ben, though her interest seemed to have shifted more to Danny than before. "What about you, Ben? What do you do?"

He pursed his lips together as he picked up his ball, probably deciding how honest he wanted to be. "I'm an assistant manager at O'Reilly's Fun Center," he said with a chuckle. "I mostly work the mini golf counter."

Hannah was far cozier with Danny after that, as if she hadn't realized Danny owned his own business rather than working for someone else like Ben did.

Though Madi was a little annoyed that Hannah wasn't nearly as interested in Danny until after she learned he was successful, she hoped things worked out between the two of them. From what she could tell, Danny was really into Hannah, and he deserved to be happy.

At the end of the first game, Danny and Hannah went to grab some sodas for everyone, and Madi wrapped Ben in a huge hug. "You are the best kind of friend a girl could have," she told him. "You really didn't have to fall on your sword like that."

He shrugged. "I figured it would help."

"You also don't have to be ashamed of your job. Maybe it's not the most glamorous, but it's a job."

Except for during his college semesters, Ben had worked at the same place since high school, and he had been at the same level as assistant manager since he was eighteen. His easy enthusiasm had slipped away after he mentioned his job, which probably meant he was thinking about how his life hadn't really gone anywhere. They'd had conversations about it over the years, though he always lied and told her he was fine with his current situation.

Madi had tried to tell him so many times that he deserved a job where he was appreciated and valuable, but she had never known what to say to him. To be honest, she didn't even know what he wanted to do with his life, and she wasn't sure if he did either. He had a degree in illustration, but she hadn't seen him draw in years.

"You'll find a great job someday," she told him and kissed his cheek, hoping she sounded genuine.

He gave her a little smile as the other two returned. "Yeah," he agreed. "Someday."

Madi hoped someday came soon, because all of her brothers deserved the best in life.

TEN

APPARENTLY KIT THOUGHT BEING STEALTHY meant they had to be in disguise, which was why he and Oliver showed up to the bowling alley in baseball hats and sunglasses.

"You're an idiot," Oliver said for the fifth time that evening, and he pulled the glasses off his face when they reached the counter because he couldn't see a thing with them on.

Kit scoffed. "It works in the movies."

"I can't believe I ever thought you were smart," Oliver replied. It wasn't like they were superheroes on the run from their villains, and wearing sunglasses inside had only drawn more attention their way instead of the opposite, as Kit had planned.

The looks-too-young-to-have-a-job kid behind the counter seemed to think they were there to cause trouble, glancing between the two of them before sending a quick look toward his manager over at the bar.

"We're here to bowl," Oliver said before Kit could open his mouth and say something stupid, like, "We're here to investigate some of your patrons."

Kit had done it before, and something told Oliver he would do it again. The guy really was intelligent—he had to be, to teach third graders—but sometimes he took things a little too far. Kit rarely did anything halfway, and there was still some mischief lurking beneath the calm and collected adult.

Oliver tried to get the old Kit out now and then, but now was not the time for shenanigans.

"You'll get the last open lane," the employee said with obvious relief. "How many games?"

Oliver glanced at his watch. Madi and Ben had been here long enough that they had probably already bowled one game, and he couldn't imagine Madi would be able to play more than two. She was likely already behind in her work after three dates in a row.

"Just one," he said, rolling his eyes when Kit ducked behind the counter as someone who looked similar to Madi walked past. "Will you stop embarrassing yourself? I thought that was my job."

"We just have to make sure we keep our distance," Kit muttered as he straightened back up and adjusted his hat lower over his forehead. "My sister is a lot of things, but spontaneous is not one of them. She's doing this for a reason."

Madi had never done anything without a reason, and it was one of the things Oliver loved about her. "Will you relax?" he told Kit.

"You'll be on Lane Thirteen," the teenage employee told them, then asked for their shoe sizes.

They were halfway to their lane when Kit grabbed Oliver's collar and dragged him to a choking halt. Oliver was about to ask why when he saw them.

Ben and Madi were on the lane right next to theirs.

"Cheese sticks," Oliver muttered, and he wondered if there was a way he could convince someone to switch lanes with them. But from the looks of things, everyone was in the middle of their games, so that wasn't going to work, and they couldn't sit at the bar and watch the proceedings without looking like total creeps.

"Gonna have to call an audible," Kit said.

"I don't know what that means."

"You really need to brush up on your football."

"I'm good." Oliver had never gotten into sports, and thankfully he had always had Madi to hang out with on Superbowl Sundays and the World Cup. "So, what's the plan?"

"We'll have to play it off as coincidence." Kit grimaced at that, looking around the bowling alley as if hoping for some other solution to present itself. There were very few circumstances under which Kit was willing to stray from the plan like this, and those situations always involved helping someone else. Although, Oliver wasn't entirely sure if this was helping anyone. "Or we could go back home and let Ben handle this."

Oliver might have agreed if Ben hadn't put his arm around Madi just then. And Madi didn't stop him. In fact, she took hold of his hand on her shoulder and laughed at something he said in her ear before she dropped her head onto his shoulder. Whatever happened to her personal bubble?

"What's he doing?" Kit asked.

Oliver's hands slowly curled into fists, and he had the strangest urge to punch Ben in the face because he was blushing and clearly enjoying himself. This was *definitely* going against the rules. "I have no idea."

Kit growled a little and pulled off his hat. He was clearly as unenthused by Ben's actions as Oliver was. "I think it's time to do some bowling."

"I couldn't agree more," Oliver replied.

They each grabbed the first ball they saw and hurried over to their lane, ignoring the four people to their left as if they had no idea they might run into someone they knew. They would have to bring attention to themselves at some point, though. Madi and Ben seemed a bit too cozy to notice anything around them.

"Oh hey!" Kit was the first to acknowledge what was happening, and Ben and Madi both jumped and broke apart at the sound of his voice. "Fancy running into you guys."

While Kit was fully focused on his sister, Oliver glanced at Danny to see what he thought about the interruption. The man hadn't noticed yet, as he was busy helping Hannah improve her bowling approach.

Madi rose to her feet. "What are you guys doing here?" she hissed through clenched teeth.

Ben offered a glare, even though he had already known they would be showing up. He'd probably hoped they had forgotten or changed their minds.

Oliver lifted up his ball, regretting the motion because he hadn't exactly recovered from yesterday's training session. Why had he grabbed the heaviest ball there? "We're bowling."

"Oh, hey Oliver." Danny had returned, and he gave Oliver a wary smile. "What a fun coincidence." He glanced at Ben and offered a brief shrug of sympathy because Madi was on a date with someone else.

Oliver tried to look sad about it instead of angry. "Hi, Danny. Nice to see you again."

At Danny's side, Hannah seemed unable to decide what to make of the current circumstances, especially because Madi was completely red. Maybe this whole thing had been a bad idea.

No maybe needed. This had *definitely* been a bad idea.

"Hey," Danny said, holding out his hand to Kit. "I'm Danny Camper."

Kit had to pry his jaw open, apparently, because it took him a second before he managed to speak. "Kit Morgan."

"My brother," Madi offered weakly.

Danny brightened a little. "Oh, what a crazy coincidence. You said you and Oliver met at a photoshoot, right?"

"Yeah," Oliver and Madi said at the same time. They really should have gotten their story straight before they showed up at the barbecue, and Oliver was regretting this decision to come to the bowling alley more and more with every passing second.

This was awkward. Ben looked like he wanted to chase them from the alley, but he couldn't because he was supposed to have no idea who Kit and Oliver were, and Danny glanced between Oliver and Ben like he couldn't decide who to root for.

"I didn't realize you guys were so into bowling," Madi practically growled. "Isn't it a school night, Kit?"

Oliver spoke without thinking. "We're starting a bowling league."

Kit whacked him in the back of the head.

And for some reason, Oliver was suddenly starting to enjoy himself. He figured he was already in deep water so he might as well swim a little farther from the safety of Honesty Shore. "You guys should join us!" he said. "Madi, I know how much you love bowling."

If looks could kill…

"Thanks for the invite," Ben said, "but I don't have time to join a bowling league."

Madi jumped right on that excuse and said the same thing, punctuating her remark with a glare that made Oliver want to laugh. He'd missed those glares of hers, though he wasn't usually on the receiving end.

"Maybe we should get back to our game," Danny offered. "It was nice meeting you, Kit. Your sister is one of my best friends at these weddings we work together, and she's awesome."

"Uh huh." Kit narrowed his eyes. Clearly he didn't know what to make of Danny Camper, just like Oliver, and he was going to use this game of bowling to his advantage.

"Enjoy your game," Ben growled.

Oliver intended to.

Not that Oliver had been much of a bowler before, but being completely sore from his training session with Cam hadn't improved his game. In fact, he was doing so poorly that he really was tempted to grab one of those little ramps that the kids used because he could barely lift the ball, let alone throw it.

Then there was the fact that Ben and Madi weren't being subtle about how much they were enjoying their little "date." Their laughter and banter were completely distracting, and Madi was a whole lot more outgoing than she usually was. Was she putting on an act for Danny's sake? Or was this the real Madi when she was extra comfortable with someone?

Ben had spent almost as much time as Oliver had at the Morgan house, but Oliver couldn't remember him spending all that much time with Madi specifically. When did they get so close? Or maybe Oliver had just been completely oblivious. Had he taken his Madi time for granted over the years? That could have been him sitting there next to Madi, discussing the rules of bowling and laughing about each failed roll. But instead, he was on another lane entirely, stuck with a guy who analyzed each approach with careful calculation.

And not just his own approaches.

When Oliver rolled his eighth gutter ball in a row, Kit walked up to his side and watched it roll down the gutter and disappear.

"Spill it," he said, clapping a hand on Oliver's shoulder.

Oliver cringed. "What?"

"What's bothering you?" Kit had relaxed during this first half of their game, so he must not have seen Danny as a threat anymore, and that had given him a chance to pay more attention to Oliver, apparently.

Oliver figured it wouldn't work, but he tried it anyway. "Cam really messed up my shoulders yesterday."

Narrowing his eyes, Kit tried to figure out the real answer by staring at him, but at least he didn't push the issue. He knew Oliver well enough after all these years to know that there was little point in trying to get him to talk if he didn't want to.

They weren't as close as they used to be, but they were still friends. That would never change.

It wasn't like Oliver didn't want to open up to Kit. They used to talk about all sorts of things, and Oliver had rarely been afraid to tell Kit things that he wouldn't tell anyone else. But this was different. Oliver wasn't even sure what was bothering him, though he suspected it had something to do with the way Madi was acting.

Actually, no. It was with the way *Ben* was acting.

Oliver watched as he gave her a congratulatory hug when she got a strike, and to an outsider it would look like a couple of people on a date, exactly as it should. But Ben should have known better.

Ben had made the pact, just like the other two.

So far, all of them had kept that promise. But Ben was really pushing that line, and it made Oliver's blood boil. This was exactly the sort of thing they'd wanted to avoid.

When Madi and Ben got into a sort of tickle fight at the end of their game, Kit put a tight hand on Oliver's shoulder and seemed to be thinking the same thing.

"I'm calling a group meeting," Kit said, already reaching for his phone.

Oliver didn't always agree with Kit, but he was absolutely on his side with this one. They had to protect Madi at all costs. Even if it was from themselves.

ELEVEN

HANNAH HAD AN EARLY CLASS in the morning, so Danny took her home shortly after they finished their second game. Kit and Oliver left quickly too, and though Madi was tempted to suggest they play one more game, her arms and hips were pretty sore from doing an activity she hadn't done in so long. That, and her guilty conscience was reminding her she had a lot of work she'd been putting off.

She was a lot more relaxed now, though, as opposed to during the game. Knowing Oliver was right behind her had made her nervous, to the point where she was pretty sure she had acted completely over-the-top, pretending she was having the time of her life. For some reason, she'd wanted Oliver to think she was enjoying herself with Ben. Which she was. But she'd wanted Oliver to have no reason to think she would have preferred him over Ben.

Even if that wasn't exactly true.

Ben walked her to her car, and when they reached it, she threw her arms around his shoulders, holding him tight in the way she'd done for years. Ben had always given great hugs, though they never came close to what her dad had described. Ben's hold didn't shut out the world, as nice as it was. "You were amazing tonight," she told him. "And I had so much fun. It's been forever since I did something like that, and I really needed it."

"I thought so." He gave her his signature smile, the one that apparently made girls swoon. Madi had always loved that smile, but not for the same reason. That smile meant Ben was genuinely happy, and it had taken a while after she first met him before she saw it.

Most people didn't think much of Ben. He was good at fading into the background once people got over the initial shock of his attractiveness, and no matter how many women giggled when he was around, they hardly ever talked to him because he never made a first move. Without a fancy job or an outwardly strong personality, he generally kept to himself because he thought it was better that way. It wasn't, and Madi had always loved his quiet warmth. Hopefully someday soon someone else would too.

"Whatever happened with that girl you were crushing on a while back?" she asked him.

He immediately turned bright red and dropped his gaze to the ground.

It was still going, then? "Have you even talked to her yet?" she asked with a laugh.

Shoving his hands into his pockets, he shrugged. "The only time I ever see her is at the grocery store, and it's not like I know anything about her except she likes to shop on Tuesday mornings. What would I even say?"

Madi deeply wished Tuesdays weren't her busiest studio day. She would totally go shopping with him so she could see the mysterious beauty and help him find a way to start up a conversation. "You say hi," she told him, poking him in the ribs. "It's not that hard."

"Easy for you to say."

It wasn't, considering she hadn't made any vendor friends until the day she met Danny. But she wouldn't tell Ben that. "Come on, Ben," she said. "You're handsome and charming and the sweetest guy on the planet. There's no way she would turn you down if you asked her out. She's single, right?"

Another shrug. "She doesn't wear a ring, and she only seems to buy food for herself."

"See? You know more about her than you think. If you can make date night with me this fun, imagine what you could do with her when you're actually into her!"

Ben shrugged yet again, clearly not as convinced as Madi was that he had a chance. "Yeah, well, you're easy. And you already know me. I have nothing to prove to you."

"If you think you have to prove anything to the person you love, then she's not the right person for you."

His head snapped up. "Who said anything about love?" he stammered, turning an even deeper red than before. He was saved from Madi's teasing when his phone buzzed, and he pulled it out of his pocket with a frown. "Apparently I'm late for a club meeting," he said, then lifted the phone to his ear. "Will you guys calm down? I'm coming."

Madi couldn't hear enough to tell who was on the other end, but he sounded angry. It was probably Kit since Kit was a major stickler for rules; he liked to be in control. And he was growing increasingly angrier as Ben got more and more annoyed while he listened.

"I know," Ben almost snapped. He listened a moment longer, then rolled his eyes. "I know that too." When Kit said something else, Ben closed his eyes as if he'd never wanted anything more than to be done with this conversation.

When he finally hung up, he looked weary to the bone.

"What did my brother do this time?"

Ben smiled a little. "Nothing. He was making sure I understood something."

"What something is that?"

This time he gave her a full grin as he said, "Under no circumstances am I allowed to kiss you."

Madi snorted a laugh. *Oh, Kit.* "Is there any danger of that?" she asked Ben, mostly to get him to blush again. "Calm down. I know your heart is taken by the angel in aisle five, and you've already exceeded my expectations for tonight."

He understood what she meant, glancing at the bowling alley as if Danny and Hannah were still inside. "Do you think she'll give Danny a chance?"

"I hope so. He's a good guy; he's just not the smoothest. And it's hard to tell from the outside because he'd never try to talk himself up. So thanks again for coming tonight. It really means a lot."

She unlocked her car door and let Ben pull it open for her, but before she could climb inside, he placed a gentle hand on her arm. "I would kiss you, you know," he said quietly. "If you wanted me to."

Madi grinned. Once, when she was fifteen, she asked him what it was like to hold hands with someone. She hadn't ever been on a date, but there was a boy in her history class she liked. She hadn't been brave enough to ask the kid out, but on the off chance he read her mind and realized she was crushing, she wanted to be prepared for the date that would hopefully come.

Though they'd been doing homework together, Ben had smiled at her and offered to hold her hand the rest of the night so she would know firsthand. Literally.

Madi snorted in the bowling alley parking lot. "I hate to break it to you," she told Ben, "but someone beat you to the first kiss a while ago."

Ben raised an eyebrow. "Was it any good?"

"No."

"Then my offer still stands."

Madi shook her head. "Even I know Kit would go berserk over that. Besides, that's not really something I would do just because, as much as I like you, Ben. If I'm going to kiss someone, it's because I really want to." She put her hand on Ben's arm and squeezed. "You're going to make someone very happy someday."

He immediately blushed scarlet, taking a step away from the car. "Someday," he agreed, though he didn't seem all that confident. "Have a good night, Madi."

"Goodnight, Ben."

When she got home, she reluctantly turned on her computer to get some editing in before she crashed. "No more dates this week," she told herself as it booted up. And she would probably have to put next week off-limits as well just to get her focus back. As much fun as she was having with the Wonder Boys, she couldn't afford to slack at work.

She'd made a name for herself by being extra quick to send finished photos to her clients. If Danny's bet ruined her reputation, having her photos on his website wouldn't do her much good. Bowling and ice cream were fun, but so was having a thriving business.

Though, perhaps she didn't want her business to thrive quite as much as she'd used to. If she cut back a little, or found a way to make the editing stage faster, she could do more things like tease Ben about the girl he'd loved from afar for several weeks now. She could talk to Cam more and figure out why he was so against commitment. She could hold Oliver's hand again and understand why she still felt the tingle of his touch a day and a half later.

"*Focus*, Madi." She'd already been staring at her computer for a few minutes without doing anything.

But then her phone buzzed with a text, and she let out a sigh. Maybe she should just resign herself to not getting any work done tonight.

> Danny: You seemed really happy tonight. Are you going to go out with Ben again?

Her comfort level with Ben was going to make things more difficult than she wanted. Danny might think they were getting serious, and that could jeopardize anything Ben might start with the grocery store gal. "Friendzoning" Ben would limit her options for these fake dates, but she had already gone on four of the ten dates. It wouldn't be long before she won the bet.

Something told her Danny would take her familiarity with Ben and try to push her into something more if she didn't do something about it now, and she really needed a break. However small.

> Madi: I don't know about Ben. He's a great guy, but I don't think we would work well together romantically.
>
> Danny: There was some serious chemistry tonight, Madi.

Otherwise known as Madi's panic-induced flirting because of Oliver…

> Madi: I do like him, but he feels more like an older brother than anything.
>
> Danny: Ouch. Pretty sure that's worse than the friendzone.

> Madi: Ben seems like a level-headed guy. I'm sure he'll
> be fine.

And he *would* be. Though they spent so much time together doing homework while the other Boys goofed around, Ben had never been anything more than an adopted older brother. He could have made an excellent fake boyfriend if that had been what she needed—the benefit of having no risk of real feelings getting in the way—but Ben didn't do casual.

The guy had too big a heart.

Madi sighed, shutting her computer down and heading to the bathroom to get ready for bed. She would have to get up early now to edit before her studio hours in the morning, and she was already dreading that alarm.

Danny texted again as she brushed her teeth.

> Danny: Thanks for helping me out with Hannah, by the
> way.
> Madi: I don't know what you're talking about.
> Madi: Are you going out again?
> Danny: She's coming to the Gilbert wedding this week-
> end.
> Madi: Wow! I thought bringing your girlfriend to work
> was a fifth date kind of deal. Way to kick things up
> a notch!
> Danny: *GIF of someone rolling their eyes*
> Danny: She wants to see what I do. Apparently Ben
> made it sound really interesting.
> Madi: And you're going to prove him right and show her
> how awesome you are. With or without your job. If
> she doesn't realize you're a catch by next week,
> she's not worth your time.

Settling on the edge of her bed, Madi looked around her little bedroom. She had been living in the same apartment since she was nineteen, when she had a stroke of bravery convince her she was perfectly capable of living on her own. With so many weddings using up her social stamina, she'd liked coming home to silence and solitude.

After spending so much time with her Wonder Boys this week, though, the small space seemed to expand around her, leaving her a tiny speck in the vast world. She had been on a trajectory most of her life, shooting for the stars. Everything was shiny and bright, but she had left everyone else behind.

Maybe Danny was right. Maybe it was time she stopped pretending she enjoyed the loneliness that came from her life.

His last text came in just as she settled beneath the covers and hugged her spare pillow.

> Danny: Thanks again for doing all of this, Madi. You're the best.

TWELVE

IT FELT SO GOOD TO run and work out his sore muscles, and Oliver wished he had done this days ago instead of waiting until Saturday. He might have worked out his pain way earlier and saved himself the trauma of trying to haul his groceries up to his apartment with unusable limbs. Next time, he was using a delivery service.

He also might have saved himself two days of his thoughts getting the better of him.

He'd hit the pavement hard this morning, blasting music in his headphones and trying to think of nothing as he focused on each step. Technically, he should have showed up for a training session with Cam this morning, but he'd needed to blow off some steam, not tear his body apart while being shouted at by a guy whose arms were too big for his own good.

According to his watch, he had already logged ten miles this morning and hit a personal best mile, which meant the run wasn't helping. It also meant he was running out of steam and was still a few miles from home. He hadn't been paying attention to where he was going, and he paused at the edge of a park to catch his breath and try to figure out where, exactly, he was. Maybe he would order himself a ride home instead of trying to run all the way back.

As soon as he stopped, though, his thoughts caught back up to him, and he really didn't like it.

For some reason, he was still thinking about Madi and Ben. Mostly about how he didn't know Madi as well as he thought he did since he had no idea she and Ben were so close. Oliver had known her since he was six, but she'd never sat arm in arm with Oliver like that before. She'd never flirted with him.

Ben had spent the good part of an hour Thursday night assuring them all that he had no intention of pushing things with Madi beyond what they'd always been. Apparently, he and Madi had had "plenty of discussions" about how they were and always would be friends and nothing more.

Oliver believed him. Mostly. He just couldn't get over how familiar the two of them were with each other, and the fact that the two of them had even talked about being more felt wrong. What about the pact? Regardless, Ben had gone off to college for four years, just like Oliver, and they'd all been in town for the six years since graduation. They'd all had the same amount of time with Madi.

Sure, Oliver had been pretty busy with his company for those first three years after college, but he didn't remember Ben spending all that much time alone with Madi. Ben would have said more about that if that were the case. Right?

Not that they were all that close to begin with. Oliver had accepted Ben and Cam into the group, but he rarely did anything with them if Kit wasn't around. Kit was the commonality between them. Kit and Madi. Without either of them, they were just three guys awkwardly standing around waiting for their shared interest to show up.

How stupid was that? They were supposed to be *friends*.

Grabbing his phone, Oliver dialed Ben's number before he could talk himself out of it. "Wanna hang out tonight?"

The sounds of the arcade around Ben were almost deafening. "Just a second," he said. He was quiet for a moment until the arcade was suddenly muffled, though not entirely gone. "Sorry. Hang out? Do you need something?"

Oliver didn't like that Ben's first thought was that he wanted something from him. Maybe it would be best not to address that issue. "I thought you didn't have an office. Where are you?"

"Hiding in the supply closet where we keep the extra prizes. You okay?"

"Can't a guy hang out with his friend once in a while? We used to do that all the time."

"Yeah, when we were twenty and you didn't have any dates to keep you occupied. Look, I've only got a second. There's a nine-year-old having a birthday party today, and he looks like a food fighter. He was eyeing his cake pretty hard."

"How in the world—"

Ben laughed. "You're asking that question when you're still known for that fight you started sophomore year? You all have the same look, Oliver. It's a demon look."

Oliver tried and failed to not be offended by that comment. "Are you free tonight or not?"

"Not. Did you even look at the calendar?"

Oliver had definitely forgotten about the calendar they set up for Madi, mostly because he didn't have anything to put on it. Yet again, an uncomfortable pinch settled in his gut as he considered how little he had done with his life the last three years. He still didn't have a plan for the future despite trying to come up with new ideas. Nothing had felt right yet, and Oliver listened only to his gut when it came to the important stuff. The mind couldn't be trusted.

"Look," Ben said, "I gotta go. Maybe sometime next week we can—I don't know—catch a movie or something."

Oliver barely stopped himself from saying how lame that sounded. "Yeah," he said instead, his mood dropping even lower than it already was as he hung up the phone. Was he even friends with Ben anymore?

After glancing at the calendar and discovering Cam and Kit were both busy, Oliver was almost tempted to see if there were any singles events happening nearby so he wouldn't have to be alone with his thoughts. The idea made him squirm.

But then he heard a familiar laugh, and he spun in a half circle, lifting his eyebrows high when he realized Madi was on the other side of the park taking pictures of a young couple. It was probably an engagement shoot or something, based on the two of them smiling and kissing. The background behind them didn't look like much, but Madi seemed thrilled every time she glanced down at her camera.

Intrigued, Oliver jumped back into a light jog with sudden renewed energy and pretended not to see her as he ran past. He paused at a park bench just beyond her to stretch his quads and glance at his watch, hoping she wasn't so into her shoot that she didn't see him.

"Oliver?"

He grinned, then tucked his smile away as he turned and pulled out his earbuds. "Mads? What are you doing here?"

Apparently Madi decided she had enough shots because she told the couple they were done. Oliver hoped she hadn't stopped on his account, but he was so glad to have *someone* to talk to that he couldn't bring himself to worry too much.

Once she had explained to the couple that they would get their edited shots in a few days, Madi wandered a little closer to Oliver and took in his sweaty tank top with a look he hadn't seen before. Appreciation?

He stood a little taller.

"Do you run in this park a lot?" she asked. "I don't think I've seen you here before."

That was because Oliver had never tried this hard to distract himself before. "I was lost in my head today," he admitted, though a part of him wanted to boast about how far he ran most mornings. Thankfully, he remembered arrogance did nothing to impress Madi Morgan. "I forgot that however far I run, I have to run the same distance back. I'm working up the courage."

Glancing at her watch, Madi considered that for a moment. "I could give you a ride, if you're tired. I'm heading back home anyway. Where do you live?"

Oliver had to laugh at that one. "Wilson Court."

Her eyes went wide. "That's just down the street from me!"

"I know. When Kit gave me your address the other day, I almost slapped myself for not learning about it sooner." He might have had someone to hang out with more often if he had only known.

That was the problem with only ever hanging out at Kit's house. Oliver still didn't know where Cam and Ben lived, which made him feel like the worst friend in the world. He would try to fix that, assuming he ever found nights where they were free.

"All these years we've lived so close to each other," Madi said, shaking her head. Did she look as disappointed as he'd been when he found out?

"What are you doing tonight?" Oliver spoke the question without really thinking about it, and he told himself that he wanted to reconnect with his old friend. Spending so much time with her lately had made his life feel normal, and he craved more of that.

If he was really being honest with himself, though, he was pretty sure there was more to his question based on the way he held his breath as he waited for her response. He just wasn't sure what that *more* was.

Madi bit her lip and seemed genuinely sad about it when she said, "I have a wedding to shoot tonight."

"Another one?"

She laughed. "It's the middle of May. Do you know how many weddings are in May? All of them. Though, now that I think about it, next month will be even worse." She shuddered a little. "Come on. I need to change and grab my extra lenses for tonight, so I'll drop you off."

As he followed her through the park, Oliver marveled at the way Madi had handled her clients. She seemed so confident—a rare occurrence for her—and she talked about her job in a way Oliver hadn't really seen before. It made sense, though. At this point, she'd been doing photography for ten years, which was way longer than anything Oliver had ever committed to. No wonder she'd asked him what was next.

Oliver took charge of her camera as they got into her car, and he took the liberty of flipping through the photos she'd taken of the couple this morning. Not that he was surprised, but they were exceptionally good, and she'd framed the photos so well that it didn't matter that the background was a bit boring. A little bit of editing, and the photos would be perfect.

"Do you do your own editing?" he asked as he continued to look through the files.

Madi chuckled. "Of course. I can't trust anyone else to do that except me."

She had so many photos in here. Not only would she have to go through and pick out the best ones, but then she would also have to work her magic and get them to the level of perfection he had seen on the walls in her studio.

He frowned down at the camera. "That has to take forever."

"Sometimes, yeah."

No wonder she didn't have time to date. "Would you ever consider a program to do it for you?" he asked. "I mean, one where you could set whatever parameters you want, and it could learn your process and adapt to your style to make things easier."

"Like some magical editing robot?" She let out a deep, weary sigh. "Sounds too good to be true, so I'm pretty sure it doesn't exist. Or if it does, it's probably way out of my budget. I do well for myself, but not that well."

The wheels had already started spinning in his mind, but Oliver tried to stay focused a little longer. "What if I built one for you?" he muttered.

Madi glanced at him in confusion. "Built one? Just built an artificial intelligence photo editor in your free time? Right."

"I'm serious!" In fact, Oliver was deadly serious, and he was already mapping out the sort of research he would need to do to start on the coding for something like that. He grabbed his phone out of his pocket and pulled out the stylus so he could start scribbling notes before he forgot any of the ideas flying around in his head.

It felt like only seconds had passed when Madi cleared her throat. Oliver looked up, surprised to see his apartment building. He thanked her for the ride and wished her luck at the wedding, but he could barely concentrate because his computer was calling his name.

Finally something had caught his attention, and he had no intention of letting it go.

THIRTEEN

MADI COULDN'T REMEMBER THE LAST time she had seen Oliver that excited about something, and though she was trying not to get her hopes up, she was really into the idea of a program that could do the bigger editing processes for her. She could easily picture all the things she could do in her free time, like finally cleaning the grout in her shower or getting takeout from the Thai place across town that was too far away for regular trips.

It wasn't like she didn't enjoy editing, and she would never give up full control of that. But it took up *so much time,* and it was a good chunk of the reason she hadn't had a social life since starting up her business in high school.

She just hoped Oliver didn't give up when he couldn't figure it out in a day or two. He never did like when things didn't come easy to him—it was the reason he had given up guitar and never learned to whistle. He generally stopped trying when presented with a real challenge. Luckily for him, he was so good at so many things that it didn't matter. Most of the time.

Madi tried not to think too much about Oliver as she worked, because then she started thinking about his idea for an editing program, and that made her sick to her stomach because she wanted it so badly but would probably never get it. So she focused on taking photos of the bride's bouquet while the bride and groom had a private moment to themselves before the reception.

"Admiring my work, Miss Morgan?"

Madi grinned as Danny came up behind her and adjusted the bouquet to give her a better shot. "You didn't arrange the flowers."

"Of course I didn't. I would never take credit for Laura's work. But I *did* convince the bride to go with daisies instead of roses, and I think they fit her better."

"You are the master of weddings," she said, rolling her eyes. "How's Hannah doing?"

They both glanced over to where Hannah was laughing with one of the bridesmaids.

"They knew each other already," Danny explained with a grin. "So I think she's having fun."

It certainly seemed that way, especially because she kept throwing smiles toward Danny, even with Madi standing right next to him.

"I don't know, Madi," he said, pulling his eyebrows together. "There's something really special about Hannah, and I don't want this thing to end."

"So don't let it." Smiling, Madi gave him a little shove. "Go ask her to dance, loverboy."

He laughed. "Please never call me that again. But I think I will." And he did, marching right up to Hannah and taking her by the hand. Though they didn't move to the dance floor since they weren't technically wedding guests, they danced behind the tables and seemed to be having a really great time.

If the expression on his face was to be believed, Madi was pretty sure Danny was falling in love with Hannah, even if it had been less than a week since they met. She wondered what that would feel like, being so comfortable with a person after so short a time. Being immediately compatible.

Outside of the Wonder Boys, Madi had never felt that way with anyone. Not that she'd dated much to begin with, but with everyone but her adopted brothers, relationships of any kind always took a lot of time and energy, things she usually had in short supply. Thank goodness for people like Danny and Oliver, who immediately put her at ease.

Unlike most other men she met.

She was in the middle of taking photos of the bride dancing with her father when a familiar cologne suddenly filled her nose, and she tensed.

"Well, hello there. What are the odds of us both being in a place like this?"

Madi stopped herself from saying his name, knowing Terry from the singles barbecue was probably the sort of guy who would take a lot of pride in being remembered. *Of course* he would show up to a fancy wedding, and *of course* he would recognize her. Madi was just angry with herself for not recognizing *him* earlier, because based on the flower in his lapel, he was part of the wedding party. He had probably been watching her all day.

"Excuse me, I have photos to take."

"You're really good," Terry said without moving away. As his eyes traced the length of her body, she tried to stay focused on the dance. "I saw the bridal pictures you took for Kinzie. No wonder you charge so much."

A shudder ran through her, and she shuffled through the crowd to get some shots from a different angle.

Terry followed. "It's too bad you can't take pictures at your own wedding, huh? But we'll look so good together that it won't matter who takes them."

Madi froze. "Excuse me?"

He grinned when she finally turned her attention to him, which meant that had probably been his goal when he said what he did. He probably thought it was some funny joke, not realizing he had pushed a little too far. "Come on, Mandy. I'm sure you felt our connection just like I did. Come dance with me."

"I'm working." And since that probably wouldn't be enough for him, she added, "And I would rather not."

"I don't think Zack would mind if you took a quick break. He's too busy dancing with his pretty new wife. Just one dance."

Madi twisted out of his reach when he tried to take her arm. "Please leave me alone. I'm not interested."

"It's okay if you're shy."

"I'm not—"

"I'm more than happy to make the first move, if it'll make you feel more comfortable."

Madi shifted out of his reach yet again, but she had to be careful. Alienating a good friend of the groom would reflect poorly on her, and she needed to make sure her client went away from this event wholly satisfied. She relied entirely on word of mouth for new business, and if Terry was petty enough, he could do a lot of harm. "I'm sorry, but it's just not going to happen. If you'll excuse—"

"I thought we had a moment the other day."

This felt like the time she wanted to audition for the school play but got so nervous when it was her turn that she hyperventilated and ran from the room, and Oliver found her and stayed with her until she could breathe again. But Oliver wasn't here, and Madi didn't know what to do.

"Madi, you okay?"

Relief flooded through her when Danny appeared, Hannah right behind him. "Fine," she breathed, though she hated that she'd needed rescuing in the first place. She should have been able to get rid of Terry on her own.

Terry narrowed his eyes, sizing Danny up. "You're the wedding planner, right? You actually did a decent job."

Danny's forehead creased. "Uh, thanks? So how do you know Madi?"

For a second, Terry looked confused, but he made the connection pretty quickly and turned a bright red when he realized his mistake. "No wonder you didn't want to go out with me," he chuckled. "You could have told me I got your name wrong."

Madi flinched when he shifted closer, as if he thought his apology was enough to get her to like him. "It's okay," she said, even though it was anything but okay.

"Well hey, now I know who to talk to when it's our turn to plan, right?" Terry chuckled again, though no one else laughed.

Danny was still looking at Terry like everything about him was off, and Hannah seemed to be inching closer to Madi, just in case. Madi was desperate to get away from the situation, and she hoped Danny and Hannah would be enough to keep Terry where he was.

She cleared her throat. "Look, I don't want to go out with you Terry." Before he could argue, she added, "And I'm already dating someone. If you'll excuse me, I have to go take pictures." And she ran, pushing past people to get to the other side of the dance floor to get a few measly photos of the bride and groom sharing their first dance. She had missed most of it already.

At least she'd escaped.

Danny found her after the wedding had ended—she'd been avoiding him as much as she avoided Terry—and he helped her gather up the last of her supplies without saying anything. Only when he walked her to her car did he open his mouth.

"Guys suck."

At least it brought a smile to her face, though it didn't really make her feel better. She was exhausted. "Not all of you. Where's Hannah?"

"Saying goodbye to her friend." Danny shifted, clearly uncomfortable. "That guy you were talking to—he was at the barbecue, right?"

She nodded.

"I think I understand now why you don't like those things as much as I do. I've never had a girl get all creepy like that. Like, take a hint, buddy." He was quiet for a second, leaning against her car, and then he let out a deep sigh. "Look, I'm sorry for pushing you with this dating thing. The bet was stupid, and you don't need me getting all up in your business like that."

As glad as Madi was for the apology, she didn't like the way it sounded like he was giving up on her. Was she really so hopeless that he thought one bad encounter with a not-so-great guy was enough for her to be defeated? She was stronger than that.

But Danny also deserved a better friend than her. Things seemed to be going well with Hannah, but Madi had known Danny long enough to know what that tension in his shoulders meant. He was still nervous about dating, probably worried he was going to mess something up if left on his own too soon.

"You're not backing out, are you?" Madi asked, fighting the grimace that threatened to break her teasing.

He'd given her an out, but Madi couldn't bring herself to back down from the challenge. Not when this was as much for Danny's benefit as it was for hers. "I expected more from you, Camper."

He scoffed, definitely relaxing as he stood a little straighter. "That's not what I said."

"It's what it sounded like. I *will* be taking new photos for your website, and you're going to love them. Even if you don't love the check you write me."

Thankfully, his easy grin made an appearance as he shook his head. "I'm sure I will, but what makes you so certain you'll get full price for them? You still have six more double dates. Though, I guess you could go on your own dates. It's not like I don't trust you."

The way he said that told Madi he really hoped she argued. "A bet's a bet, Danny. I agreed to ten double dates."

The poor man relaxed even more. "Well, that's settled then. Though, maybe don't find dates at singles events. I don't want you finding another creep like that guy."

"Oh, I don't have to worry about that." Only when the words were out of her mouth—and Danny narrowed his eyes with interest—did Madi realize her mistake.

He lifted one eyebrow. "What does that mean? Do you already have dates lined up? I know you told that guy you were dating someone, but I thought that was just to get him off your back."

That *had* been the reason, but the more Madi thought about it, the more she realized this was probably her best plan. If she kept going out with the same three guys, she was going to have to admit that all of her dates had been fake unless she wanted Danny to think she was stringing them all along. She'd already friendzoned Ben, and Cam had barely made it through their one and only fake date, nearly blowing everything. Madi didn't like lying to Danny—hadn't from the start—but she was doing this for him. Helping him get comfortable enough with Hannah before setting him free.

There was really only one way Madi could see around this, and she opened her mouth before she could talk herself out of it. "I'm kind of dating Oliver."

The rush of heat that ran through her was a strange side effect of lying, one she'd never experienced before.

Danny's eyebrows shot high. "Wait, really? Since when?"

She *really* hoped Oliver would be okay with this.

"Oliver and I started working on some editing software together the other day," she said quietly. "Things just sort of clicked, but I had already set up that date with Ben."

"That would explain why Oliver was so cool at the alley on Thursday. He's a better man than me for keeping his jealousy so low key. I would have been ready to explode if I had to let Hannah go out with someone else."

"Oh, I'm definitely not going out with anyone else," Hannah said behind them, grinning as she crossed the parking lot.

Danny's whole bearing changed, like a fire had ignited inside him. "Really?"

Laughing, Hannah slid her hand into his and gave him a wide smile and a shrug. "I like you, Danny."

"I like you too."

And Madi hoped they would step away from her car before they started making out. "Well, I should get going," she muttered.

Thankfully, that was enough to pull Danny's attention from Hannah. "See you around, Madi. Oh! Hannah, you'll never believe this, but Madi just told me she and Oliver are dating."

"I could have told you that," she replied with an eye roll.

Danny and Madi spoke at the same time. "What?"

Though a little confused, Hannah shrugged again. "I see the way he looks at you, Madi. He was burning a hole through Ben the whole time we were bowling."

Danny and Hannah were both crazy, and Madi couldn't understand why either of them would think Oliver was acting jealous at the bowling alley. Still, when she agreed to text Danny about going out as couples next Wednesday and slipped into her car, that strange heat still pulsed through her, and she wondered if maybe it had nothing to do with lying at all.

FOURTEEN

IT HAD BEEN TEN MINUTES since she started pacing the hall outside Oliver's apartment, and Madi was pretty sure she was going to chicken out if she waited any longer. It was late Tuesday afternoon, and she had plenty of editing she needed to be doing right now. But she hadn't talked to Oliver yet about tomorrow's double date, and this seemed like the sort of thing she couldn't do over a phone call.

"You can change your mind," she said out loud, shuddering as soon as she did. Madi Morgan did not *change her mind*. Besides, if she went against what she told Danny, that would mean even more lying than she'd already done, and she wasn't sure she had the energy to come up with a reason why her "relationship" with Oliver didn't last long.

No, she had to do this. At least for now.

She knocked on Oliver's door, considered running away, and then held her breath as she waited. What if he wasn't home? What would she do then? She had asked Kit for Oliver's apartment number, and her brother had wanted to know why. When Madi wouldn't tell him, he got suspicious, and she half wondered if Kit had lured Oliver away from his apartment so she couldn't do what she planned.

And what if Oliver said no? He had been a good sport with the dates so far, but Oliver was an incorrigible flirt and would definitely not like being tied down to something that wasn't even real. He liked his freedom, which had always made Madi wonder how he and Kit were such good friends when Kit was all about rules and structure. Maybe they balanced each other out?

Regardless, this boyfriend thing was going to be rough when it came to Kit, and that was assuming Oliver even agreed to it.

It took so long for Oliver to open the door that Madi had been about to leave and try again in the morning, but suddenly he was there, blinking in the sunlit hallway as if he hadn't expected it to be daylight. "Hey," he said, squinting with one eye mostly closed. "What are you doing here?" It looked like he hadn't shaved in a few days, and there were dark enough circles beneath his eyes that he clearly hadn't been sleeping well.

Madi gulped. Maybe this was a bad idea. He was obviously going through something and didn't need added stress. But could she back out now? No. Not if she didn't want to hurt Danny. Even if they postponed the double date, Madi would lose her nerve and never be brave enough to ask Oliver to help.

She was nervous enough as it was, her heart racing as she gazed at the man in front of her.

She took a deep breath. "Can we talk?"

"That's a terrifying sentence. Come on in."

Madi had never been to Oliver's house, apartment or otherwise. Though she should have expected him to have all the nice things, she was still surprised by how expensive all of his furnishings and appliances looked. These apartment buildings weren't necessarily the best in town, though they were high on the list, but Oliver had turned his into something impressive. Impressive, but in a livable way. He clearly had his life together, way more than she'd expected.

Madi had thought he was lost, but that didn't seem right anymore. Oliver wasn't lost; he was stuck.

He gave her a quick tour of the clean and organized space, opening blackout curtains as he went to let some light in, then grabbed a couple bottles of water before they settled on the comfiest couch Madi had ever sat on.

"So, what's going on?" he asked as he opened his bottle and lifted it to his lips.

Though slightly distracted by the enormous TV in front of her, Madi tried to stay focused and jumped right into it. "I need you to pretend to be my boyfriend."

He choked, spitting water all over her, and grabbed a blanket from the arm of the couch so she could dry herself off. "Sorry," he coughed. "I just… What? I thought that's what we were trying to avoid."

She gave him the condensed version of what happened at the wedding on Saturday, including telling him about the bet and the double date stipulation, and ended with her reasons for saying what she had. "In the end, it helps both me and Danny, and hopefully it gave Terry a reason to stop trying so hard."

Oliver listened without saying much, though he'd gotten a hard edge to his expression as she talked about Terry. "Why didn't you say Ben was your boyfriend?" he asked when she finished.

That was his first question? "Because pretending to date Ben would feel the same as dating Kit."

Oliver's eyes darkened.

"Besides," Madi added as her heart kicked up a faster tempo, "I didn't want to mess anything up with the girl he likes."

"What girl?"

"At the grocery store. Hasn't he told you about her?"

"Oh. Right. That one." Oliver clearly had no idea who she was talking about as he frowned at his water bottle, and he quickly changed the subject. "And Cam would open his big mouth and ruin things if given a chance to say more than three words, so that left you with me."

Madi couldn't tell if he was disappointed by that or not, but she really wouldn't have trusted either of the other two with something like this to begin with. Oliver was the only one she didn't worry about hurting; they had never been anything but friends.

For some reason, that was starting to bother her. She'd held hands with Ben in high school and was his date to his sister's wedding, and she and Cam had gone out to dinner after his college graduation. Both dates had been fun but weird, making them all surer than ever that they were better as friends. But Oliver had never even asked her out, so the question still lingered in the back of her mind.

Were they better as friends?

She let out a sigh. That wasn't important, even if her pounding heart seemed to think it was. "Am I a terrible friend for all of these dates being fake? I feel like I'm being a terrible friend."

"Madi, a terrible friend wouldn't feel bad about any of this. In fact, I'm pretty sure Danny's the bad friend for forcing you into this."

"He didn't force me into anything."

Oliver raised an eyebrow.

"Okay, yeah, so he's been kinda pushy with the whole dating thing, but it's not like he's wrong. I do want that kind of happiness, and I'm not going to find myself a partner if I'm always by myself."

"And how's 'dating' me going to help with that?" He made quotes with his fingers, that lone eyebrow still high on his forehead.

Madi didn't really have an answer to that question. "It won't," she admitted, "but it'll buy me some time and help me win the bet. Once summer is over, I'll have more time to figure out what I'm doing when it comes to dating. But until then…" She sighed. "None of this has been part of the plan."

He scratched his scruffy cheek. "You Morgans and your plans."

"Don't you dare compare me to Kit."

"That's not a bad thing, you know. Your brother is my best friend."

It wasn't like Madi had forgotten that, but adulthood had shifted their friend group enough that things didn't feel the way they used to. She missed how they used to all spend a ton of time together, and she knew her own schedule was a big part of the blame for that not happening very often. She had needed something to fill the gap when the Boys went off to college, so she had turned to photography. And things hadn't really changed since, even with them all back.

But what was the cause of the rift between Kit and Oliver? She was pretty sure they barely ever saw each other anymore, and she missed the days when it would be the three of them against the world. Maybe her "dating" Oliver would remind him how little time he spent with Kit nowadays.

"I know this is a lot to ask," she said. "It doesn't have to be for long. Just until I win the bet."

Oliver chewed his bottom lip as he considered that. "You don't know that," he said eventually. "If we break up too quickly, Danny might try to set you up with every seminormal guy he meets. Though he'd better not keep trying to put you in Terry-ble circumstances."

Madi hadn't thought of that. "You're probably right," she sighed. Just because he felt bad about creepy guys existing, it didn't mean he was going to stop trying to find her a happily ever after.

Oliver grunted, probably thinking about Terry based on the way his expression darkened. "By the way, you do know you're allowed to punch a guy if he won't take no for an answer, right?"

"Not when that guy is the best man to the guy who signs my paycheck."

He winced. "Oh."

"Yeah. So, will you do it? Please?" Madi was starting to feel desperate; under no circumstances was she willing to tell Danny the truth and put a rift in their friendship. Not while he was still trying to figure things out with Hannah. She had to see this one through. She grabbed Oliver's hand, leaning closer to make sure he understood how much this would mean to her if he helped her. "If you do this for me, Ollie, I promise you can ask me to do anything you want."

He raised an eyebrow again and looked down at their hands. It was the second time she'd grabbed his hand, and he seemed fixated on their fingers together. Or maybe that was just Madi projecting since she couldn't focus on anything else. His hands were soft and warm, a strength to them she wouldn't have known without these fake dates giving her a reason to touch him like this.

She didn't want to let go.

"You're giving me a blank check favor?" he said after a long while. "That's a pretty steep price for you, don't you think? You have no idea what I might ask you to do."

He was teasing her, which was a good sign, but Madi didn't relax just yet. "I trust you," she said.

He really seemed to consider that, his almost-green eyes boring into hers as he thought it over. "I guess this'll give me something to do, before I die of boredom," he said slowly, like he was trying to find a reason to say yes. Then he shifted their hands into a handshake and grinned. "Of course I'll do it. You know I'd do anything for you, Mads."

Madi almost squealed. "Really?"

He laughed, and suddenly Madi couldn't remember the last time she had heard Oliver laugh like that. It had been so long since she really spent any significant time with him that she was realizing how much she had missed this man and the easy light he brought into any situation. He used to laugh at everything, and he always made Madi feel better no matter what anxieties she was facing. That had been absent in her life the last decade, and she was glad to have it back.

This whole fake boyfriend thing was going to be good for *all* of them. Danny got his double dates, Oliver got something to keep him busy, and Madi got the website photos and a chance to spend more time with one of her best friends in the whole world.

"I think it'll be fun," Oliver said with a shrug. "But you should probably be the one to tell the Boys so they know this was your idea. Otherwise, they might kill me."

He wasn't wrong about that. All of the Wonder Boys were highly protective, and this fake relationship would be a big deal. She wasn't too worried about Cam or Ben since they would probably understand if she explained the situation, but Kit… There was no telling what her brother would do if he found out she was "dating" Oliver.

Kit had never come right out and said she couldn't date his friends, but the implication had always been there. She wasn't sure if he thought the guys weren't good enough for her or the other way around, but he had been obvious about how much he disliked the idea of anything more than friendship between Madi and the Wonder Boys. Anything beyond what they already were would break Kit's most solid part of his life, and that wouldn't be an easy change for him.

"What if we don't tell them?" Madi suggested quietly. "This is only going to make them worry, and they'll probably try to talk me out of it like Kit did with the fake dates thing in the first place. I'm honestly surprised *you* haven't tried to talk me out of it."

Oliver gave her a lopsided grin. "So am I," he admitted. "But I get it. You don't want to hurt your friend, and Danny seems like a decent guy. Besides…" He adjusted his grip, making Madi realize she was still holding onto his hand. "I've missed hanging out with you, and I don't want to give that up."

So, they were in agreement. A strange thrill ran through Madi at the thought that maybe Oliver liked being around her as much as she liked being around him. She'd never wondered what he thought of her—she'd never needed to—but now she wished she was brave enough to ask him. Did he mean it when he said he'd missed her like she'd missed him?

"By the way," she said, knowing she should keep the conversation going before she asked something she might regret, "we have a double date with Danny and Hannah to-morrow."

"Nice of you to spring that one on me." He didn't seem to mind, though; he hadn't stopped smiling since agreeing to the plan.

Well, that was that. Madi glanced around the room, feeling as if they'd just discovered something big but had no idea where to put it. Oliver had made the whole thing so easy, but it was only going to get harder from there. Theory and practice were two very different things.

"I guess I should get out of your hair before you get sick of me." Madi got to her feet, planning to give Oliver all the space he might want since she was asking so much of him.

But he grabbed her hand again and held her back, his eyes shining brighter than ever as he said, "I could never get sick of you, Mads. I want to show you something."

Pulling her over to his ridiculously complex computer setup, he nudged her into the insanely comfortable chair in front of the desk. He had to lean over her a little to reach the mouse, but she didn't complain when she caught a tiny hint of his cologne or soap or whatever it was that smelled so good. He wore it so much better than Terry, even when he wasn't trying.

"It still needs a lot of work," he said, pulling her attention back to the computer. "Obviously. And I'll probably need some input from an actual editor like you since I don't know what I'm doing. But it's a good start, I think."

He opened up a program that looked pretty simple and somewhat similar to the editing software she usually used, but the longer she looked at all the features listed on the side panel, the more she realized what this was. "Wait," she said, leaning forward. "Is this…?"

He'd actually built it! A program that could do the basic editing stuff she hated doing.

With a massive grin on his face, Oliver walked her through the different templates and demonstrated how the program adjusted itself based on whatever changes he made, learning his techniques. "You can save settings as well, so you can have a bunch of different presets you start with for different kinds of shoots, but the main part is teaching it how you edit so it can pretend to be you. Hopefully save you some time. So, what do you think?"

What did she think? Madi was in love. "Ollie, this is amazing! When did you have time to do all this?"

"Oh, I haven't slept in three days," he said with a laugh. "I'm running purely on energy drinks at this point, and you caught me at a sweet spot. I'll crash in an hour or so, and I'll be dead to the world until tomorrow."

He had come alive as he walked her through the software, and Madi stared at him with wonder. He was probably like this in college too, while he was creating his company, and she suddenly understood why most people thought he was lazy. If he dedicated this kind of energy to everything he did, there was no way he could sustain it, so he probably did all his work in bursts but had incredible results.

Oliver Hamilton was brilliant, and Madi couldn't believe she'd forgotten that. He'd been like this as a kid too, mastering things quickly and getting bored easily if he wasn't properly inspired. Kit had hated this side of him—it meant Oliver never studied but always aced his tests—but Madi had always found it fascinating.

"You're incredible," she whispered, turning in her chair so she was facing him. With one of his hands on the desk and the other on the arm of the chair, they were suddenly just a few inches apart, and she didn't mind in the least. In fact, she would be content to stay right there forever, under the gaze of one of the most amazing men she knew. He looked at her the same way he looked at the program, like she was the only thing that brightened his life.

He looked good with facial hair, even if he didn't look like the Oliver she knew. The Wonder Boys had all always been clean-shaven, but the reddish scruff made Oliver look older. Different.

Too curious not to, she reached up and brushed her fingers against the scruff, and then she touched the shadows beneath his eyes. He'd lost sleep for *her*. No one had ever been so dedicated to her.

He grasped the back of his neck, his other hand still holding his weight on the arm of the chair as he turned slightly red. His lips parted, as if he was about to say something. But nothing came out, and he leaned a little closer as his hand fell, and Madi wondered if it would really be all that hard to pretend they were a couple if he kept looking at her like this.

In a way that made her whole body spark with electricity and heat.

His eyes slid down her face and rested on her mouth, making her heart pick up speed. He wasn't going to… Was he? But why would he…?

The moment stretched on a few seconds longer until Oliver blinked, shook his head, and then drooped as if he'd hit an energy wall. He wasn't kidding when he said he would crash, and his eyes fluttered as he struggled to keep himself from collapsing right on top of her. "There it is," he muttered, and he took a deep breath before he pushed himself up straight and ran a hand down his face. "What time do you want me tomorrow?"

She told him the details of tomorrow's date, then pulled him in for a hug. He really leaned into it as if he might fall asleep in her arms. It wasn't as if she'd never hugged him before, but this was an especially good hug.

"Goodnight, Oliver," she told him, reluctantly pulling away. Just like with their hands, they fit so well together. How had she never noticed that?

He gave her a smile as his eyes followed her to the door, making her want to linger. "Goodnight, Mads."

She couldn't wait until tomorrow.

FIFTEEN

I F OLIVER WAS BEING HONEST with himself, he wasn't sure if yesterday had been real. Odds were high he had dreamed up a scenario where he was secretly dating Madi Morgan, and he was not looking forward to learning he had made it all up. He didn't dare text the guys about it—that would be suicide whether or not it was real—and he couldn't ask Madi and risk embarrassing them both if he had imagined it.

He figured showing up to the art gallery where the alleged date was happening was his best option; he would lose nothing but time if it turned out to be a fevered programming dream. And it had given him a reason to dress up a bit, even if he hadn't had the energy to shave, so there was that.

He'd slept for nearly sixteen hours straight, and he was pretty sure most of those hours had been filled with thoughts of Kit's sister.

Why would he dream about dating Madi, though? They'd never dated in the past, and there was that whole pact thing with the Boys. Not that he'd never thought about it, but since she had always been off-limits, he had never let his thoughts stray beyond idle wonderings. He had known her for so long, practically his entire life, so of course he'd thought about it. He'd even compared dates in the past to Madi Morgan, holding them to her impossible standard. Probably why he never went on more than a few dates with anyone.

No one could really compare.

She was smart, driven, and kind in a way no one else could be. She could never hide her smile if something was making her laugh, and she was the kind of person who felt bad for the smashed box of noodles that had been ignored by everyone else at the grocery store. She never let anyone fight her battles for her if she could help it, and she was the most determined person Oliver had ever known. The girl had started her photography business at sixteen, after all. And there was something about the way she saw the world, like there was a little bit of good in everything if she looked hard enough. Even in Oliver. He'd known that since the day he met her.

Okay, so maybe it made sense that he would dream about the chance to date Madi… He just hoped it wasn't actually a dream. Talk about disappointment.

But Madi was there waiting for him when he turned the corner to the gallery, and she seemed entirely relieved to see him as if she was worried about the same thing he was. She immediately hugged him, which surprised him, but then he saw Danny and his lady friend in line to buy tickets and realized their game had already begun.

"So, what's our story?" he asked, slipping his hand into hers without thinking. He felt her tense at his touch, and he was about to pull away when he realized that they were supposed to be dating and that would just look strange. *Not* holding hands in general would be strange. They really should have set some ground rules yesterday, though he may not have been lucid enough to remember them if they had. He was lucky he had made it to the right gallery at the right time.

"You're okay with this, right?" he asked quietly and held their hands up in the air. And *that* was strange, so he tried to fix the situation by touching his lips to her knuckles and giving her a sheepish grin.

She returned his grin with a confused look but seemed to realize like he had that they would have to do more than they had before, when they were just going on casual dates. "Holding my hand is fine," she decided. "I just…" She frowned at their hands, which Oliver still held up in the air between them like a weirdo. Then she kissed *his* knuckle.

Both of them burst into laughter a second later.

"We're going to be terrible at this," Oliver decided out loud before they joined up with the other two at the doors. Now that they'd gotten over that awkwardness, though, he was pretty sure they would be fine. This was no different from the games of make-believe they'd played as kids, and they could pull this off as long as neither of them thought too hard about what they were actually doing.

More specifically, as long as *he* didn't think too hard. These blurring lines were going to be difficult to keep an eye on, especially while his brain was still lagging from the coding haze of the last few days.

"Hey Danny, how's it going? It was Hannah, right?" Oliver barely gave Hannah a glance so Madi wouldn't have any reason to think he was flirting. He hadn't been flirting the last time, either, but he wasn't about to slip up again by being too friendly. He would be a good boyfriend. A *perfect* boyfriend. Exactly the kind of guy Madi deserved.

He cringed. A guy worthy of Madi Morgan was a big role to fill.

Danny slipped his arm around Hannah's waist as he greeted Oliver, and Hannah leaned into his touch. The two of them were a whole lot closer than they'd been a week ago, and Oliver tried to remember what Madi had told him yesterday. Had she said Danny and Hannah were an actual couple now? He didn't think so. He wondered what that would mean for Madi since things could go either of two ways:

Either Danny got caught up in his own love life and left Madi alone once the bet was completed, or he would be so blissfully happy that he wouldn't rest until Madi was as well.

Oliver really hoped it was that first option, or things were going to get a little crazy.

But not too crazy tonight, considering their date spot. If given the option, he never would have gone to an art gallery, but he could easily see why Madi would like a place like this. Her eyes took everything in all at once as they stepped inside, and she practically bounced at his side, like she couldn't decide where she wanted to start.

She probably can't, Oliver thought with a laugh. Madi had never been good with decisions, and she tended to freeze up if faced with too many options. It didn't matter if deep down she knew what she wanted; the only decisions she made without waffling were the ones she had zero hesitations about.

"What if we go this way?" he suggested, nudging her to their left to go along that wall first.

She sent him a grateful smile, then turned her full attention to the art.

Like Oliver, Hannah seemed only mildly interested, but Danny seemed just as fascinated by every new piece as Madi. The two of them even made comments to each other that made no sense to Oliver, and he wondered why those two had never dated. They seemed pretty well-suited to each other.

"So, do you know anything about their history?" Oliver asked Hannah at one point. Madi and Danny had both been standing in front of the same painting for five minutes, neither of them saying a word.

A smile played on Hannah's lips as she glanced over at him. She definitely didn't seem interested in Oliver anymore, which was a good thing. As much as he liked the attention, he wanted it from…someone else… He wasn't sure who that someone was, but it wasn't Hannah.

"Danny didn't tell me all that much," Hannah admitted. "I know they went on a date once, back when they first met."

"They did?" Madi could have mentioned that little tidbit at some point…

Hannah nodded. "As I've been discovering, Danny is a head-first kind of guy, and he probably came on to Madi a little strong. He said she was nice about it, but it sort of ruined the chance of anything romantic, from what I gathered. Danny keeps telling me they're too similar to have worked anyway, so I'm not all that worried. You shouldn't be either."

"I'm not," Oliver said immediately, but it felt a bit like a lie. Madi deserved the best, and Oliver would do whatever he could to make that happen.

It was one of the reasons he'd worked so hard to get her editing program up and running. He wanted to give her some freedom to actually go out and have fun without worrying about the amount of work she needed to get done. Oliver knew from experience how dangerous that obsessiveness could get, and he and Madi were very similar when it came to work.

Madi turned around just then and hurried over to him, grabbing his hand as if she'd been doing that their whole lives. While it wasn't like they'd never touched, this was…different. "There's a photography exhibit up ahead," she said with excitement, and Oliver couldn't help but grin as he let her drag him forward. He hadn't seen her this animated in a long time, and it was nice to see some of little Madi coming back into the woman she'd become.

The photography exhibit, he discovered, was a lot more interesting than the paintings. These, at least, were real things, not just stripes of paint on canvas, and the more he looked at them, the more he could see some of the editing techniques he had implemented into his software. The way these artists used lighting and framing was fascinating, even for a code and numbers guy like Oliver, and it was like a whole new world had suddenly opened up to him as he wandered the gallery.

He was so fascinated, in fact, that it took him several minutes of staring at one photo in particular to realize Madi was no longer at his side and had moved on without him. Oliver may have been a fake boyfriend, but he would not be the kind of boyfriend who left his girl alone for too long.

There she was. She stood on the other side of the room, talking to an official-looking woman in a maroon pantsuit, probably about the photo between them. She smiled and nodded, clearly passionate about the subject, and there was something different about her while she stood there. That passion wasn't little Madi; it was something new. And Oliver couldn't look away.

As he watched her, a sudden realization hit Oliver straight between the eyes and left him feeling numb and electrified at the same time, like he'd just been struck by lightning.

Madi was *beautiful*.

She had always been pretty, but this… This was him fully realizing just how much she'd grown up, and it stole the breath from his lungs as he watched her without even really knowing what had changed. It was the deep red dress she wore and how it accented her curves. It was the way she'd done her hair up in an elegant bun of sorts and a braid that crossed over the top of her head like a crown. It was the heels she wore—higher than he'd ever seen her wear—and her simple but elegant makeup that definitely didn't make her look sixteen anymore.

That was it. Oliver had inexplicably still seen her as sixteen, the age she was when he left for school. He hadn't spent enough time alone with her—away from the Wonder Boys—to realize how desperate he was to get to know this new, older Madi. He had missed a decade of her life through his inaction, and there was so much to learn about her.

He sank onto a plush bench and spent the next twenty minutes admiring *her* instead of the art, drinking her in and telling himself that this changed nothing. They were still only friends, like brother and sister, definitely not a couple despite telling everyone they were.

Nothing had changed.

But Oliver knew that was a lie, and he was afraid of what that meant.

By the time Madi returned to his side, Oliver was completely tongue-tied. It was like he was seventeen again, only instead of crushing on the school choir's lead soprano who'd just moved to town, he was standing next to a girl he'd known his whole life. He'd never been in this situation before, and he didn't know if it was a fleeting thing, brought on by the fake date, or if this was a real attraction.

Of course it was a real attraction. Oliver could barely breathe every time he looked at her, and every male glance in her direction made his blood boil. Though he couldn't say why something had suddenly shifted inside him, he knew he'd stepped over a threshold and would have a hard time going back. Assuming he even *wanted* to go back.

This was bad. Whatever *this* was. Some space would be a good idea, and Oliver made a plan to book out the next few days with anything that could keep him away from Madi so he could figure out what had snapped in his brain to make him see this girl in a way he hadn't before.

"You okay?" Madi asked, slipping her arm through his and making him tense for half a second.

So much for space. He smiled, hoping it didn't look as forced as it felt. "Just the after-effects of my coding craze. I'll be fine after another good night's sleep."

But as Madi led him to the next photo, Oliver wasn't sure he believed his own words. If the high speed of his heart was any indication, he wasn't anywhere close to being fine.

SIXTEEN

OF ALL THE THINGS TO go wrong today, it had to be this. Madi was in trouble, and she had no idea how to fix it.

Today was the biggest wedding of the year—of the century—and all of her assistants had bailed on her. She tried calling Emily again, but the girl had stopped answering her phone after their last conversation, in which she told Madi that in no uncertain terms could she come to work today because she had the stomach flu and had spent the morning curled up on the bathroom floor.

And of course Pedro had flown to Texas for his uncle's funeral yesterday and wasn't willing to hop on a plane to come back, and Gina couldn't leave her newborn with a babysitter while her husband was at work.

Which left Madi completely on her own, and that was going to be a disaster. There was no way she could keep things organized by herself, and her parents were on their yearly anniversary trip in Hawaii, and Kit...

Madi stabbed at her phone with her finger to call Kit. Surely he would help her.

"Hey, Mads."

"Oliver?" Why had Oliver answered Kit's phone? Madi glanced at her screen, realizing she had called *Oliver*, not her brother, but she was too panicked to try to explain why he wasn't the person she needed right now. He had helped at the studio, so maybe... "Are you busy for the next six hours?"

He laughed a little. "Uh, I feel like this is a trick question."

Madi explained the situation as quickly as she could, then held her breath, waiting for him to tell her he was busy and couldn't help her. If this wedding went poorly, everyone in the city would know about it. Dr. and Mrs. Jennings weren't exactly celebrities, but they were rich and powerful enough that they controlled a good deal of the social scene. This wedding would make or break Madi's career.

She heard Oliver take a breath, and she worried her heart would stop beating in anticipation.

"What kind of boyfriend would I be if I didn't help you, Mads?"

Madi barely dared to hope that meant what she thought it meant. "Really?"

"Tell me where to be and when."

Madi almost broke down into tears, and she would never think a bad thought about Oliver Hamilton again. Not that she usually did. He was as close to perfect as they came. "Can I come pick you up in half an hour? Dress nice. Do you have—never mind. It's stupid." She plugged in her curling iron, though she worried she would be too on edge to do her hair properly.

"Do I have what?" Oliver asked.

"A tux. See, I told you it was stupid. Just wear a nice—"

"I do have a tux, actually."

Madi paused in the middle of grabbing all her makeup from the drawer. "Wait, you do?"

He laughed, and the sound sent a shiver through her for some reason. "I do. Assuming it still fits, of course. It's been a few years."

Why would Oliver have a tux? Madi didn't even care. "Wear that," she told him, hanging up before he could come to his senses and change his mind about coming to help her.

Twenty-five minutes later, she pulled up outside his building just as he was coming down the outside staircase, and her jaw dropped.

He looked incredible.

Oliver Hamilton was born to wear a tuxedo. He'd shaved since the art gallery, and though his sandy hair was still damp from the shower he must have just taken, he looked ready to walk the red carpet. His tux definitely still fit, and Madi couldn't believe she had never taken the time to admire the cut of Oliver's torso. He was always next to Cam, so he generally looked pretty small, but it wasn't like the man had nothing going for him.

He wasn't the skinny kid she'd known back in the day.

In fact, he had already built up some muscle in the last couple of weeks training with Cam, and the tailored fit of the tux highlighted all his best features.

He smelled amazing when he slid into the passenger seat, and Madi took a moment to breathe him in and just look at him. She hadn't seen him this dapper since their prom days, when all of the Boys danced with her because she never had an actual date. As a droplet of water fell from his hair onto his shoulder, she watched it slide down his back, wondering if she should brush it away before it ruined the dark fabric. She was tempted to run a hand over his shoulder just to feel how solid he was.

"We're in a hurry, right?"

Face burning, Madi muttered a quick, "Uh huh," then turned her focus to the road and the impending wedding madness. At least, she turned *most* of her attention to the wedding.

She still couldn't get over how attracted she was to Oliver. *Oliver*. The boy who had lost both his front teeth at the same time one summer and spoke with a lisp for months. Now that he was grown, his teeth were perfect. So was the rest of him, and she had no idea how it had taken her so long to notice.

He was like red velvet cake. She'd thought for years she didn't like it, no matter how pretty it looked, but as soon as she had a taste of the subtle chocolate flavor, she realized she'd been missing out all along and couldn't get enough of it.

He smelled amazing. Had she noted that already? She had. But it was worth noting again because it was that good.

She needed to start up a conversation before she blurted something out to embarrass herself. Suddenly dying of heat, she fumbled with the air conditioning before she asked, "So, am I allowed to ask why you own a tux?"

He gave her a crooked grin, but he wouldn't really look at her. Was he embarrassed? Madi wasn't sure if she'd ever seen him embarrassed before. *Nothing* bothered Oliver. "There's a chance I may have gotten an award or two," he said slowly.

"What kind of award?"

"The kind where I have to stand up in front of six thousand people and try not to mess up my speech and make a fool of myself because it's, uh, televised."

"Seriously?"

He laughed, filling the car with light. "Don't sound so surprised. I was kind of a big deal in the coding world once upon a time."

Madi could easily picture Oliver standing on a stage, his confident smile firmly in place and the whole room waiting with bated breath to hear what wisdom he had to share.

"That doesn't surprise me, actually. I always knew you would do great things."

He bit his lip as he grinned at her, and she spent a dangerous amount of time looking at that lip. What was wrong with her? It wasn't like the tux had accented his *mouth*, for crying out loud!

"It sounds like more than it is," he assured her, though Madi wasn't about to believe that. "You look amazing, by the way."

Madi glanced at her formal blue gown. She felt ridiculous, but that didn't mean she hated the praise. Especially from him. "This wedding is kind of a big deal," she said, though that hardly explained why they had to look so impressive. It wasn't like she was going to be in any of the photographs, but the groom's family had insisted. "If this doesn't go well, I'm dead in the photography industry."

His eyebrows high, Oliver seemed to be trying to figure out who could be important enough to demand something like this. "Who's getting married?" he asked when he couldn't figure it out.

"Todd Jennings." Not that she expected Oliver to know who that was.

Though she was busy watching the road and forcing herself not to look at him, she was pretty sure Oliver turned a little pale. If nothing else, the air seemed to thicken with tension. "As in the son of Dr. Jennings, the wildly successful surgeon, and his wife, the hospital administrator at the biggest hospital in the city?" he asked.

Madi laughed a little as a pit formed in the base of her stomach. That response wasn't helping her nerves. "That was oddly specific."

"Yeah, well, that's what happens when your mother is also a wildly successful surgeon and your father runs the

ER at said hospital. They've worked with the Jennings duo for years and might even consider them friends. Assuming they're capable of having friends." He said that last part in a growl.

"Do you think they'll be at the wedding?" Madi asked as she pulled into the venue. She tried to remember if she knew anything about Oliver's parents outside of their wealth, but she was coming up blank. She didn't even know they were doctors. He never talked about them, but he was always so much happier when he spent large chunks of time at the Morgan house. She had a feeling the Hamiltons weren't the best of parents.

Oliver looked slightly nauseous as he shifted in his seat. He waited until Madi offered her ID to the guard at the gate—they were legitimately checking in vendors and guests, apparently—then grimaced as she pulled into her designated parking spot. "You never met my parents, did you?" he asked.

"No." Not even at the Boys' high school graduation. Madi hadn't questioned it at the time, being so used to having the guys around, but not even Ben's parents had been there that day. (Apparently they'd mixed up the days.) And Cam's parents had died when he was little, so his elderly aunt was at the ceremony but didn't stay beyond that.

What was the Hamiltons' excuse?

Madi climbed out of the car and hurried to gather up her stuff, even though she wasn't anywhere close to being late. She wasn't willing to risk anything with this wedding.

After Madi loaded Oliver up with camera supplies, he rolled his shoulders and looked like he was preparing for battle. "I'm glad you didn't have to meet them," he muttered. "Let's pray it stays that way."

Danny had given her a spot in the vendor tent to keep all her spare batteries and emergency supplies. Having Oliver to help out was a blessing on its own, but knowing Danny was around here somewhere kept Madi from slipping into a full-blown panic. He'd dealt with so many nightmare clients that he could stay calm in the worst of circumstances.

Madi was about to run out and find Danny for a pep talk when Oliver put his arm around her shoulders and gently pulled her against his side.

"You'll be fine," he said, though she had no idea how he knew she was panicking a little.

She liked to think she could hide her emotions pretty well. But when he kissed the top of her head, her body relaxed. Maybe she wouldn't need Danny after all. No one had ever read her as well as Oliver.

"Tell me how I can help," he said.

She explained all of her gear and gave an estimate on how long her batteries and memory cards would last. Her ridiculous dress didn't have any pockets to hold those, and she couldn't afford to miss any moments.

"I will happily be your errand boy," he told her. "And I'll be right here in case anything goes wrong."

She threw her arms around him in a hug and held him tightly, wishing she had a way to make him understand how glad she was that he was there. And suddenly she didn't want to let go. It was like he shut everything out so she could breathe. As the pressure of his arms protected her from the growing stress of the day, she leaned in a little tighter, pressing her cheek into the smooth fabric of his tux and using the opportunity to take a deep breath.

Seriously, he smelled *so good*.

"Oh good, you're here!" Danny appeared at the door of the tent, his eyes wild. He must have been putting out fires all morning. "We're going to have a team meeting really quick and make sure everything is good to go."

He took her by the hand and practically dragged her from the tent, pulling her toward a huddle of vendors. "Alright, now that everyone is here, we can go over the schedule to ensure we pull off *perfection* today. Anything less, and it will be all our heads. Now…"

Madi had memorized this schedule weeks ago, but she tried to pay attention in case something had changed. It wasn't easy, though, because when she glanced back over to the tent, Oliver was going through her bag and loading up his pockets with everything she could possibly need at a moment's notice. Even granola bars. He looked so entirely calm. And attractive. And *strong*. Like he would never crack under pressure, which was exactly what Madi needed today.

"Now, go make magic!" Danny said, and all of the vendors hurried off to fulfill their parts. He gave Madi a quick smile before rushing off toward the area where the ceremony would be, leaving Madi to walk back to the tent on her own to grab her camera and start photographing the venue before the bride arrived and started getting ready. She was far less steady than she'd been before the meeting with Danny and the vendors, and her legs shook while her lungs stuttered.

Before she'd even touched her camera, Oliver took her by the shoulders and made sure she was looking at him when he said, "Breathe, Madi. You'll be great." Then he tucked her into another hug that seemed to shut out the world entirely.

It was just like when she was little and too scared to try out for that play. After catching sight of all the people who would be watching her audition and completely forgetting all of her lines, she'd run and hidden in the band room, be-hind the tubas. It was Oliver who found her—all of the Wonder Boys had been looking for her—and he had wrapped her up in a tight hug that hid her from all the scary things making her panic. He hadn't minded that she sobbed into his shoulder and got his shirt all wet with her tears, and he had stayed with her until she calmed down, even though it had taken close to half an hour.

"We can put on the play for your parents," he'd said as he held her. "It won't matter if you don't have the lines memorized because you'll be playing a bunch of parts any-way since there aren't enough of us. This way you can still be an awesome actress, but you don't have to deal with all the jerks in the school who don't like artsy things and can't act to save their lives."

That had been several months before Madi's embar-rassing birthday party. Before the boys all claimed her as a little sister. Like Kit, Oliver had always been there for her, and Madi couldn't believe how lucky she was to have him in her life.

"You're amazing," she breathed into his collar.

He stepped back and gave her a wide smile. "You're going to slay this wedding, Madi Morgan."

Camera in hand, she stepped out into the sunshine and felt like nothing could go wrong tonight. She knew that would quickly change, but for now, as she snapped her first picture—Oliver standing at the tent entrance looking like a million bucks as he grinned at her—she felt like she was on top of the world.

SEVENTEEN

OLIVER HAD NO IDEA THAT being a photographer could be this stressful, and he wasn't even the one taking pictures. He had to give props to Madi, because if this was what she went through at least once a week, she was a whole lot stronger than he'd realized. And he already thought she was pretty strong.

Halfway through the wedding, Madi was still full of energy, zipping around the reception in her heels and inter- acting with guests and capturing candid moments as if she knew they were going to happen.

All Oliver had done was fix a few bow ties and hunt down missing family members, and though he was proud of himself for being able to supply fresh batteries when needed, he hardly thought he should be as exhausted as he was.

Perhaps that came from keeping Madi calm. Though she looked perfectly calm and relaxed, he had known this girl long enough to know when the wheels were turning in her mind. She kept imagining what could go wrong and how she could fail, and every once in a while she must have pictured her jobless future because she would pause and get a far off look in her eyes, one filled with terror and misery.

That was why Oliver had decided to start following Madi around. He pretended to be a wedding guest and blend in—easy enough to do in his tux, as long as he looked disgusted enough whenever he looked at someone under-dressed—and he kept at a decent distance. He didn't want to distract Madi or give anyone a reason to think she wasn't professional, but he stayed close by in case she needed him to keep her from slipping into a panic.

Any time she looked like she was faltering, he gave her a smile.

Every time she smiled back, his stomach twisted a little tighter.

He really had planned to give himself some space and figure out why his thoughts about this girl had changed, but when she'd asked him if he could help... How was he sup-posed to say no? He would have committed murder for her if she'd asked, so it was a good thing she wasn't the vengeful type.

Madi was definitely in her element out here taking pic-tures, and Oliver couldn't bring himself to look away as she did the one thing she was clearly born to do. Not that he wanted to look away. Her navy dress made her look like one of the fancy, glittering guests, but she had the benefit of being a humble, selfless person and stood out because of it. That, and everything about her shone so brightly that she drowned out everything else around her. It was like she came alive when behind her camera, and Oliver had never seen that kind of passion in someone before.

He wondered if he would ever feel that.

"She's amazing, isn't she?"

Oliver jumped when Danny appeared out of nowhere. "What? Oh. Yeah. She is."

Chuckling, Danny adjusted one of the flower center-pieces on the table next to them, and he seemed to be avoiding looking at Madi. Oliver appreciated that, even if he wasn't actually dating her. Danny was good about not making him wonder if he harbored any feelings for Madi. Mostly.

"You should see her when she isn't on edge," Danny said. "I work with a lot of photographers, but no one fits the role quite as well as she does."

"She was born to do this," Oliver agreed. "She got her first camera when she was twelve, and she's never considered anything else as a career since that day."

"So, you know her pretty well?"

Oliver tried to decide if Danny was questioning his story or just trying to get some backstory on the new couple. How much had Madi told her friend? "Sometimes it feels like I've known her forever," he said.

Across the venue, Madi glanced down at her camera screen and looked around. Oliver snapped to attention.

"Duty calls," he said, eager to get away from Danny in case he accidentally said something he shouldn't. When he reached Madi, he grabbed a couple new memory cards from his pocket since she had recently replaced her battery.

The smile she gave him made his head spin a little, though he tried to ignore that. He *couldn't* ignore the way her hand lingered against his when she grabbed the cards. Every bit of skin that touched hers was on fire.

"What would I do without you?" she asked quietly, then swapped out the cards and went right back to taking pictures.

Oliver stumbled back toward the tent to stow the full cards in her bag, but a laugh—a very fake laugh—stopped him dead. He'd been so hopeful, but as usual, luck was not on his side.

Maybe they hadn't seen him? But he only made it one step before a quiet voice said, "Oliver? What are you doing here?"

Taking a steadying breath, Oliver turned and found himself face to face with his father. "Dad." A familiar sense of itchy failure trickled over him, though he tried to keep it from sinking into his skin like it usually did.

Dr. Kent Hamilton looked so much like him that Oliver had once been mistaken for his father, and it had taken a good deal of explaining (and a reminder of what year it was) to correct the mistake. The biggest difference between them was Dad's inability to smile; he only did that when truly overcome with happiness.

Dr. Faith Hamilton was the opposite in that regard and smiled all the time, only it was hardly ever real and never reached her eyes. Eyes that didn't even glance in Oliver's direction despite her sitting only a few feet away. She would have had to be painfully oblivious to everything around her to not know Oliver was standing right there, and the city's best surgeon was no fool.

She was ignoring him. And that didn't surprise Oliver in the least.

"You know Todd?" Dad asked. He was probably trying to figure out how Oliver could possibly be at the same event as them when they ran in the highest of circles and Oliver…didn't.

Oliver wasn't about to explain the truth, in case it somehow hurt Madi. "Yeah," he said, stuffing his hands into his pockets. "Though I don't know him well." He was going to hate this, but Oliver would have to be polite to his parents if he didn't want the whole table thinking too hard about him and raising questions. "How have you guys been?" he asked.

"Never better," Dad said. Mom didn't even look in his direction. "Your mother and I just returned from a medical conference in Prague."

"Sounds informative."

Mom huffed a short laugh but seemed wildly interested in her salad. Oliver shouldn't have let himself hope, but this whole encounter was making it very clear that she still hadn't forgiven him for selling his company. In her mind, it could have led him to fame and fortune and a pretty wife on his arm, and he had thrown it all away.

Oliver had no regrets about his decision, but sometimes he wondered what his mother would have done if he had carried on with it all. It wasn't like she had been all that thrilled with him before he sold the company, so would things have been any different? He had become a failure the moment he went to the wrong school with the wrong major.

Probably before then. He couldn't actually remember the last time they had been proud of him.

He really needed a way out of this conversation without reflecting poorly on his parents and further disappointing them, but he was drawing a blank.

"Hey Ollie, I have a break coming up." Madi to the rescue. She touched his arm and brought some life back into him, and he wanted to pull her into his arms and relive their moment in the tent earlier. Holding Madi and keeping her fears at bay had made him feel important for the first time in years, but he couldn't hold her here.

Before Oliver could make his excuses and get both of them out of there, his father spoke. "Miss Morgan, I presume?"

Madi's eyes went wide, and Oliver didn't think it was because a stranger knew her name, though he was as surprised as she probably was. Dad must have inferred her identity because she looked a lot like Kit. No, she likely stood there in shock because she had inferred just as easily who stood in front of her, and she had no idea how to react.

Unfortunately, Dad recovered more quickly, glancing down at the camera in her hands and narrowing his eyes. "I see you've upgraded. I don't suppose I'll ever see mine again?"

Oliver winced and slid his arm through Madi's before she could ask what that meant. He would explain later, but that was not a conversation for now. "Don't waste your break," he whispered to her and tugged her away. "Dad, Mom, nice to see you, as always."

The lie tasted as bitter as it always did.

When they got a decent distance away, Oliver could practically feel the questions bubbling up inside Madi. He wasn't ready for that, though, so he led her over to the vendor tent where Danny was standing and watching over his flowers. "I'll tell you everything later," he promised, and then he hurried off in the direction of the bathrooms.

Just to have a moment to breathe and ease the tightness in his chest.

Oliver tried not to let things get to him, but run-ins with his parents were never easy. They always left him feeling drained, like it took all of his energy just to stand up straight like his mother always told him to. Every time he saw them, he felt ten years old again, the age he'd been when he'd realized nothing he did would ever be good enough. After winning an award at school for getting top scores in math, he had brought the trophy home with pride. Dad had patted him on the head without breaking away from his phone conversation, and Mom had barely even looked at the thing before telling him he needed to do better in science.

It didn't matter how many times Oliver told himself their opinions didn't matter; the eighteen years of disappointment since that day had left their mark.

He just needed a second to recover, to remind himself that their expectations did not define his worth. And he needed Madi to be done working so she didn't turn her focus to him when it should be on her work. If he could keep his cool for now, she wouldn't pick up on his emotions the way she always seemed to. Once the wedding was over, he would explain everything and hope she still looked at him the same way.

After so many years of having Madi in his life, he couldn't bear the thought of losing even a small part of her friendship. Their relationship was one of the few good things he had in his life, and he would hang onto it as long as he could.

Because Madi was everything.

EIGHTEEN

SHE'D MADE IT. MADI OFTEN lost track of time while working, but this particular wedding had been a doozy, and she was more than ready to be done with it. She still had all the editing to do, of course, but Oliver had sent over his software the day before, and the little bit she had played around with had given her high hopes for the future.

A future with some actual free time in it.

All of the guests had gone, and just a few last vendors were left cleaning up. Madi probably should have left long ago, but she'd barely gotten to see Danny, and she was eager for an update on Hannah. He was probably busy getting everything closed up, though, so Madi settled herself on the stage where the little orchestra had been playing. She would call him in the morning; for now, she wanted to take a moment to breathe.

"Is it always like that?" a soft voice asked.

Oliver materialized out of the darkness, and as he came into view under the twinkling string lights that were the only light left in the whole outdoor venue, he still looked so good. Madi felt like she was an absolute mess, jealous of his ability to keep himself together. Even after an encounter with his parents. Just like she'd been doing all day, she relaxed at the sight of him and wondered how he could be so calming all the time.

How had she gone so many years not spending as much time with him as she could?

"Pretty much," she said, giving him a tired smile.

As he sat next to her, he held out two different slices of cake. A raspberry cream by the looks of it and a dark chocolate. "Danny saved these earlier," he said. "And you don't have to choose, by the way. They're both for you."

Madi's heart swelled with gratitude. She was most definitely lucky to have Danny and Oliver in her life.

"He's a really good friend to you, isn't he?" Oliver handed her the raspberry first without even asking which one she wanted. She always saved the chocolate for last. He knew her so well, and she grinned at him.

"He may be a little pushy," she said, "but he's an amazing friend. And so are you, Ollie. I'm sorry your parents were here tonight."

He shrugged. "I have to see them at some point, I suppose. Might as well be in public so they're less inclined to shout."

"I'm not sure your mom was inclined to say *anything*. Is she always so quiet?"

He laughed a little, anything but amused by the question. "My mother has never been quiet in her life."

"So why—"

"Why was she ignoring her one and only son?"

Madi grimaced at his bluntness, though it wasn't like he was wrong. "Well, yeah."

Sighing, he tugged his bow tie loose and let it hang on either side of his collar. He looked more like Oliver this way, and though Madi didn't have any complaints about the tux, she liked him better when he was more like the boy she'd known her whole life.

Though, perhaps *boy* wasn't the best description. He was absolutely a man, and a handsome one at that. She had seen plenty of attractive people at today's wedding, but none of them held a candle to Oliver and the way he drew her eyes to the skin beneath his open collar. She couldn't help but wonder what the rest of him looked like beneath the starched shirt. She'd gotten a peek when she found him on his run, but she had a feeling there was a lot more to see.

It wasn't like she hadn't seen him without a shirt on before, but she'd never paid attention before. Not like she was now, as her eyes traced every inch of him.

"My dear mother thinks I'm a disappointment," he said in a breath, pulling Madi back to the conversation.

How could anyone think that? It was basically impossible for Oliver to disappoint anyone. The guy was as close to perfect as anyone could get. "Why?"

He shrugged. "Because I sold my company and therefore ruined my life."

Madi didn't know how to respond to that. "And your dad?"

"Dad always wanted his son to be a doctor, but all he got was a kid who liked playing with computers."

Setting aside her cake, Madi took hold of his hand and held it tight. "There's nothing wrong with that, Oliver."

"I know."

She wasn't sure he *did* know. He kept his eyes on the ground and looked completely miserable, and she hated that. Oliver was the happy one. The one who was never bothered and always up for a good time.

Though she wanted to tell him as much, her curiosity beat out her compassion this time. "What did your dad mean? When he mentioned my camera?"

Luckily, Oliver grinned and looked over at her, filling her with relief because it meant he wasn't entirely disheartened. There was still some happy Oliver in there.

"He was referring to the fact that I may have stolen one of his cameras to give to you for your birthday."

Madi's breath caught in her throat. Ben had handed that camera to her on her twelfth birthday, the day she gained three more brothers, but she'd always thought it was a gift from her parents since it was a nice enough camera that four teenage boys couldn't have afforded it. Her parents had denied being a part of it, but she'd just thought they were teasing her.

Tears filled her eyes as she thought about all the years she should have been thanking *Oliver*. She would probably return the camera now that she knew it didn't belong to her, but that didn't change the fact that it had changed her life in the best possible way. "You got me my first camera," she whispered. "Oliver, my whole life is the way it is because of that camera, and you..." She dropped her head onto his shoulder and shivered a little when he put his arm around her. She felt so safe and wanted in his hold. "Do you know how much I needed that present that day?"

"I figured you should have a way to remember the good parts of the day," he said. Though he spoke casually, there was an edge to his voice. Like he had made some sort of discovery, just like Madi had. He pulled her in closer, his cheek resting on her head. "It's not a big deal, Mads, and I know you're thinking about returning it. Don't. He had three others, and he never used it. I didn't even get in any real trouble for taking it, even though Dad threatened to lock me in the house for the rest of my life. He never went through with it."

Madi's heart sank at the thought of a parent treating their kid like that. Her parents had gotten angry with her and the Boys plenty of times, but they never made threats. They taught right from wrong and walked them through how they should have acted instead of what they'd done. Oliver's parents had clearly had high standards, and Madi suddenly understood him so much better.

She still had that camera tucked away in a box at home, and it had always been one of her most treasured possessions. "You risked a lot. For me. You shouldn't have—"

"I don't regret taking that camera for one second." He gently pushed her upright again so he could meet her gaze. His eyes were more of a brown than a green today, and Madi wondered what was going through his head as he looked at her with very little expression on his face. "I wouldn't have made my parents proud even if I didn't constantly disappoint them, so it wouldn't have changed anything if I hadn't stolen it."

She didn't believe that. Maybe his parents were a little harsh, but Oliver had done so many great things in his life that they had to think well of him. "I'm sure your parents are proud of you, Ollie."

"I like when you call me Ollie." He took both of her hands, running his thumbs over her knuckles as he looked down at them. "It reminds me of when we were kids. Did you ever wonder why I spent so much time at your house?"

Madi shrugged. "You and Kit are best friends."

He smiled at that, but it wasn't a real smile. It was a halfhearted twitch that didn't reach his eyes. Was he really questioning whether Kit thought of him as his best friend? Or was Madi just making conjectures? There must have been a reason Oliver wasn't around as often as he used to be.

"My parents are the kind of people who expect nothing less than the best," he said with a small sigh. "They pushed me so hard—too hard—and I would have cracked under the pressure if not for you and Kit. And before you say they must have been proud of the company I built from scratch, you might be right." He shrugged. "But as soon as I sold it, all of that went out the window. I don't think my mom has even said a word to me in the three years since I sold it."

Madi couldn't imagine a mother going so long without talking to her only child, and her heart ached for Oliver. She was pretty sure Kit didn't know that part, or her brother would have worked a lot harder to make sure Oliver was doing okay. She had never asked Kit about it, but she'd wondered why the Wonder Boys weren't all together as often as they used to be, even though they lived within fifteen minutes of each other. Oliver had the most open schedule of all of them, but it was Oliver who was most often missing.

Had Kit even tried to keep him as close as he used to be?

"Why did you sell your company?" Madi asked quietly. Maybe that would help her understand why this man in front of her was hurting so much. Until this moment, she hadn't even realized he was hurting, and she hated herself for being so unaware.

Taking a deep breath and letting it out slowly, Oliver seemed to debate answering her question. He lay down on the stage and looked up at the string lights overhead as if they were stars. If they turned those lights off, they would probably even be able to see a few actual stars. But Madi wasn't about to leave Oliver's side, not when she was pretty sure he was about to share a secret with her.

She didn't know how she knew that, but she lowered herself down next to him and took hold of his hand to let him know she was there to listen.

Oliver turned and gave her a small smile, this time a real one, and then he lifted their hands and rested them on his chest. "My company was doing so well," he began softly. His thumb traced little circles against hers as he spoke, making her shiver. "The software I built helps hospitals read X-rays and MRIs and analyze incoming data quickly, and we were expanding like crazy into other aspects of the medical field. It was everything I had hoped for in a career, and I was on top of the world.

"But it was sucking the life out of me. Literally. I spent four years building that thing from the ground up, going from just me to twenty employees, and it completely consumed me. I barely saw my friends, never had time for dating, and my health was going downhill because I was always at the office. Sometimes for days straight. And when I wasn't at the office, I was working on my phone or at my home computer because I felt like I couldn't abandon my baby."

He looked up at the night sky above them, his eyebrows pulling low as he frowned. "Eventually, I started getting sick. I figured it was just a cold or the flu, so I worked through it. And kept working through it. And then I woke up early one morning with a raging fever and could barely move because I was so sick. I thought..." He swallowed, and his voice went hoarse. "I honestly thought I was going to die."

Madi's heart twisted itself into a knot, tears blurring her vision. She blinked them away, but more came, and she wished she had some way to comfort him as he kept talking. Holding his hand could only do so much.

"I spent three days in the hospital before I was strong enough to go home," he said. "And when I came back to the office, I realized everything had kept moving without me. In fact, my team barely even cared that I'd been gone because they actually had a chance to do what I'd hired them to do, and they loved it. I'd been working myself to the bone for nothing. If I had taken a step back and seen how incredible my team was, I might have…"

He shook his head and turned to look at Madi. "I could have been enjoying my life all those years. I can't remember looking forward to my days back then. Not a single minute of them. I only remember needing to be the best. It was all just work. And stress. And anxiety. In the hospital, I couldn't remember why I liked what I was doing, and I couldn't even look at a computer without getting sick. Two days after I got out of the hospital, I sold the company. I'd been getting offers for months, so that part was easy, and the new owner has turned it into a thriving enterprise. And I've never looked back. Why should I try so hard to be something for someone else when it won't change anything?"

He let out a little sigh. "I just want to be me. The way I am with nothing to prove."

Still crying, Madi tried to imagine what that must have been like for him, but she couldn't. How had he gone through all of that on his own? "Why did no one tell me you were in the hospital?" she asked.

"Because no one knew," Oliver replied. "I didn't want anyone getting mad at me for being classic, overachieving Oliver. They would have been angry, not worried, and that would have made everything worse. I already disappointed my parents; I didn't want to disappoint my real family too. It's better if no one has any expectations."

Though she had no idea how he would react, Madi reached over and pressed her palm to his cheek. It wasn't like they had to pretend for anyone right now when they were entirely alone, but it felt right to be lying here holding his hand. She wasn't sure what that meant, but she wasn't complaining about the situation.

"I would have worried about you, Ollie," she said with a smile. "And I've always loved who you are."

He pressed his hand against hers as he met her gaze. There was something in his expression that felt like he was trying to tell her something, but she didn't know what he was trying to say. "That's because you're special," he muttered, his eyes saying so much more.

Soon after, a security guard kicked them out, and Madi drove Oliver back home, though she wished they could have stayed there all night. Something was happening between them, something new. Though she wasn't sure what it was, she really wanted to find out.

"Thanks again for helping me today," she said when they reached his building. "I would have fallen apart without you there."

Grinning, he brushed her cheek with the back of his finger. "You would have been fine. You're Madi Morgan. You can do anything."

He stepped out of the car, but Madi couldn't leave it at that. He had been entirely raw with her tonight in a way he'd never been before, and that deserved something. Fumbling with her seatbelt, she followed him out and threw her arms around his shoulders before he got very far.

And the hug he gave her was unlike anything she'd ever felt before. He held her so tightly, like he wanted to protect her from the world, but there was something else there too. He buried his face in her neck as if he hoped she could protect him right back. No one had ever needed her like that before.

It felt like coming home.

NINETEEN

When Danny suggested the four of them go mini golfing, Oliver had been wary. The city only had one miniature golf course, and it happened to be at the fun center where Ben worked. So he'd opened up the calendar to check Ben's schedule and picked his night off, because even though Ben knew perfectly well that Madi needed fake dates, Oliver wasn't so sure this one *was* fake.

It certainly hadn't felt fake when Madi gave him a greeting hug when he picked her up from her apartment, and she was the one who took his hand as they walked into the fun center to meet Danny and Hannah at the front.

Then there was that wedding over the weekend. It had been four days since they lay on the stage and talked, and the only contact Oliver had had with Madi since then had been fixing a few bugs with the editing program and setting up tonight's date. So he really had no idea what she thought about everything he'd told her, and a small part of him wondered if all of that had been a dream.

I've always loved who you are.

She hadn't judged him. At all. After years of his father calling him a coward and his mother refusing to even look at him, Madi had given Oliver a sense of peace about his decision to let go of his company and move on. Even Kit wouldn't have let him off so easily, which meant Madi was the one and only person who truly understood Oliver. And that meant…

He didn't know what that meant.

"Looks like we both survived the Jennings wedding," Danny said when Oliver and Madi met up with him and Hannah at O'Reilly's Fun Center. "Any bad news?"

Madi shook her head, and she looked so alive and happy. Oliver hoped a part of that was because she had been telling him on the drive over that his editing program had saved her literal hours and was the only reason she was even free to come out tonight.

"I hope this means we're only going to get busier from now on," she said brightly.

"I hope you're wrong about that," Hannah replied with a laugh, and then she tugged Danny down for a kiss.

Oliver raised his eyebrows. Those two had certainly moved forward with things if they were already to the public affection stage. While he was happy for Danny—he really was a decent guy—he still wasn't sure what that meant for Madi and these fake dates. And that made him squirm a little. He definitely liked things better when he had all the answers, and right now he had none.

"Should we go play?" he said with a little cough, breaking the two lovebirds apart.

Danny chuckled and turned to Madi. "Bet you I'll win."

Madi narrowed her eyes. "I bet *Hannah* will win. Loser has to tell Sophie Jensen's mother-in-law she can't wear hot pink spandex to the wedding."

Though Danny's eyes went wide, he clenched his jaw and nodded. "Fine." Then he turned and led the way to the back, where the mini golf was.

Oliver raised an eyebrow as they walked. "So making bets is a regular thing with you two?" he asked.

Grinning, Madi leaned into him a little and seemed perfectly happy with the way the night had started. Apparently she had no reservations about this date, unlike Oliver. "It's how we became friends. One of my first weddings, I was completely on edge and terrified that I was going to mess things up, and Danny was the wedding planner. He could tell how nervous I was, and he bet a hundred bucks that I couldn't get a shot of every wedding guest."

"And?"

"And I did. All two hundred and fifty of them. Not all of the shots were great, and some of the guests were in the backgrounds of other photos, but I was so determined to get all of them that I forgot how scared I was. And I had so many good photos to send to the bride and groom that they tipped me extra. Plus, I got that extra hundred bucks from Danny."

That was surprisingly cool of Danny, and Oliver's opinion of him rose even higher. He'd been good for Madi, and Oliver made a note to thank him sometime for being her friend. Not only had he helped her become the incredible photographer she was today, but he was also the reason Oliver was here tonight with these dates.

Oliver was even starting to relax a bit the longer he held Madi's hand.

But when he saw Ben standing behind the mini golf counter, all hope of relaxing flew out the window. Oliver stopped dead, stopping Madi with him. When she gave him a questioning look, he nodded toward the counter and searched for a place to hide. "He wasn't supposed to be working tonight."

Madi grinned. "He probably had to switch shifts with someone. He does that all the time."

"Yeah, but now he's going to see…" He lifted their hands. "What is he going to think?"

"He's going to think we're on our fourth date, so naturally we would probably hold hands at this point." She touched her lips to one of his fingers, and though it wasn't like she hadn't done that before, it still caught him off guard and sent his heart racing. The unnecessary gesture wasn't helping his uncertainty about whether this date was fake or not.

Oliver reluctantly let Madi pull him onward, though he searched his annoyingly empty brain for some way to explain why he was a lot closer to Madi physically than he usually was. That part was both for show and because he *wanted* to be closer, and it was going to be a delicate balance all night. He didn't need the stress of knowing Ben would be watching, and he was determined to tell his friend as much.

"Oh hey. Ben, right?" Danny had recognized him, which only made things more awkward than they already were, and Oliver did his very best not to make eye contact with Ben.

Ben shook Danny's hand, his eyes lingering on Oliver's hand around Madi's.

Oliver would have let go if Madi hadn't tightened her own hold.

"Good to see you again, Danny," Ben said. "You guys here to golf?"

"Yep."

Danny paid for him and Hannah, then they stepped off to the side to give Oliver and Madi their chance.

Oliver leaned in immediately. "What are you doing here?" he whispered.

Ben lifted one eyebrow and barely looked at Oliver, going about his business and ringing the two of them up. "I work here."

"You were supposed to have the night off."

This time Ben frowned, pausing long enough to let Oliver know he'd said the wrong thing. Now he was suspicious, and it was all Oliver's fault, and Madi was going to decide they couldn't fake date anymore and he had totally blown his chances. Chances at what, he didn't know, but he didn't like blowing them all the same.

"It's pretend," Oliver said forcefully.

Ben shrugged. "I know that. And you know that."

Was that an accusation?

"Here are your balls and clubs," Ben said, and his expression shifted a little. He was a subtle man in general and rarely did anything surprising. It was why Oliver liked him. But he was also super smart, and he seemed to think he knew something he shouldn't know.

When they got to the first hole, Oliver glanced back at the counter and saw Ben with his phone in hand, and he almost shouted at him in panic. Thank goodness for Madi, who clearly sensed his worry and said something about wanting a different color of ball. She ran back to the counter, said a few things to Ben—he frowned and nodded once— then returned with a new ball and slipped her hand back into Oliver's.

"Should we get started?" she asked as if nothing had happened. As soon as Hannah went to make her first stroke, she pulled Oliver closer and whispered, "We're fine. Ben's not going to tell the others for now, so relax."

Oliver swallowed. Technically, that would be helping Oliver break Kit's rule about everyone knowing about each date. "For now?"

The grin she gave him didn't exactly help him make sense of the next thing she said. "Depends on how well you play your part."

Did that mean he should play up the boyfriend thing? Or was he supposed to hold himself back so Ben could tell it was definitely pretend? He couldn't decide, and he had a feeling Madi wasn't going to enlighten him.

His phone buzzed, and as if he knew exactly who had just texted him, Oliver pulled his phone out with a good deal of trepidation.

> Kit: Next time you go on a fake date with Madi, will you
>   keep an eye on her? I'm worried this whole thing
>   isn't going to be good for her.

Swallowing, Oliver glanced back at Ben one more time to make sure he was busy working instead of sending condemning texts to Kit. So far, he seemed to be safe, but he wasn't sure how long that would last. Especially with how protective Kit could be.

> Oliver: Madi's strong enough to handle anything. I think
>   she'll be fine.
> Kit: Even so, I know I can trust you to set her straight if
>   she starts confusing fact with fiction.
> Kit: I'm counting on you.

Oliver stuffed his phone back into his pocket without responding, doing his best to ignore the way Madi watched him with curiosity. He was not about to tell her that her brother was checking up on her through the Boys; she would hate that. So he plastered on a smile and pretended to be incredibly interested in the way Danny was holding his putter.

When it came to Oliver's turn to hit his ball, he took a deep breath and tried to calm himself down. But something told him he was going to remain in a state of perpetual anxiety the rest of the night.

It felt good to do something normal for once. Casual. After three years of feeling like he was on the outside watching other people actually live their lives, going miniature golfing with people who were only there to have a good time made Oliver feel alive again.

The sad part? He hadn't even realized he had fallen so far from reality until now.

To no surprise, Madi was a huge part of that normalcy when she upped her teasing as soon as they got to the third hole. It reminded him of all the times she and the Wonder Boys would hang out and play games, and her little jabs and insults were paramount to getting him to relax.

The problem, though, was every time the two of them touched, it sent a jolt of electricity through him, and he didn't know what that meant. And he was pretty sure Madi had no idea what she was doing to him every time she bumped his shoulder or touched his arm. Or if she did know, she was having far too good a time torturing him like this.

Danny and Hannah were flirting up a storm, constantly holding hands or tickling each other or stealing kisses to distract each other from the game. And while this was supposed to be a double date for two couples who had been dating for about the same amount of time, Oliver couldn't bring himself to cross the friendship line and follow suit.

Not while Ben could see.

Holding Madi's hand was one thing, but anything more than that—anything breaking Kit's rules—would certainly raise questions. Questions Oliver wasn't equipped to answer.

Even if he was mildly panicking the whole game, Madi seemed to be having a good time and was completely relaxed. She hadn't smiled this much in a long time, Oliver was pretty sure, and he could practically feel the stress lifting from her shoulders as the night went on. Even if he was freaking out and hyper aware of how close he was to her every second—not as close as he wanted to be—her happiness was enough for Oliver. It would have to be, because otherwise he wasn't going to survive the night.

"Looks like Hannah wins with twelve over par," Danny said after the last hole, making a face at Madi because he'd lost the bet. Oliver was surprised he had even managed to keep track of the score with all the flirting he was doing. "Madi was second at fifteen over. Then me at sixteen. Which leaves Oliver…" He pursed his lips, trying not to laugh as he looked down at the total.

Madi looked over his shoulder and snorted. "Forty-seven over? Oh, Oliver."

Oliver tried not to be embarrassed by his abysmally low score, but the look of pity Danny gave him didn't help anything. He was usually pretty good at mini golf, but with Ben over there watching his every move and Danny and Hannah locking lips every ten seconds and his heart leaping from his chest every time Madi bumped into him, it was a miracle he had put the ball in the hole at all.

It didn't help that he kept expecting Kit to suddenly pop up in the arcade or something with judging eyes and a ready fist, even though that was ridiculous. Kit didn't even know Oliver and Madi were on a date right now.

He'd better not know.

"Oo, I just had the best idea!" Hannah said. She dumped her club onto the counter—Ben had thankfully disappeared—practically bouncing up and down as she waited for the rest of them to do the same. "We should go stargazing!"

Oliver's stomach dropped.

"I love that idea," Danny said, reaffirming his response with yet another kiss. Why was he so intent on double dating when he would do a whole lot better on his own? He was clearly doing just fine. "What about you, Madi? You probably have editing to do."

Yes. Thank you, Danny.

But Madi grinned and shook her head. "Actually, I have this fancy new program that does a lot of the work for me, so I have some free time for once. And my first client isn't coming until ten tomorrow."

What would they think of him if Oliver said he didn't want to go? Danny would think he was crazy, and Madi would think he was lying. And she would be completely right. Oliver *desperately* wanted to go stargazing with Madi because it would mean time with her away from anyone who would suspect this thing between them might be real when it shouldn't be.

That was the problem. It *wasn't* real, and pretending otherwise was only going to get one or both of them hurt. Probably him. Because every time he looked at Madi, his heart beat a little faster, and every time he touched her, it was like something woke inside him, like a long-asleep half of himself that he didn't even know existed until now.

When they reached the parking lot and paused to make a plan, Madi turned to face Oliver and looked up at him with eager anticipation. "We don't have to go if you don't want to," she said quietly, which meant he was not as subtle about his wavering thoughts as he'd hoped. She seemed to be begging him to deny it. "I don't want things to get weird."

"I want to go," he replied. He just wasn't sure what would happen if he did.

Things would definitely get weird.

Madi brightened, practically glowing with excitement and leaving Oliver dizzy with that perfect smile of hers. "I have a ton of blankets and stuff at my apartment," she told the others, apparently completely unaware of the heat that spread into his face as he watched her. "Let's go grab them since it's pretty close by."

"I'll drive," Danny offered, and they were off.

It was too late for Oliver to back down.

And he worried he wouldn't be able to stop himself from crossing a very large, very important line.

TWENTY

"So, you and Madi, huh?" Danny leaned against the side of his car, folding his arms as he watched Oliver pace. The girls had gone up to get the blankets, leaving the two of them down in the parking lot as night settled in. "She's seriously awesome."

"Tell me something I don't know," Oliver muttered. Pacing wasn't exactly subtle, but he was so full of pent-up energy that he had to get rid of some of it somehow before he was stuck in a car for the next forty-five minutes until they got up to the top of the nearby mountain. He was desperate to go for a run, but that was not in the cards. Pacing would have to do.

"I mean it," Danny said. "You're a lucky guy."

That made Oliver pause. Maybe he could get some actual answers tonight. He doubted it would help his current predicament, but it would certainly satisfy his curiosity. "So why haven't you dated her?"

Danny turned red and shrugged, his eyes on the ground. "I tried. But when Madi gets something into her head, it's hard to convince her otherwise. She decided we would work better as friends, and at the time I didn't agree with her."

A twinge of queasy jealousy sprouted in Oliver's stomach, and he clenched his jaw as he tried not to picture Danny and Madi together. The hardest part was knowing they were totally compatible. Danny had Hannah now, but if Madi hadn't done the whole fake dates thing, would she have eventually ended up with her wedding planner friend?

"She was right, though," Danny added with a smile. "We're too similar, and I think we would have driven each other crazy by now if she had let me take her on a second date."

That was a relief. Sort of.

"Can I make an observation?"

Oliver stopped pacing again and turned to him. "Depends on what it is," he growled, though he should probably be nicer to Madi's friend. Danny was the reason this whole thing had started in the first place.

Danny shrugged one shoulder. "I was really surprised when Madi said the two of you were dating, and it's still a little hard to believe it."

Oliver's palms started to sweat, and he stuffed them into his pockets before Danny noticed his fingers shaking. "Why's that?" he asked, barely managing to get the words out clearly. Was everything going to be ruined before it really had a chance to begin?

"Because you don't act like you're dating," Danny said.

"Cheese sticks," Oliver muttered under his breath. Danny had figured it out. He was going to accuse Madi of lying to him, and their friendship was going to be ruined, and Madi would hate Oliver for blowing the secret.

"I know you're still pretty new as a couple," Danny continued, "but dude. If you want to keep her, you're going to have to up your game."

It took a good five seconds after Danny finished talking for Oliver to realize what he had just said. And another three to realize what that meant. He thought Oliver was nervous. Or shy. Or straight up cowardly for not making a move yet. And while that stung, it was so much better than Danny thinking the whole thing was a ruse. Oliver leaned his hand on the car, his heart slowing back to a normal rhythm. He could work with this.

"Not gonna lie," Danny said. Apparently he didn't care that Oliver had barely said anything during the whole conversation, though he frowned a little before he kept talking. "It sounds terrible, but there was a part of me that thought all these dates Madi was going on were fake."

Oliver's hand slipped. His shoulder hit the car, and he wanted to run away and hide forever when Danny looked at him with wild concern. He tried to cover his tracks by choking, "All these dates?"

Thankfully, Danny realized what he'd said and how it sounded, and he winced with solidarity. "Sorry. Probably shouldn't have said that. It's not a ton of dates, but compared to how many she was going on before, it... It doesn't matter. Pretend I didn't say anything. I mean, she picked you, so you probably don't need to worry."

"Probably," Oliver repeated. If he had actually been dating Madi, he wouldn't have cared about her going on other dates before because Danny was right. She'd picked him. But that wasn't the situation. She had picked him by default, and Danny had suspicions that it was all fake, and Oliver was going to have to do something to convince him that Madi hadn't lied to him even though she definitely had.

How was he supposed to accomplish that when he couldn't actually do anything with Madi without breaking the pact he had made with the Wonder Boys?

"Seriously, don't worry," Danny said, putting his hand on Oliver's shoulder. "I'm really glad I was wrong about the fake thing. It's clear Madi likes you."

Was it? Or was Madi just a good actor? Oliver wouldn't know since they had never actually put on that play that he told her they would do, after she had that panic attack in junior high. Why had they never performed that play? What if things would have been totally different if he hadn't been such a flake and had spent the time rehearsing with her?

An ache settled in Oliver's chest as he thought about the million and a half possible futures he might have missed out on because he'd been too blind to see what was right in front of him.

The girls returned a moment later, ending the horrible conversation but leading to increasing stress on Oliver's part. He didn't want to tell Madi what Danny had told him because that would make Madi worry and maybe even back out of stargazing. Oliver didn't want that. But neither could he follow Danny's advice and *up his game*. Things with Kit were strained enough as it was, and he had no idea where Madi stood on the subject. What if he put himself out there, and she told him she didn't feel the same way? They would never be able to go back to the way things were after a confession like that, and he couldn't lose Madi from his life.

He couldn't.

Since they took Danny's car, that left Oliver and Madi in the backseat. That would have been fine, if Danny didn't keep looking at Oliver in the rear-view mirror and raising his eyebrows at him as he and Hannah sang along to the music. *Subtle.* The worst part was Danny was right, and it definitely didn't seem like Oliver and Madi were dating. As far as

Danny knew, they had been going out pretty regularly for two weeks now. Plenty of time for Oliver to at least be past the scared-to-touch-her stage. Holding hands was one thing, but Danny clearly didn't think it meant much, and that meant…

Oliver scooted a little closer to Madi and put his arm around her, hoping she didn't think he was pushing an unspoken boundary. Why had they never talked about the rules of being a couple? Going on individual dates was one thing, but now Oliver was her boyfriend. What, exactly, did that mean?

It didn't help that Oliver had never taken a date stargazing, so he didn't know if there was some sort of protocol he was supposed to be following. Was it like parking, and they were supposed to make out the whole time? He certainly hoped not. Or maybe he did want that. But he couldn't do that, because Kit would kill him if he ever found out, and he would probably panic the whole time anyway and be terrible at it because this was *Madi*.

For all the dates Oliver had been on in high school and college, he had never really gotten to know any of the girls, so he'd never been put in this sort of situation because he rarely went on more than a couple of dates with any one person. There was never any risk of vulnerability. What was Madi going to expect from him? What was *Danny* expecting? Why did so many people in his life *expect* something from him when he really had no idea what he was doing? With anything.

He never had.

His stomach churning, he thought maybe it would be a good idea to say he was sick and needed to go home before they got too far.

But then Madi rested her head on his shoulder and slid her fingers into his other hand, her eyes closed and a little smile on her lips. "Do you remember that night we camped out in the backyard?" she asked quietly.

Camped was a loose term, certainly, and Oliver had never actually been camping with Madi. But it would have been impossible to forget that night. It had just been the three of them—Oliver, Kit, Madi—and it was the first time his parents let him spend the night away from home, outside of the time he had chickenpox. The three of them had spent the night out on the trampoline surrounded by blankets and pillows.

It had taken Kit months to convince Oliver's parents to let him do it, and he had promptly fallen asleep as soon as it got dark.

Madi hadn't, though. Nor Oliver. They'd lain there with their heads pressed together and looked up at the stars for hours.

"How many do you think there are?" Madi had asked. "More than a thousand?"

"Probably more than ten thousand," Oliver had said.

She'd been eight at the time, and Oliver had never understood why Kit complained about her hanging around. Sure, she was two years younger, but she had never acted like it. She was really fun, and nice, and she always gave Oliver happy smiles that made him feel wanted, something he never got at home. She had done that from the very beginning, and he had never come up with a way to repay her for making his life brighter.

"If I could give you a star," he'd said that night, "I would do it."

"I would give you one too."

So, they'd picked out stars for each other. Oliver had chosen the brightest one, but Madi had gone for a smaller one. She'd had to take Oliver's hand and point it out for him so he could find it among the thousands of others. And she wouldn't tell him why she picked that one, saying it was a secret.

He hadn't minded. It was the first thing he'd owned that hadn't been given begrudgingly or with any expectation, and he had treasured that star. And that night.

"How could I forget?" Oliver said, resting his cheek against her hair. Whatever shampoo she used, it smelled amazing, though he resisted the urge to breathe in deeply. That would be creepy, and he was still trying to navigate this whole "dating but not really" thing.

Madi's fingers tightened around his as she scooted a little closer, at least as far as the seat belt would let her. "Do you ever wish you could go back to how things were when we were kids?" she asked.

He didn't know how to answer that question. Yeah, they had been a lot closer before they all went off into their respective careers, but going back to their teenage years would mean never experiencing this feeling of being next to Madi in a way he'd never been before. They'd watched plenty of movies as a group, and she even sometimes shared the bean bag with him when the other guys took up all the couch space. But this was different.

Way different.

Swallowing, Oliver lifted his head and waited until Madi looked up at him, though his words stuck in his throat when he realized they were only a few inches apart. They'd never been this close before. Not like this. "I like things the way they are now," he said eventually, and at some point he'd cut the distance between them in half so he could see the dark ring of brown around her honey-colored eyes, even in the darkness of the car.

His own eyes traced her whole face in the silence, noting each freckle and curve and the slight part in her pink lips as she gazed back at him. She was entirely beautiful, far lovelier than anyone he'd ever met, and he couldn't help but wonder how no one had noticed enough to do something about it. How had Madi stayed single this long? Under different circumstances, Oliver would have fallen in love with her the day he met her.

Hannah said something up in the front seat—at some point they had stopped singing—reminding Oliver they weren't alone, and he glanced forward and caught Danny's gaze in the mirror. He looked far too pleased with himself, and Oliver stifled a sigh. He reminded himself that none of this was real, and when Madi put her head on his shoulder again, he was glad for it. It was better if he stopped gazing into her eyes and fantasizing something more, erring on the side of caution until he knew exactly what *Madi* expected from him.

Her expectations were the only ones that mattered.

Though Madi didn't say anything else as they drove up the mountain, she kept her head on his shoulder and seemed perfectly content with the way the night was going.

Oliver hoped it stayed that way.

TWENTY-ONE

WHEN THEY REACHED THE TOP of the mountain and parked at the overlook, Madi was practically shivering with anticipation. It had been so long since she'd done anything like this that it was all a lot more exciting than it should have been. She didn't care, though, because she was having a lot more fun than she'd had in a long time, and she didn't want it to end.

Most of that was because of Oliver. He had been…surprising. The good kind of surprising, not the kind where he jumped out from behind a bush and scared the living daylights out of her. (He'd done that too, but not for years.) No, while Ben had been the favorite with the ladies, Oliver had always been the flirty one, constantly trying to charm the girls in school. Ben had told her once about how many dates Oliver went on in college, and she imagined he had a kiss record so long he'd lost count.

Not that she was thinking about Oliver and kissing. *Mostly*.

So the fact that the most he'd done tonight was hold her hand really said something. What that something was… That was a different story. He probably didn't want to cross any lines and push their fake relationship any deeper than it needed to go, which was really gallant of him. But the later the night went, the more Madi was starting to realize something.

Madi *wanted* him to cross those lines.

That thought alone was completely ridiculous. Madi had known this man almost her entire life. She had only been four years old when she first met him! She had never even considered crossing friendship lines like that. Not once. And it wasn't like he had changed all that much over the years, so there wasn't some magical new reason for her to start thinking about him differently. Outside of maturing a bit, which he'd done years ago, he was still Oliver.

So why had she thought about kissing him on the drive up? She might have done it, too, if Hannah hadn't said something and pulled her attention away.

Beneath the twinkling sky, the four of them laid out blankets in the grass behind the dirt parking lot, where a large meadow stretched out and gave them a fantastic view of the stars. Hannah sat in Danny's lap without hesitation, and though Madi was tempted to copy her, she had no idea how to navigate this moment. Did she take his hand? Follow Hannah's example? Keep her distance because this definitely wasn't a real date even though she *definitely* wanted it to be?

Despite everything Danny believed, it wasn't like she and Oliver were actually a couple.

A pity.

Madi almost slapped herself for that thought. What was she thinking? Oliver had been one of her best friends her whole life, and she was the one who was stupid enough to get them into this fake relationship mess. She wasn't about to make things worse by snuggling up when he probably had no intention to make any of this real.

She *did not* like Oliver. She was just caught up in a game of make-believe, and she didn't think of Oliver as anything but a friend. That was just her imagination taking hold. It wasn't like Oliver was handsome, or calming, or sensitive, or utterly adorable when he got excited about a project, or…

Oliver took hold of her hand and tugged her down right next to him. He put his arm around her as if he'd been doing that their whole lives, his touch sparked a tingling sensation that spread through her whole body, warming her to her core.

Uh oh.

"Aren't stars amazing?" Hannah said, breaking Madi out of her spiraling thoughts. "I could sit here and look up at them for hours."

"They make me feel small," Danny said. "But in a good way. Like there's a whole universe of possibility out there, and I'm just a part of it."

"They make me feel big," Oliver said, so quietly that even Madi barely heard him. He was looking up at the sky as if he might find some answer to a mystery up there. "Yeah, there's a whole universe out there, but the important stuff is right here." And he turned his gaze to Madi.

A shiver ran through her. No one had ever looked at her like that. Like she was important.

She was suddenly aware of so many things, like a switch had been turned on. Oliver's thumb caressing hers, their legs pressed together, the cool breeze that made her want to shift closer and curl up against his chest. He was so warm. How had she never noticed how warm he was? Without thinking about it, she reached out and pressed her hand against his chest, feeling the way his muscles moved beneath her fingers as he breathed.

His heart was racing, the same rhythm as hers.

Before Madi could say or do anything else, she caught sight of Danny and Hannah on Oliver's other side jumping into a kiss that wasn't likely to end anytime soon. She cringed.

"Let's give them some space," Oliver suggested with a grin, though his voice was a little breathless.

As quietly as they could, they grabbed their blankets and moved several feet away to their own little patch of grass. This time, they lay on their backs like they had on the stage, once again linking their hands together as if they'd been doing that their whole lives. They could better see the stars this way, and Madi shifted her position until her head rested right against Oliver's.

It reminded her again of the trampoline when they were kids, only so much better.

They lay there in the meadow for a long time in silence, both of them content to look up at the night sky and appreciate how big it all was. Oliver was right, though. Unlike in the emptiness of her apartment, Madi felt like, with all that expanse above her, she truly mattered on this planet. Right here. Right now. It wasn't a foreign feeling, exactly, but she wouldn't call it familiar either. She had always just…existed. Moving from one thing to the next, always on her own because she didn't even let the Wonder Boys in too deep when she was capable of handling things herself. Independence had kept her from getting hurt, but it had also kept her from experiencing life the way it was meant to be.

She didn't want to just exist anymore.

She wanted to *live*.

And she wanted to do it all with the man lying next to her.

She'd spent her whole life around Oliver, but she'd never noticed that he could sit so perfectly still when he was lost in thought. She'd never synced her breathing up with his just to see what it might feel like to be him. Before this whole fake dating thing, she never would have been acutely aware that her hand fit so well within his, like their fingers had been molded that way. It was such a strange thing to notice, but she could feel every curve of her fingers lining up with his.

She breathed in time with him for several minutes, wondering how she could have gone her whole life without recognizing how easily this man made her feel completely comfortable and at peace in a way no one else could. It had always been that way, so why was she only just now paying attention? No one made her feel alive like Oliver did.

"It's still my favorite star, you know," she said, her eyes on the bright ball of light overhead. She didn't even know what constellation it was a part of or if it had a name, but she loved it all the same because Oliver had given it to her.

Oliver pulled her hand to his chest again and wrapped both of his around it. It wasn't necessarily cold up there, even with the gentle breeze that smelled of pine and dirt, but she definitely didn't mind him trying to keep her warm.

"Why did you pick that star?" he asked after a while.

Madi was surprised he still remembered which one was his; it wasn't exactly bright or widely known. But he was looking right at it, and it sent a wave of heat through her to know that after eighteen years, he still knew which star she'd picked. And she had picked it on purpose, even though he probably thought she'd pointed to a random star. With the way he was looking at it now, she was pretty sure he *desperately* needed to know why, of all the stars in the sky, she had chosen that one.

"Because it's the only one like it," she said with a smile. He met her gaze again, and suddenly she couldn't breathe.

The expression on his face… His eyes were locked on hers so intently that she thought she might catch fire. For a moment, she couldn't even remember what they were talking about, and what little breath she had left slid out of her like his eyes had stolen it.

When his eyes flicked downward, panic pulled her gaze back to the sky. "Do you see how it twinkles?" she asked, still breathless. "All these other stars look the same to me and are a part of a bigger piece, but that one reminded me of you because it's on its own. It doesn't need any other stars to be beautiful. It's special in the best way."

She turned to tell him how silly it was to think a star reminded her of him when suddenly his lips were on hers.

Oliver was kissing her? Oliver was kissing her. *Oliver was kissing her!*

Finally.

As all of her thoughts vanished at his touch, Madi dove into that kiss, threading her fingers into his hair and breathing in that fresh scent she loved so much. He responded in turn, his palm sliding over her cheek and to the back of her neck as he twisted closer and deepened the kiss. She sank further into his hold, not close enough, and she was enjoying every surprising second until he pulled away with a jerk as if he had just realized what he'd done.

And then they stared at each other in the darkness, both of them out of breath and at a loss for words. Madi had never been kissed like that, and she was pretty sure it meant something. Something big.

TWENTY-TWO

Oliver crossed the line.

He hadn't slept a wink last night because he crossed a line he was never supposed to cross, and now he didn't know what to do.

He *kissed* her. He kissed *Madi*. He hadn't meant to do that. He had planned to get a little closer, maybe cuddle a bit to get Danny off their backs, at the very most kiss her cheek or forehead. Anything to prove to Danny that Madi wasn't lying to him (even though she definitely was), and their relationship was real (which felt more accurate than it should), and Oliver wanted to kiss her (that much was definitely true).

He had *wanted* to kiss her, and that was a problem because he very much wanted to do it again.

He tried telling himself that it was all part of the game and Madi had played along with things for the sake of her lie. But Danny had been plenty busy off on his own blanket, so there was no one to pretend for. And while Oliver had kissed Madi, which was crazy enough, Madi had definitely kissed him *back*.

She had caught him as much by surprise as he'd caught himself, and if that had only been a pretend kiss, he couldn't imagine how much better a real kiss would be.

Oliver could practically still taste her as he paced his living room the next day. He could feel her soft lips against his, and the way her fingers played with the hair at the nape of his neck as she pulled herself closer. It hadn't even been that long of a kiss, but every second of it had stuck with him and replayed in his head all night long, leaving him exhausted and confused and desperate to experience it again because it hadn't been enough.

He wasn't sure if anything would ever be enough. It was like he hadn't realized he was hungry until he had a taste, and now he was starving.

Oliver cringed. "Don't compare Madi Morgan to food," he snapped at himself.

She was so much more valuable than that.

If only Madi wasn't busy with that photoshoot this morning, then Oliver could talk to her and figure out exactly what was going on. After that kiss, they really need to clear the air. Oliver needed to be honest with her—with himself—about what was going through his head and heart, and until she was free, he was stuck with pacing.

He should have talked to her last night after he dropped her off and helped her carry all her blankets back to her apartment. He should have told her *why* he'd kissed her, even if he didn't have much of an explanation. Not one he could articulate. But he'd chickened out and hadn't even given her a goodnight hug for fear of kissing her again.

He'd wanted to kiss her again, but that was the sort of thing reserved for a real boyfriend, not a fake one. But was he really fake now?

He needed to do something to get his mind off of things, so before he could talk himself into a panic, he changed into workout clothes and headed over to Cam's gym. A good muscle-tearing workout was exactly what he needed right now.

Thankfully, Cam was there and waiting for him, though he seemed surprised to see Oliver despite this being his scheduled time. "I thought you'd given up already," he said with a chuckle.

It hadn't been that long since Oliver's last session. He narrowed his eyes but said nothing. He was really getting sick of his friends seeing him as lazy, but he would only be able to change their minds with actions, not words.

The opposite of how he needed to do things with Madi. "Let's do this," he growled.

Cam started with the bench press, which was fine by Oliver because he would have to put his full concentration into it; daily runs didn't exactly give him any arm strength.

"So, how's the whole fake dating thing going?" Cam asked as soon as Oliver had the bar in the air.

Oliver scowled. Why did Cam always want to talk at the worst times? Oliver lifted the bar a few times before he answered, annoyed that his arms were already burning. "It's fine," he grunted.

Cam folded his arms, looking way too casual for a guy who was supposed to be spotting. "Has Madi had to set up any dates since bowling? She hasn't asked me, but you're the one who doesn't do anything so you're the obvious choice."

Oliver gritted his teeth, but it was good to know Ben hadn't blabbed. "We went mini golfing the other night." Why did he think coming here was a good idea? He needed to talk to Madi and figure out what was going on before he accidentally said something stupid.

And if Cam started asking questions Oliver couldn't answer, he had nowhere to run. He was trapped beneath

130 pounds of metal, at the mercy of a jacked Hispanic who liked to make his friends—Oliver in particular—miserable.

That wasn't true, and Oliver reprimanded himself for thinking it. Cam had one of the biggest hearts he knew and considered all of them family since he didn't have his own. Oliver couldn't take his frustrations out on Cam just because he'd been too scared to do anything last night.

"I hear Danny has a girlfriend now," Cam said.

Where in the world had he heard that? Did Madi tell him? How long was her shoot going to be this morning, anyway? They *really* needed to talk.

"He does," Oliver said through his teeth. How many reps had he done? It was probably ten, but it felt like a hundred.

"That was fast."

"Was it?" Oliver felt like this whole thing had been dragging on for weeks, and he'd completely lost track of time since his first date with Madi. After that kiss last night—had it only been last night?—it felt like they'd been a couple forever.

Fake couple. Until he talked to her, he had to remember that distinction.

But would a fake girlfriend kiss him like that?

Memories of the kiss resurfaced, and Oliver's arms wobbled, threatening to drop the bar on his chest and probably kill him. Thankfully, Cam took hold of the bar until he was steady again.

"Pay attention, Hamilton. You've got a few more reps in you. So does that mean Madi's off the hook?"

"It's hard to say." Partly because Oliver's arms were not made to handle this kind of weight and he was out of breath. Partly because that depended entirely on the conversation he needed to have with her.

"Nice work. Squat time."

Oliver groaned. The last time he'd done squats with Cam, his backside hadn't forgiven him for a week. But he knew better than to argue. Cam would only push him harder, and he would be even worse off than if he sucked it up and did as he was told.

"Help me move these weights over," Cam added with a wicked grin. He knew exactly how little Oliver wanted to do these, which meant he was probably going to add even more weight than he would have for someone else.

"You take too much pleasure in other people's pain," Oliver muttered as he slid the weight plate from the bench press bar.

"I take pleasure in helping people become better," Cam corrected. "You've spent the last three years doing the bare minimum, and I know you can do more. You know it too. So let me help you get your body working, and your brain will be quick to follow. Maybe then you won't be so lost anymore."

That response surprised Oliver, and he studied Cam for a second as if seeing him for the first time. Maybe they needed to spend more time together and try to be actual friends for once. He hadn't really paid attention before, but there was apparently more to the guy than his muscle. Not that Oliver would ever tell him that. He had his pride, after all.

"By the way," Cam said with a smirk, "I had a question for you, but I'm not sure you're going to like it."

"That is a terrible way to start a topic."

He snickered. "Maybe. But this question is important."

Oliver was probably going to regret this, but he asked anyway. "What?"

"Have you ever wondered why Madi never really dated anyone for real?"

Oliver froze, though he wasn't sure how this particular conversation could be dangerous. It was more intriguing than anything, and he didn't even know if what Cam said was true. "Madi's dated people."

"No, she hasn't, and you know it. She's too shy for that, and too busy. She started taking photo clients in high school and never stopped, and you know how stubborn she is when it comes to doing things by herself."

That much was true, but it seemed ridiculous that someone as amazing as Madi Morgan would be on her own for so long. Was there really *no one* who had seen how incredible she was? "Is there a point to this conversation?" Oliver asked, sliding the plate onto the squat bar before he went to grab another.

"There is definitely a point, and I'm getting to it, but I'm curious about how much you know."

"I've known Madi my whole life, Cam. You've only known her—"

"Since I was thirteen. That's a long time, Oliver. And Madi is the most genuine person I know, so she's not exactly hard to read."

Oliver paused with his next weight, holding it in his fingers and wondering if it would do any damage if he tried to throw it at Cam to shut him up. With how weak his arms were at the moment, he probably wouldn't be able to throw it in the first place. "Can we not talk about Madi dating people?" Not until he knew if he even had a shot with her.

Cam laughed. "This is *why* we're having this conversation."

"Get to the point faster, then."

"You have never been good with patience, have you?"

Oliver shut his eyes tight, willing himself to stay calm. He was on edge enough as it was, and he didn't need his friend trying to psychoanalyze him or whatever it was Cam was doing. He needed a workout, not a therapist. "I'm going to go run on the treadmill," he muttered and went to put the weight on the bar.

"Madi's never been interested in anyone else, and I'm not sure she ever will be."

Those words hit Oliver like a weight in the gut, and he gripped the plate in his hands as he tried to figure out what that had to do with anything. "Else?" he asked quietly. Did Cam mean Madi wasn't going to be interested in anyone at all, or she was already into someone and would never feel for another? Either way, he didn't like it.

Laughing, Cam leaned one elbow on the bar and watched Oliver as if he had just figured something out. "You know," he said, "I always thought you were pretty street smart, even if Kit never did. He thinks your intelligence is limited to books and numbers. But I'm starting to think he's right."

Oliver's arms burned with the effort of holding the plate, but he couldn't bring himself to move. Whatever Cam was about to say, it felt important. Like, it would change his life, important. "What are you talking about?"

Cam shook his head. "How have you not figured out yet that Madi's in love with you?"

Oliver dropped the weight, and excruciating pain shot through his foot as the plate landed directly on top of it.

And then he passed out.

TWENTY-THREE

MADI WASN'T SURE WHO SHE was angrier with: Cam for letting Oliver break his foot, or Kit for laughing about it when he told her. Her brother had called as she was finishing up a newborn photoshoot, and he was laughing so hard that he could barely get the words out.

"They brought him to my house because it was easier to carry him in on the ground floor," Kit had said when he could breathe again. "He keeps asking about you, so you'd better get over here."

Madi had left for Kit's little townhome as soon as she was free, and she marched up to the door ready to smack all of the Wonder Boys if they didn't take this matter completely seriously.

Kit let her in with a grin, and Madi took a moment to take in the scene. Oliver was in his usual place in the giant bean bag, his foot raised up by some pillows and his focus on an intense video game. Cam and Ben were playing with him, and all three of them were throwing out some pretty vigorous trash talk, which meant Oliver wasn't in too much pain.

That was good.

"How bad is the fracture?" she asked Kit, though it wasn't like she knew anything about broken bones. She just wanted to know how much this would affect Oliver when he was already having a hard time as it was.

Kit shrugged as he closed the door behind her. "I understand bones about as well as you do, so I'm not sure. But he's fine, Madi."

Madi certainly hoped so, because otherwise Cam was going to get the verbal beating of his life. How had Oliver even managed to drop a weight on his foot? Wasn't it Cam's job to move those?

She figured she had better ask Oliver what happened, because the other guys would probably just make a joke about it. But as she approached the living room, she wasn't sure where she should go. She wanted to get close to Oliver—and she would have to, to ask what happened—but she didn't want to get *too* close in case the other Boys got suspicious. But she also couldn't act weird around Oliver since the guys would get suspicious about *that*. And she had no idea if that kiss last night had been real or not—it had certainly felt real—so she wasn't sure if Oliver even *wanted* her to get close.

Why hadn't she talked to him last night? She had tried. Multiple times. But she didn't want to bring it up in the car, in case Danny heard, and she'd lost her nerve when he dropped her off at her apartment, so she had gone inside before he hugged her or kissed her again or whatever he might have done.

Besides, she'd been riding pretty high all night after that kiss, so she might have said something dangerous if she hadn't given herself some time to think things through. She might have asked him to date her for real, and that was next-level crazy. Oliver didn't want to date her.

Right?

If he didn't want to date her, nothing about that kiss made sense. So maybe he did?

She wouldn't know unless she asked him, and they were in a strange limbo until they could actually talk. She hated it.

Madi decided to sit on the floor next to the bean bag since the Boys were on the couches, and a blush spread across her cheeks when Oliver stopped playing as soon as he saw her. Though he immediately died in the game, which normally would have gotten him pretty riled up, he grinned at her.

"Hey, Mads," he said softly.

Every inch of her felt electrified under his gaze, like her body hadn't realized it had more than a couple senses before now. It was like she was attuned to Oliver, and the closer she got, the higher the frequency until she was ready to explode. She needed to look away from his handsome face before the other Boys noticed how red she'd turned, so she looked down at his foot. "How is it?" she asked.

"Could have been worse," Oliver replied.

"That's not really an answer."

"I'm trying not to think about it. I have never wanted to go for a run as bad as I do right now, and it's driving me crazy."

Grinning, Madi glanced back at his face and regretted it when she found him still smiling at her like everything was okay now that she was here. "I'll be honest," she said, hoping she sounded normal. "I would hate it. But would it make you feel better if I went for a run for you?"

He lifted his hand, as if he might stroke her cheek, but he must have changed his mind halfway because he scratched his forehead instead. "It definitely wouldn't make me feel better," he said with a little chuckle.

Madi was staring way too intently into his eyes, and it took everything in her to look away. They were extra green today, and she had no idea what that might have meant. She was sure his eyes were greener when he was happier, and he couldn't possibly be happy about breaking his foot. So, what had gotten him so cheery? Was there any chance it was because of her?

"So, how's the Danny situation?" Kit asked, plopping himself onto the couch and stealing Oliver's controller out of his hands, seeing as he was no longer playing.

Madi and Oliver exchanged a look, and she was pretty sure he was telling her they still needed to keep their thing a secret. She couldn't agree more. "Well, he's dating some-one now," she said, trying to decide how much she should say. Ben already knew that part, and based on his eyebrow-wiggling reaction, so did Cam.

"Is that good or bad?" Ben asked. He looked more suspicious than the other two as he gazed at Cam. Madi hoped it was because he knew she and Oliver had been on a couple more fake dates, not because he actually suspected something about their little pretend relationship.

At least, Madi thought it was still pretend, but she'd been wrong before.

"I'm not sure," she said, referring both to her thing with Oliver and to Ben's question. "He's a lot happier now that he has Hannah, and he's spending more of his free time with her."

"But he keeps wanting to go on double dates," Oliver threw in. How did he sound so casual when their secret was right on the edge of being blown? At least he hadn't said anything about the bet. "I think he's worried about how he'll act if left alone."

Kit narrowed his eyes, and Madi couldn't fathom why he was looking at Oliver like that. Like his best friend had just betrayed him somehow. Did Kit know something Madi didn't? "Are you suddenly an expert on Danny?" he asked.

Oliver rolled his eyes as he shifted in his bean bag. "We've doubled a few times now, so of course I've gotten to know him better. I'm the lazy one with no job, remember? Madi has needed some dates recently, and you all have your lives together."

Madi knew Oliver said that because it was what the guys expected him to say, but she couldn't help but wonder if he felt some truth to what he said. Did the Wonder Boys actually think he was lazy? Did Oliver believe them? He looked perfectly at ease and unconcerned by his comment and the role he'd apparently been given, but that didn't mean much. Madi knew how hard Oliver had fought to make his parents proud and be someone who mattered.

She knew what that fighting had cost him.

Yet again, she wondered why Kit always gave Oliver such a hard time when Oliver had never had it easy. The two of them used to be so close.

"Just don't go thinking any of this thing with Madi is real," Kit muttered, and it seemed like he said it more to himself than to Oliver.

Madi met Oliver's gaze again, but she couldn't tell what he was thinking. Either he was reaffirming Kit's thought and making sure she didn't read into last night's kiss, or he was telling her it was definitely real and Kit was entirely wrong.

Not knowing which one it was was going to drive Madi crazy, but without a chance to talk to Oliver alone, she was never going to figure it out. She would have to wait, but first she needed to change the topic before any of the Boys started getting crazy ideas. Ben and Cam were already throwing each other looks as they played their game, having their own little silent conversation.

"Do you know what this reminds me of?" she asked, looking around the room. All the guys were in their usual places, the places they'd adopted when they were teenagers. Kit had even arranged his couches this way to keep things the same as they'd always been.

The Boys were pretty focused on the game, but they knew better than to ignore Madi, something she had always loved about them. She could command their attention with ease.

Three of them spoke at once:

"When Ben's sisters all got the flu," Cam said.

"That time Kit was grounded," Ben said.

"When Oliver broke his hand like an idiot," Kit said.

Oliver didn't say anything until the others had, and he said it so quietly that only Madi heard him: "Chickenpox."

A warmth filled her, starting at her chest and moving outward until even the ends of her toes were warm. "You remember that?" She didn't think he had since he had never talked about it. Madi had begged her mom to let Oliver stay longer than the week it took them to heal because Oliver was so much happier that week than he usually was. She hadn't understood why back then, but now she did. Oliver had had some time away from his awful parents.

Oliver gave her a little smile. "Best summer of my life."

She was pretty sure he meant that, even though Oliver and the Wonder Boys had had some pretty epic summers as they got older.

She settled a little deeper onto the floor, resting against the side of the massive bean bag. Though she thought about pretending to watch the guys play their game, the aliens they were shooting at weren't nearly as interesting as the man next to her. She could almost feel him because she was so close, but the others in the room had basically built a wall between them, keeping them apart until they could figure out what was going on between them.

"So, does it hurt a lot?" she asked quietly.

"Would you kiss it better if I said yes?"

He may have said that to make Madi blush, but she didn't think so. He turned slightly pink too when he said it, and he said it so softly, as if he wanted to make sure no one else heard him. For a man who had always wanted to be the center of attention, that had to mean something.

But *what* did it mean? Madi didn't know, and until she and Oliver were alone, she wouldn't be able to find out.

"I'm glad you're here," Oliver said.

Madi smiled. "So am I."

TWENTY-FOUR

THE WONDER BOYS STAYED AT Kit's pretty late, and it felt like old times for the first time in years. They must have all realized how much they had been missing quality time with all four of them, and they'd abandoned their video games to eat pizza and argue about stupid, pointless topics the way they used to.

If breaking his foot was what it took to get them all together like this, Oliver was glad he could make that sacrifice. At least this time it hadn't been intentional, though he would never admit out loud to breaking his hand to take the attention off of Madi and her stuck finger at the bowling alley. She had never liked being noticed for things out of her control, so Oliver had gone with the first stupid idea that had come to his head. It had definitely worked, but Oliver still occasionally got a dull ache in his left thumb and forefinger from the Whack-a-Mole incident. Extreme? Maybe. But it had given the Boys something to laugh at that wasn't Madi.

It was worth it, just like tonight.

Especially with Madi there with the guys, Oliver was feeling more relaxed tonight than he had felt in a really long time. Who needed supportive parents when he had three awesome brothers and Madi? Though the guys teased him about selling his company, they had never judged him. Not like his parents did. If they knew the truth, they might even applaud his choice, and that was not something he would get elsewhere. The Wonder Boys were the best people he knew, and thanks to them, life was pretty good.

He hoped it would only get better. Kit might not think so, but change was important. And with the way things had been moving with Madi, Oliver was so ready for this change.

Eventually, Cam and Ben decided they needed to head out. Both of them wished Oliver a speedy recovery and gave hugs to Madi, and they continued discussing the pros and cons of using hair gel as they walked each other outside to head home.

"You sticking around, Hamilton?" Kit asked after the door closed. He yawned, up way past his bedtime. Once he became a teacher, he'd lost all sense of night life.

Oliver raised an eyebrow at him. "Unless you want to carry me home, then yeah. I'm still pretty dizzy from the pain meds, so if you don't mind, it's probably best if I camp out in your guest room until I'm a little more mobile."

Kit looked confused by the way he'd worded that. "Of course I don't mind."

Oliver glanced at Madi, who gave him a pointed look, and he added, "Besides, I have to challenge your sister to a rematch in *God of Battle*." At least that bit was true. She had beaten him quite soundly in the video game an hour ago, and the defeat still stung a little. When did she even find time to practice games like that? Maybe she was naturally gifted.

Yawning again, Kit nodded. "Madi, don't let this idiot keep you up too late." Though he lingered a moment, glancing between the two of them, he headed up the stairs to his bedroom and shut the door.

Oliver practically felt the tension leave the room, though it was quickly replaced by a new kind of anxiety. He and Madi were finally alone, and that meant… It meant he had to be brave, and he was not feeling all that confident at the moment. Not when every time he looked at Madi he was tempted to kiss her, something he couldn't do until he was sure she wanted him to.

Cam had said she was in love with him, and it was high time Oliver figured out if there was any truth to that.

"You…" He swallowed as the rest of his words stuck in his throat. "You don't have to stay, you know." But he wanted her to. She had already spent most of the evening making sure he was comfortable since the Wonder Boys weren't all that helpful.

Madi smiled from Ben's loveseat, where she'd been for the last couple of hours. "I know."

A spark of hope came to life in his chest, but he wouldn't let it grow beyond that. Not yet. "I know you're busy and probably have a lot of editing to—"

"I actually have this fancy new program that does a lot of the work for me," she said with a grin. "Some weirdo programmer made it for me, and I'm pretty sure it's smarter than me."

If she was trying to give him a big head, it was working. "I'm pretty sure it's not," he said, and it came out as a whisper because his self-control was dwindling. The only reason he hadn't moved over and mauled her with a kiss was because he wasn't sure he *could* move without causing himself a whole lot of pain. Now that the pain meds from the hospital had worn off, the boot on his foot only helped so much to curb the ache of the fracture he'd caused with that weight. He wasn't quite ready to put moving to the test.

Madi got up, moving back to the floor where she'd started as if she knew exactly what was going through Oliver's head. She rested her shoulder against the bean bag, and she was close enough that Oliver would have run his fingers through her hair if his hands weren't shaking.

"Actually," she said after a moment, "I was planning to use tomorrow to edit all those photos from the wedding last weekend. But I already finished those."

Oliver swallowed again. "Which means what?"

She turned, resting her arms on the bag and dropping her chin onto her wrists, putting herself only a few inches away from where he lay. "Which means I have an unplanned day off for the first time in years. *Years*, Oliver. Thanks to you. You have no idea what that means to me."

Oliver couldn't stop himself. He reached out and hooked his finger on hers, and his heart started racing when she opened up her hand so they could slide all their fingers together. That was not the action of someone who was only pretending. It couldn't be. "Mads," he whispered. "What—"

Kit's door opened, flooding the hall with light, and the two of them broke apart right as he appeared at the top of the stairs in pajamas and mid-yawn. "I forgot," he said as he made his way to the fridge and grabbed a bottle of water. "Mom and Dad are flying back in tomorrow from Hawaii, and they're coming over for dinner. You'll probably still be here, Oliver, so you're welcome to join us."

Though he was eager to see the Morgans again since it had been a while, he was a little distracted by the look on Madi's face. Why didn't she look excited about the news of her parents coming back?

"Why didn't I get an invite?" she asked after a moment.

Oliver's heart sank a little. She hadn't known about dinner?

Kit chugged half his water before he answered. "Because you're always busy on Fridays."

"But I'm not tomorrow."

"Oh. Well, dinner's at five. I'll pick up a couple more pizzas, and—"

"No way," Oliver said forcefully. "You are not feeding Duke and Lydia *pizza* as their first meal back from a long trip. I'm cooking."

Kit rolled his eyes. "You can't even walk, Hamilton."

"I'll help him," Madi offered.

"You're a terrible cook," Kit said. "We need them not to starve if we want to keep them around."

That was probably a little harsh on Kit's part, but he wasn't wrong. Madi had never been very talented in the kitchen, and they all knew it.

"I'll coach her," Oliver said before Madi could take too much offense to her brother's comment. "We'll take care of it, Kit."

Kit looked like he might try to argue, but another yawn cut him off. Then he shrugged and muttered, "Fine," before he headed back upstairs and shut his door behind him, throwing them back into semi-darkness.

Only the kitchen light made it possible for Oliver to see Madi, though he didn't mind the mood the low lighting set.

He *did* mind when Madi said, "I should probably go." But then she didn't actually move. She just sat there, her chin on her arms and her brown eyes locked on his. She was right, though, and she looked tired enough after two late nights in a row that she would do better to go to sleep.

"Will you come back?" he asked, hating how needy that made him sound but not caring at the same time. He wanted her to come back. He didn't want her to leave in the first place. He wanted her next to him every minute of every day. He always had, and he would have been stupid to argue otherwise.

Madi smirked. "Of course I'll come back."

That was a relief, and Oliver hoped she knew that. He worried he would mess up his words if he tried to say as much, so he went for a different comment. "Are you okay with the whole dinner thing?" he asked gently. "I can't believe they wouldn't—"

"Kit was right. I'm always busy on weekends. And they usually do invite me, but I guess they got tired of me saying no. They've finally given up on me."

Oliver's heart ached for her. He knew exactly how hard it was to start up a business, even harder to run a successful one, and he wanted to make sure she knew she was not alone in all of this. "I would never give up on you, Madi Morgan."

She sighed and glanced toward the stairs. "I think Kit gave up on me years ago," she muttered. "He clearly doesn't care if I'm here or not."

Blood pounded in Oliver's ears as he thought about that one. She thought Kit didn't care about her? Was she insane?

"I know it was a while ago," he said carefully, "but do you remember the first year Kit and I went to junior high?"

Madi bit her lip, and the urge to kiss her was so strong that Oliver bit his own lip as she spoke. "I was so scared to go to school that year because it was the first time I didn't have Kit there with me," she said.

Oliver chuckled. "Me too."

"What?"

"My parents decided I should go to a fancy private school where I could 'apply myself' better, and I hated every minute of it. I skipped half my classes and wouldn't pay attention the rest of the time, and when I failed my first semester, they thankfully agreed to let me come back to school with Kit."

"That's why he was in such a good mood over Christmas break that year!"

Oliver grinned, amazed that she had even noticed. He and Kit had been friends for so long at that point that being away from him had killed all of Oliver's motivation. And maybe a part of that was being apart from Madi too since his private school was too far away for him to walk to Kit's after school, so he never saw her. "Yeah. We were always better as a pairing. Cam and Ben made things even better."

Those early days had been some of the best of Oliver's life. Having that feeling back again had reminded him how much he missed his group of friends.

"Hey," Madi said, and she seemed hesitant to ask whatever question had popped into her head. It must have been quite the question if she was so disinclined to ask it.

Oliver grinned. "What?"

"What did Kit and Cam fight about when they met? No one ever told me, and it's been driving me crazy for years."

He had all but forgotten about that fight. He'd been stuck in an advanced math class that happened after school, but word had spread quickly. Kit Morgan was in a fist match with the new kid.

Oliver hadn't believed it at first, but when his teacher ran out to help, he figured he should make sure Kit was okay.

He hadn't been. Though Kit was taller, Cam definitely had the advantage in sheer bulk, even back then. Kit's face had been covered in blood, and Cam hadn't even been hit. And when Oliver showed up, Cam chose that moment to back off. Both of them ended up in detention for three weeks, and somehow they were super tight after that, like the fight had never happened. While Oliver knew what had caused the fight, he had never been able to figure out how the friendship had come about.

"I'm not sure it's my secret to share," Oliver muttered. If Cam wanted Madi to know why he'd thrown that first punch, then it would have to be Cam who told her. "But I can tell you Kit was being stupid, and Cam put him in his place."

"Oh," Madi said, clearly disappointed, and Oliver was tempted to tell her anyway. But he wouldn't.

"We Wonder Boys have always been idiots," he said with a shrug. "Sometimes more so than others. I'm sure Cam and your brother would be happy to explain if you asked. Anyway, that whole semester that I was gone, Kit drove me crazy whenever he called me because all he could talk about was you."

Madi frowned, and Oliver shook his head. "Not because I didn't want to hear about you," he assured her. "He was so worried about you because he wasn't in the same school as you, and he wouldn't believe me when I told him you were strong enough to survive on your own. And he never worried about me, as much as I wanted him to. All of his thoughts were for you.

"It's always been like that, Mads. When we were in college, anytime one of us came back home for a weekend or whatever, he demanded updates about you. Half the time when we have our club meetings, it's because of you, even now. Believe me when I say no one cares about you the way Kit Morgan cares about you."

To his surprise, Madi took hold of his hand again, her gaze fixed right on him. "No one?"

There was no way she was asking what he thought she was asking. Because if she was asking if *Oliver* cared about her, then things were about to get really interesting.

"Well," he said, his throat tight, "I certainly hope I don't feel the same way about you as your brother does."

He leaned in, and so did she, and they were a breath apart when Kit's door opened again. Oliver considered going for it anyway, but he wasn't keen on his best friend smothering him with a pillow while he slept.

Madi pulled away right as Kit appeared and muttered, "Left my phone…" as he grabbed it from the kitchen counter.

Getting to her feet, she gave Oliver a soft smile that seemed to say so much, even if he didn't know what any of it was. "I should head home. I'll come by in the morning and see how you're doing, Ollie. And I'll help him make dinner," she said to Kit, who glanced between the two of them again as if he knew something had happened.

Nothing had happened tonight, but it almost did, and that was enough to keep Oliver going until tomorrow when they could finally be alone.

TWENTY-FIVE

MADI WAITED AS LONG AS she possibly could before she went over to Kit's house in the morning. Kit usually left for work around 7:30, to get there long before the kids did, so Madi forced herself to wait until eight. Just in case.

She had very nearly kissed Oliver last night, and if Kit had seen it before she and Oliver had even had a chance to talk about what was going on, things weren't going to end well. She wanted to be sure something was really happening before she made a big deal about it. With how big this potential was, until they knew exactly what their plan was and what their relationship meant, it was better to keep Kit in the dark before they threw him completely off balance.

She had typed up eight different texts to send to Oliver after she'd gotten home, but none of them had sounded right. This was the kind of conversation they needed to have face to face, so she'd deleted every one and hoped Oliver wasn't stressing out about the whole thing. Though, considering it was *Oliver*, he probably hadn't even thought about it. He never stressed.

At least, she hadn't thought he did, but after what he'd told her about his company, maybe she was wrong. Even though she'd known him most of her life, there was likely a whole lot more to Oliver than what she knew, and she was eager to have that deeper relationship.

As she showed up at the townhouse, she paused at the door and took a few deep breaths. All she had to do was be brave for ten seconds and tell Oliver that she didn't want to pretend anymore, and that would be that. Either he would reciprocate her feelings, or he would tell her they were just friends, and then they could move on.

All of this waiting and guessing could end.

"Good morning, Madi!"

She jumped at the sound of Cam's deep voice and turned with face flaming to find him sidling up the pathway with a couple bags of food from the closest bakery. She didn't *actually* have any reason to be embarrassed, but she was. "Uh, hi," she breathed. "What are you doing here?"

She mentally slapped herself for wishing Cam wasn't here. She should have been glad her friend was there, especially because she didn't get to see him all that often. But couldn't he have waited twenty minutes before he showed up? That was all she needed.

Cam held up his bags of food. From the smell of things, whatever was inside was deep fried and delicious. "Peace offering," he said. "I feel really bad that Oliver broke his foot on my watch. If I'd known he was going to drop the weight…"

"That's really nice of you," she said, and she almost added, "But you don't have to stay. Oliver and I will be fine." She didn't say that last part, though, because Cam was smart enough to suspect something if she turned him away for no good reason.

"Should we see if the cripple is even awake?" Cam asked with a wide grin.

It was the kind of grin that said more than it should, and Madi wondered what, exactly, he was trying to say with it. It was like he knew something. But there was nothing for him to know, because nothing had happened.

Okay, so something had definitely happened up on the mountain. Something Madi had almost repeated last night. And there had been no one to pretend for last night either, so if Oliver really had been leaning in just like Madi, then… Then they really needed to have that private conversation.

Oliver *was* awake. He had moved to the couch and was channel surfing, but when he caught sight of Madi, his lips spread into a wide smile that made Madi's cheeks burn. He reached out his hand to her as she approached, but then he caught sight of Cam and turned that reach into a stretch.

Madi couldn't help but wonder how they had managed to keep this whole thing a secret this long when they were both being completely obvious.

"Cam brought you breakfast," she said and winced, hoping he could read her disappointment.

Oliver glanced between the two of them, smiling a little, though he looked as disappointed as Madi felt. "Sweet. I can't complain about free food. So does this mean I get two nurses today?"

Cam dropped one of the bags of food onto Oliver's lap before he sank onto the other couch and held the other bag out for Madi. "Don't push your luck, Hamilton. What are you watching?"

"It's, uh…" Oliver frowned at the TV. "Some kind of soap opera, apparently. So, if you're not here to nurse me back to health, Cam, why *are* you here?"

Subtle, Madi thought, though she was wondering the same thing. There was no need for him to stay now that he'd delivered his apology breakfast.

Cam didn't seem to notice Oliver's increasing grumpiness. "Kit thought you could use the company," he said before he took a big bite of his sausage biscuit. He didn't seem to think any of this was strange, even though he and Oliver got along the least among the Wonder Boys.

That meant Kit probably *was* suspicious, though he hadn't said anything last night.

"I have the day off," Madi said, trying to figure out how to say this without somehow insulting Cam. "I was planning to stay with Oliver so he doesn't get bored. If you have things you need you do, you can—"

"I have the day off too," Cam said with a shrug. "Actually, Madi, since you're here, I was hoping to talk to you about starting a business."

Oliver paused with a hash brown patty halfway to his mouth, one eyebrow raised high.

Madi had the same reaction. "You're starting a business?"

Cam shrugged. "I was thinking of starting up my own gym, especially with that hashtag trending like it is. I figured I would capitalize on the attention, even if I hate it."

It was about time! But couldn't he have picked some other time to bring this up? Madi was totally excited for him, but she had a feeling this was not going to be a short conversation. Oliver was already gripping the TV remote so tightly that it creaked beneath his fingers, and Madi was seriously considering just telling Cam the truth at the same time she told Oliver. Maybe he would understand.

"Do you think you could walk me through where to start?" Cam asked, and he pressed his palms together and stuck out his bottom lip. It was a ridiculous look for a guy whose arms rivaled those of Hollywood superheroes, but Madi had to admit it was working.

Glancing at Oliver and trying to convey through a look how torn she was, she settled next to Cam on his couch. "Of course."

After a morning of walking Cam through the process of getting business licenses and finding premises and setting up taxes, Madi was more than ready for Cam to leave. It wasn't that she didn't want to help him, but the longer their conversation went on, the grumpier Oliver got, and Madi didn't blame him.

She'd been hoping for a whole day with Oliver, without any distractions. Madi had been planning to tell him exactly what she was feeling (or as close to it as she could get since it was all really new), and she'd been hoping she could figure out a way to tell her brothers—real or otherwise—that she was interested in dating Oliver for real.

She had no idea how they would react to that, but it was something they needed to know. Even if Oliver didn't reciprocate. She never wanted to keep secrets from the Wonder Boys.

Every time she glanced at Oliver, she reminded herself of what she planned to say. She'd stayed up far too late thinking things through, but at least she was prepared. She hadn't planned for Cam, though, and she couldn't bring herself to kick him out when he seemed so excited about starting up his gym.

At least Oliver gave her a smile every time she looked over, even though he was pretending to watch TV. It was like he knew whenever she was looking at him, and every glance he returned made her heart skip a beat.

Had he always been this handsome? Yes. Definitely yes. And Madi had no idea how it had taken her more than twenty years to consider him as anything but an older brother. All of this time she could have been seeing those little smiles of his as something meant just for her, and she'd been an idiot.

She had probably been into him for years and didn't even realize it until now. Years she had wasted.

The next time she met his gaze, Madi tried to silently tell Oliver that they would talk as soon as they got the chance. No more wasted time. It seemed like he understood, because his smile shifted into one somehow both smoldering and gentle. But Madi was probably imagining that. She wouldn't know until they talked.

Finally, after several hours, Cam glanced at his phone, then rose to his feet and stretched his massive arms over his head. "I should be going," he said. "Madi, thanks so much for walking me through things. You're the only one in the group who knows how to start a business from scratch, so it really means a lot."

The only one? Madi looked over at Oliver, whose eyebrows had pulled low over stormy hazel eyes, as much with anger as with hurt, she was pretty sure.

"You know," she said, knowing she had to approach this one carefully. "Oliver might be better with this sort of thing since you're going to have a lot more employees than I have. My business is tiny compared to what his was."

To his credit, Cam looked apologetic as he turned to Oliver. "I totally forgot," he said, and it sounded like he meant that. He wouldn't have been able to lie anyway. "I guess it's been long enough since you had it that it didn't even cross my mind. Sorry, man. Maybe we can get together sometime soon? I need to get some muscle in you, anyway, now that you can't run for a while."

Oliver nodded without saying anything, apparently speechless from that apology, and he watched Cam head out the door with a lot of emotion in his expression, both good and bad. Of the four of them, Oliver and Cam interacted with each other the least, and as far as Madi knew, they never hung out together without Kit present. Maybe working on Cam's business could fix that.

"Bye, Cam," Madi said as he slipped out.

Before the door had even closed, Oliver reached out and grabbed hold of Madi's hand. "Come here," he said and tugged, pulling Madi right off her feet and into his lap. His eyes burned with a fire that spread through Madi as they gazed at each other, leaning closer. His arm snaked around her waist, and unless she was mistaken—she didn't think she was—he wanted her as much as she wanted him. She had a feeling their conversation was going to come second to a repeat of their moment under the stars.

Well, that answered that question.

"Oh hey, Ben." Cam's voice came through the still-open door.

In the next moment, Madi was on the floor.

"Look who's here," Cam said with a grin, poking his head inside just before Ben pushed him aside to come in.

"How's your foot, Oliver?" Ben asked with a warm smile. "Madi, why are you on the floor?"

She had never been more frustrated in her life, and she didn't even bother searching for some excuse. She just crawled up onto the other couch and fell into the cushions with a huff. What would it take to get a moment alone with Oliver?

"You don't have the excuse of feeling guilty, so why are *you* here?" Oliver asked.

Madi may have imagined it, but she was pretty sure Oliver's eyes were shining with excitement despite the interruption. After so many years of being the "lazy" friend, maybe he was really enjoying all this attention. She told herself that was the case and to calm down. Oliver wasn't going anywhere, and they would eventually have time to talk and whatever else.

"I brought cupcakes," Ben said and held out the plastic container. "Mom made them. And I got you a new game. I know how easily you get bored."

If Oliver's huge grin was any indication, Ben's gesture was exactly what he needed, so Madi settled in as Ben got the video game ready to go.

She got a text a moment later.

Oliver: This isn't how I wanted today to go.

She glanced over. Though he gazed at the TV, she could tell his focus wasn't on the game, even though he was supposed to be choosing his character. She smiled and typed out a quick reply.

Madi: I tried to get Cam to leave, but you know how he
is. Once he starts talking, he doesn't stop.

A little smile quirked up on one corner of Oliver's mouth.

Oliver: What are the chances Kit put him up to it?

Madi thought about that. Kit hadn't given any indication that he knew what was going on, but he'd been acting strange pretty much since the beginning of the bet. Maybe he knew something they didn't. Or rather something they hadn't known before now.

Madi: You think Kit is the reason Ben is here too?

Oliver: I wouldn't put it past him. Don't forget, this isn't
the first time he's done something like this.

"Do you guys remember that time Kit thought it would be a good idea to stay up all night and wait for Santa?" Oliver asked out loud.

Ben raised an eyebrow. "You do remember we were in fifth grade when I met you guys, right?"

Madi matched Oliver's grin, even if it wasn't exactly a universal memory. "Technically, you weren't there either, Oliver. You were just on the phone. I was the one who had to deal with Kit."

Rolling his eyes, Oliver shifted in his seat while keeping his foot steady. "Says the girl who fell asleep at, like, eight."

"I was seven! And not nearly as obsessed with Santa Claus as he was."

"Hang on," Ben said, holding up a hand. "Kit believed in Santa Claus until he was *nine*? I only made it to four before my sister spilled the beans."

Oliver snickered. "And I had parents who thought things like the Easter Bunny and the Tooth Fairy were a waste of time. I never understood the whole Santa thing. Kit, on the other hand…"

Madi let out a little sigh as she thought about her brother and how he was back then. He wasn't good with change now, but he was just as bad as a kid, and he had staunchly refused to let go of his beliefs until he had definite proof that he was wrong. What was he going to do when he found out Madi had started to fall for his best friend?

"Kit was so sure he could prove to Oliver that Santa was real if he stayed up long enough to have a quick conversation with the big guy," she told Ben, a little quieter now. "He somehow convinced us to take shifts so at least one person was awake at all times and the Christmas tree was never left unsupervised."

Ah, now she understood why Oliver had brought this up, especially when Ben turned pink. Maybe Kit *had* put him up to this.

"I'm guessing you all fell asleep?" Ben said, though he'd gotten quieter too.

Grinning, Oliver typed out a text at the same time he spoke. How did he do that? "I was awake the whole night," he said. "Never heard a peep from Santa Claus, but I got a nice symphony of snores over the phone from the Morgan kids."

"You did not," Madi said, throwing her pillow at Oliver at the same time her phone buzzed.

> Oliver: We'll get some time alone soon. Kit's bound to
> slip up sometime.

Before Madi knew it, Kit was home again, and her parents would be arriving in an hour or so. But it was okay. They would talk later.

They had to.

TWENTY-SIX

OLIVER WAS TEMPTED. BY A lot of things, but particularly by the idea of coming right out and telling Kit that he was crushing on his sister. Crushing hard. And if he admitted it out loud—to himself as well as to the Wonder Boys—then it would all be out in the open.

But he couldn't put Madi on the spot like that. She deserved to hear it from him first, without the pressure of anyone else listening in.

That didn't mean he wasn't still tempted.

As much as he liked the Boys keeping him company today, he couldn't wait for the moment he and Madi could finally talk. At least he had the chance to talk her through making dinner while Kit and Ben were busy playing that new game. That meant they would be relatively alone, and maybe the Boys would be distracted enough that Oliver and Madi could have a conversation, if only a small one.

"I didn't know you cooked," Madi said as Oliver hopped himself over to one of the expensive-looking wooden barstools Kit had acquired last year and sat down.

He rearranged himself so he could keep his fractured foot elevated on the other stool, though he would have preferred being on the other side of the counter with Madi.

He'd done it once or twice with dates in the past, and cooking together in the kitchen was a surefire way of giving oneself plenty of flirting fodder.

He would have to do his best from the stool. At least it was fairly comfortable, though that only marginally eased his frustration. "Well," he said, "when you have a near-death experience after eating bad takeout for several years, you kind of learn to appreciate a self-cooked meal. Plus, I've had some good time to practice. Perks of not needing a job."

"So, what are we making?"

That was an excellent question. Despite Kit's slow and steady remodel of his kitchen over the last few years—which was surprising on its own—Oliver hadn't seen Kit cook much, so there was a high chance they wouldn't have a lot to work with. Oliver should have used the time Cam and Madi were talking to order in some groceries so he could impress her with his newfound skills.

This was definitely a test of Oliver's ability to perform under pressure.

"Show me what's in the cupboards," he said.

Madi did her best Vanna White impression as she did so.

Oliver frowned. Not a great selection. "Fridge?"

She listed everything in the fridge, which wasn't much at all. Did Kit ever eat anything beyond deli sandwiches and frozen burritos? Maybe he had as much luck with cooking as his sister. He had some fancy cabinets, but their contents... not so much.

"What's the verdict, chef?" Madi asked with a laugh. Oliver must have made quite the face as he tried to think of something edible.

He reminded himself that anything would be better than delivery pizza. "Lasagna casserole," he said with a sigh. "That's as good as we're gonna get." And it would be easy enough that Madi wouldn't be able to mess it up too much.

"Lasagna casserole? Why not regular lasagna?" Madi asked.

"Because Kit's a caveman and doesn't have any proper ingredients, so we're making do with what we have."

"I heard that," Kit said from the living room.

"You were supposed to," Oliver replied and gave Madi a grin. "Alright, first we need pasta."

For the first twenty minutes or so, Oliver walked Madi through the steps of cooking the pasta and warming up the sauce, and they kept their conversation strictly food related. Oliver told Madi about some of his favorite foods he'd had while traveling, and she told him about some of the worst accidents she'd had in the kitchen. It may not have been the conversation Oliver wanted to have, but it was good conversation. It made everything feel a little more normal.

But normal, as great as it was, wasn't what Oliver wanted. As dinner came close to being ready, he glanced back to make sure Ben and Kit were fully engrossed in their game, and then he slid off the stool and hopped into the kitchen.

Her eyes going wide, Madi grabbed his arm as if afraid he might fall over. She wasn't off the mark, and he was more than happy to have her take him by the waist to keep him steady.

"We need to talk," he said. Might as well get right to it.

Either she was excited about that or worried, and it was driving him crazy that he couldn't tell which. Cam had said Madi was easy to read, but he was dead wrong. She was a complete mystery tonight.

"Look," he continued, though he was a bit distracted by her eyes, which had locked onto his. Their honey color was ringed by a rich brown that had always made him think of dark hot chocolate, one of his favorite things. He could get lost in them if he wasn't careful. "Up on the mountain…"

She nodded. "Yes."

What was that supposed to mean? At least she acknowledged that something happened. Why was it so hard to ask her how she felt about him? Or even say how he felt about her? It was like if he admitted the way his heart was pounding right now, he would be risking a lifetime of friendship. Was it worth losing that if she didn't feel the same way?

"You kissed me," Madi said suddenly, and she put her hand on Oliver's chest. She had to feel his heart beating, because she leaned in close and looked down at where her fingers rested.

"I did." Those were the only words that came out despite him wanting to tell her everything. His skin burned where her fingers rested, and he breathed in the sweet smell of her shampoo, wondering again what it was.

Madi smiled a little, and she had never looked more beautiful than she did in that kitchen as she lifted her eyes back to his. "Are you going to do it again?"

Wrapping his fingers around hers, Oliver moved in closer. "Do you want me to?"

She nodded, and he almost fell apart as he took his chance.

He could practically taste her when Kit let out a shout of disappointment, hopefully because Ben had just beaten him in the game and not because he'd seen something he shouldn't. Oliver felt like he was going to explode if things kept getting in his way, but Madi bit her lip with a grin, maddening him with the temptation that presented.

Though she didn't say anything as she returned to the stove to stir the pasta, her smile said plenty, and Oliver settled back on his stool with a new hope burning in his chest.

They hadn't exactly had the conversation he was hoping for, but it was something. At the very least, Madi wanted him to kiss her again, which meant she couldn't be indifferent toward him.

He would take what he could get.

TWENTY-SEVEN

THOUGH IT HURT TO CONSIDER, Madi couldn't remember the last time she'd had dinner with her family. Her dad always took her out to eat on her birthday, and she saw Kit often enough, and her mother was always happy to help out at the studio when she needed it.

But outside of major holidays, the four of them hadn't been together like this in at least a year, probably longer, and it was nice to feel like a family again.

It helped that Oliver was there, sitting across the table from her and giving her constant little smiles. Having him there made dinner feel even more normal than it might have since it reminded Madi of all the times he would stay for dinner to delay going home.

He did that most often in high school, after he got a car and could go wherever he wanted. The only reason he ever went home at all was because his parents threatened to take the car away if he didn't sleep in his own bed on school nights. Kit had told her that part a few years ago, and now that she'd actually met his parents, she understood why Oliver would try so hard to stay away.

She honestly couldn't understand why his parents didn't see how great a son they had. Madi's parents *loved*

Oliver and always had, and they really treated him like another son. They did that with all the Wonder Boys, but Oliver had been around for so long that he was especially part of the family.

Madi hoped that never changed.

"So, Oliver," her mom said halfway through dinner. "When are you going to settle down? Are you dating any-one?"

Madi dropped her fork, and it clattered against her plate. "Sorry," she said, doing her best to laugh off the inci-dent. Her parents chuckled, but Kit frowned at her, like he couldn't figure out why she had chosen to wear green today.

It was to match Oliver's eyes, but Kit didn't need to know that.

Giving Madi a warning look, Oliver cleared his throat. "I'm waiting until the timing is right," he said with a shrug.

"But there is someone special out there?" Dad nudged.

Mom looked ecstatic until Oliver shook his head. Madi deflated.

"I don't know if there's anyone *out there* for me," Oliver said, and his eyes found Madi's. His emphasis on the words *out there* had been subtle, but it was definitely there.

Could it be that he meant that special someone was *in here*? A shiver ran up Madi's spine. A kiss was one thing; deeper feelings were another.

"Don't be silly," Mom said. "You'd be a catch for any woman out there. Just like Kit. Any of you boys, really. It's baffling to think none of you have been snatched up already."

As a bit of pink spotted Oliver's cheeks, he leaned over and squeezed Mom's hand. "Lydia, you are way more generous with your praise than you should be. We Wonder Boys are probably doomed to a lifetime of bachelorhood."

"If you put yourself out there, you'll find someone," Dad said, and he had a certain professor-like edge to his voice that he only used when he was trying to sound wise. "I keep telling Kit and Madi that."

"I'm too busy," Madi mumbled at the same time Kit said, "I'm fine how I am."

Then Kit turned pale, like he hadn't meant to say that out loud. Luckily for him, their parents latched on to what Madi had said, leaving him off the hook. Madi, on the other hand, suddenly wanted to have a heart-to-heart with her brother. Did he really want to be on his own his whole life? Surely that sort of change couldn't be *that* bad.

"You work too hard sometimes, Madi," Mom said, pulling her back to the conversation. It wasn't patronizing, for which Madi had always been grateful, but that didn't mean she liked knowing her mother was worried about her.

Taking a deep breath, Madi tried to find the best way to calm her parents' fears. "I've been getting better," she said. "My friend Danny has been convincing me to get out more, and Oliver—"

This time Kit dropped his fork, and he leveled Madi with a look that was easy to read: *Don't tell them about the fake dates.* Why would he be so concerned about their parents knowing she had gone out with their adopted sons? Particularly because none of them had even been real dates.

At least, *most* of them hadn't.

Madi rolled her eyes at her brother. She hadn't been anywhere close to telling them about her dates. "Oliver wrote me an editing program that has saved me tons of time," she said.

The conversation turned back to Oliver, who seemed thrilled to tell the Morgans all about his software. And that left Madi free to turn to Kit and raise an eyebrow at him.

"What?" he whispered. "I thought you were going to mention… you know."

"Why should it matter if I did?" she whispered back.

"Because all of your dates have been fake."

"I know," Madi said. "I wasn't going to tell them."

"Good. As long as you and Oliver are on the same page."

Madi was silent for the rest of dinner. Though she wondered if she and Oliver really were on the same page, she was content to sit back and listen to her parents recount their Hawaii adventures, especially when Mom and Dad surprised them by telling them about when they went skydiving. Despite Kit's warning, Madi was just amazed by how happy she was to be sitting here.

She could picture her future being just like this, filled with the very best people. Her parents, Kit, Oliver. Especially Oliver. In fact, she couldn't imagine anyone else sitting at the table with her. He'd been such a constant in her life, and the thought of replacing him with someone else?

Like most girls, Madi had pictured her future husband many times. She'd never been able to give him a face, though, and she always thought she would recognize him when she first saw him. That was how it happened in books and movies, but she'd never looked at someone and pictured him on her wedding day, just for fun.

But she'd pictured the things she would do with her husband. They would make dinner together, go on hikes and play video games. They would tease each other and dance in the rain, and they would tell each other secrets they wouldn't tell anyone else. He would help in the studio sometimes, and she would help him with his projects, and they would build each other up and make each other feel special and appreciated. Important.

As he talked with her parents, Oliver slid his good foot forward until it met Madi's. Though he was listening to Madi's mom with rapt attention, he sent Madi a brief smoldering look that flooded her face with heat.

When she pictured her future life over the years, she had always pictured it with Oliver as part of it, without question. And she was starting to realize why. It was more than him being Kit's best friend, and more than being *her* friend. It was even more than liking him.

She had completely fallen for him. When, she didn't know, but she couldn't even try to deny it now.

Madi was in love with Oliver Hamilton, and she probably had been for a long time.

"Well, we should be off," Mom said, sending a smile to her husband. "I'm going to need a vacation after that vacation."

Dad rolled his eyes. "This is the beauty of retirement, my dear. Kit, thank you for dinner."

"Madi and Oliver made it, actually." Kit grinned when both Morgans raised their eyebrows.

"Madi cooked?" Mom asked, patting Oliver's cheek. "You must be really talented to counterbalance her lack of talent, Ollie."

"Thanks, Mom," Madi muttered, but she couldn't stop smiling. Assuming Oliver felt the same way she did—and she suspected he did—surely her parents would have no objections. Not that she needed permission to date someone, but she would prefer her mom and dad to actually like whomever she chose.

Same with Kit, though going for his best friend wasn't going to be easy on him.

And speaking of Kit, Madi had a feeling he wasn't going to leave her alone with Oliver anytime soon, so it would probably be in everyone's best interest if she headed home too and got some rest. Her day off had been wonderful, but she had a wedding to shoot tomorrow and needed to do some prep work.

So, once her parents had driven off to head home, Madi rose to her feet. "I should go too," she announced.

Did Kit just relax?

Oliver noticed it too and frowned a little as he examined his friend. "I'll walk you out," he said after a second.

Kit's gaze darkened. "Says the cripple."

Hopping over to the living room and grabbing a pair of crutches resting behind the couch, Oliver leveled Kit with a withering look. "I have been stuck inside for two days now, and you know what happens if I get restless."

Kit cringed. "Please don't start playing golf with my mugs."

"That's what I thought. Madi, after you."

"It's raining," Kit said next. Apparently, he wasn't quite done arguing, though to Madi it looked like he was about ready to give up. She hoped that was the case, because he wasn't going to be able to keep her and Oliver apart forever. Even if that wasn't his goal, he wouldn't stand in the way of Madi going for what she wanted. "Maybe I should go out with you and—"

"Would you relax?" Madi snapped, surprising all three of them. She never snapped, but apparently her patience levels had finally reached zero. "Oliver will be fine, and it's better for him to get some fresh air than to be stuck inside for so long. Rain can be really healing, you know."

Oliver practically ran outside, unusually adept on his crutches for a guy who hadn't had to use them before today.

Madi met Kit's gaze, and for a moment, she thought maybe he was trying to tell her something. He didn't look disappointed or angry or anything, just...wary? Did he know more than he let on? Maybe he was trying to warn Madi to stay away from Oliver. Or maybe he simply sensed something was changing, and he didn't like it.

She would help him through this, just as she had helped him through other changes in his life.

"Everything will be fine," Madi said, and she followed Oliver out into the downpour.

Summer rain was one of Madi's favorite things, and she paused on the sidewalk for a moment while Oliver hobbled away. He must have really needed to get outside and wasn't just giving Kit some excuse. But Madi wanted to enjoy this rain to the fullest, so she closed her eyes and lifted her face up to the sky, letting it patter across her face and make her feel like she was in a movie.

And a sudden idea struck her.

She was not about to waste Kit's lapse in judgment in actually leaving them alone out here, so she hurried after Oliver, forcing away any thoughts trying to talk her out of doing something she wouldn't be able to take back. The time for floundering was over, and she needed to make a decision.

As soon as they were out of sight of Kit's house, Madi grabbed hold of Oliver's arm and pulled him to a stop. Then she rose up on her toes and kissed him.

Oliver responded immediately. Dropping his crutches, he wrapped his arms around her and pulled her against him. Then he slid his hands up to her head, deepening the kiss like a man in the desert finding a Madi oasis. Not that she was complaining, because he definitely knew what he was doing. His lips were soft but urgent against hers as he drank her in like he couldn't get enough, and even though she should have been cold, every bit of her glowed with warm happiness as she got lost in the moment.

The movies were right. Kissing in the rain was amazing, and she never wanted to stop.

But eventually Oliver broke away, pressing his forehead to hers as they both tried to catch their breath again. He seemed to cling to her for more than just balance, like he was afraid she might disappear if he let go.

"Please tell me it's not just me," he whispered against her mouth.

Madi shook her head. "It's not just you. I… I'm in love with you, Ollie." There. It was out in the open, and he could do with it what he would. But when he said nothing for several long seconds, she tucked her face into his chest and wished she could take it back.

No. She didn't wish that. She just wished he would say something before she ran away in embarrassment.

Pulling away, he lifted her chin so he could meet her eyes. His own were greener than they'd ever been, but what did that mean? "Madi Morgan," he whispered, brushing her cheek. "I don't have the words to tell you how much I love you."

Her heart swelled with those words, though she felt as if she were in a dream. A dream she'd been having her whole life but hadn't remembered until now. Tears building in her eyes, she wrapped her arms around his torso and pulled herself in tight. "Really?" she whispered.

His breath caught as he held her against himself. "Does that surprise you? You're the most amazing person I've ever known. I think…" He audibly swallowed. "I think I've been in love with you for years."

There was nothing in the world he could have said that would be more perfect than that. Grinning up at him, Madi took a deep breath and told herself to be brave. If he could admit as much, so could she. "Me too. It's always been you, Ollie."

Oliver bent down but stopped just before his lips touched hers, a little wrinkle forming between his eyebrows as he glanced toward Kit's house. "So, what now?" he asked.

She didn't want to think about that. Not when she'd just barely gotten something she hadn't known she wanted until a couple of days ago. Madi pushed his sopping hair from his forehead, nudging him downward to press her lips to his cold skin. If she couldn't have his mouth right now, she would take what she could get.

"I have no idea," she whispered. It wasn't like she wanted to keep it a secret from the others, but she knew it would cause some strain. Particularly with Kit. "I don't know what he'll do," she said, knowing she didn't need to say his name for Oliver to know who she was talking about.

He looked back at her, his eyes wary. "I'll talk to him." He didn't sound all that confident. Neither of them wanted to hurt Kit, but telling him the truth would not be easy. "He loves you too much to hurt you."

"But what about you?" Madi asked, and this time she ran her hand through his sopping hair, making him smile. He had such thick hair, despite its light color, and she had always wanted to do this. It was almost enough to distract her from thoughts about how her brother — whom she loved dearly but could be a bit of a pain — would react to finding out about the two of them.

Oliver bit his lip. "Let's hope he loves me too. Because I'm not letting you go." Then he finally kissed her again, long and slow until she thought steam would rise from the pair of them out there in the rain.

TWENTY-EIGHT

OLIVER SPENT ALL OF FRIDAY night waiting for Kit to call him out on going after his sister. But it never happened. In fact, Kit seemed entirely oblivious as they played video games for an hour or so after Oliver got himself into some of Kit's pajamas after spending a solid ten minutes out in the rain.

Either he really had no clue about what was going on, or Kit was a better actor than Oliver had thought. Kit had never been good at pretending, but he'd been known to surprise people. If he knew Oliver was into Madi, he was being awfully cool about it. If he didn't know… Then this was going to be an awful conversation, one Oliver knew he needed to have before he got into anything too deep with Madi.

He loved her, but he loved Kit too, and he was not about to give his best friend a reason to hate him.

It would, however, be a whole lot easier to have a conversation with the man if he would just wake up. Apparently, like the eight-year-olds he taught, Kit valued his Saturday mornings and planned to sleep the day away. The man treasured routine, and he clearly hadn't evolved past his high school sleeping patterns.

So, while he waited, Oliver made breakfast. A whole lot of breakfast. He ordered a grocery delivery and hopped around the kitchen for two hours, thanking his running muscles for helping him balance on one crutch so he didn't have to put too much weight on his booted foot as he worked on pancakes, eggs, pastries, and a quiche he was actually quite proud of.

When Kit finally wandered down the stairs in the middle of a massive yawn, he arrived at a veritable feast and came to a dead stop. "Uh." Without waiting for explanation, he grabbed his phone from the pocket of his gym shorts and typed out a text.

Oliver's watch buzzed a moment later, which meant Kit had texted the group.

> Kit: Oliver just made a crap ton of food. You'd better get over here so it doesn't go to waste.
> Cam: Oliver cooks? Is it edible?
> Ben: If it's anything like what he made in college, then no.

Oliver rolled his eyes at Kit but refused to acknowledge them this time. He wouldn't be the butt of this joke; he had done that enough lately.

> Kit: He's actually really good at it.

Oliver perked up. Had Kit just defended him?

> Kit: He was even able to coach Madi when she made dinner last night, and we all know what she's like in the kitchen.
> Cam: *GIF of a cat gagging*
> Ben: Sounds like we're coming over for breakfast.

And that was that. No more teasing, no more insults. And when Oliver looked at Kit, Kit just shrugged and started scrolling through his phone. Oliver couldn't remember the last time Kit had stood up for him instead of joining in on the jokes.

While Oliver appreciated the support, he didn't appreciate the fact that both Cam and Ben would be coming over. He hadn't worked up the courage to talk to Kit alone, and he definitely wasn't feeling brave enough for all three at once. Kit may have been Madi's only brother, but that was by technicality only. The others were just as protective of her and probably wouldn't appreciate Oliver breaking their pact without warning.

Both men arrived within fifteen minutes, during which Oliver had tried and failed six times to strike up conversation. Cam looked wary, but Ben stepped inside with his nose in the air.

"Smells good, Oliver," he said without any hint of joking. That was surprising, even though Ben was pretty much incapable of being mean. He joined in with the teasing a good chunk of the time, but he always dropped off if anything went too far. He was just as withholding with compliments as he was with insults, though, so Oliver definitely called this a win.

Hopefully it meant at least one of the Wonder Boys was in a good mood.

Oliver had almost said something to Kit right before the other guys got there, but Kit had been pounding some eggs Benedict and pancakes, and Oliver figured it was probably best to wait until Kit was full of food and a little more awake. Same with the other two. Nothing about these circumstances was ideal, but he wasn't sure he could wait much longer to really start something with Madi.

The only reason he hadn't run off to find her at dawn this morning was because of her wedding shoot. Well, that, and he wanted to come clean to the guys before they made anything official.

"By the way," Cam said as he loaded a plate with food and sat down. For a guy whose life was about fitness, he certainly knew how to eat plenty of carbs. "I'm thinking of starting up my own gym. I was talking to Madi about it yesterday, and I'm hoping Oliver can help with the business side of things."

As he hopped over to a stool and sat down, Oliver offered a brief smile—he couldn't do much more than that with his nerves—but the other two had much better reactions.

"Dude, that's awesome!" Kit said, holding his fist in the air for a fist bump.

"I'm glad you're finally doing something," Ben said with a grin.

Oliver wondered if he imagined the hidden misery in that grin, or if Ben was feeling even more trapped than usual now that another of his friends was moving on to do his own thing. Ben had been working at that stupid fun center since he was sixteen. Oliver didn't even know what Ben *wanted* to do, but the chances of him actually doing it were slim. Unless Cam's decision would finally give him that push he needed to move forward?

As Kit asked Cam more questions about his future gym, Ben chewed a danish slowly, as if he were thinking something through. Oliver held his breath. Would Ben actually be brave enough to make a decision?

"I need advice," Ben said, practically shouting it. (Though, shouting for Ben still wasn't all that loud.) But Kit and Cam both shut up and looked at him with raised eyebrows.

Ben took a deep breath. "There's this girl at the grocery store..."

Oliver sat up a little straighter. That must have been the girl Madi mentioned a while back, but he was surprised Ben would even bring anything up. He was the guy all the girls were drawn to, but he never made a move because he was too shy for that. Was that about to change?

Ben explained how he and this girl shopped at the same time every week and had similar patterns around the store, so he had been seeing her for a long time but had yet to have a conversation. "What do I even say to her?" he asked with a little moan.

"Just walk up to her and tell her you think she's pretty," Cam said with a shrug.

Kit shoved him. "We don't want him to freak her out! He has to be delicate."

"*Delicately* walk up to her and tell her you think she's smokin'."

Kit turned to Oliver. "What about you, Hamilton? You've always known what to say."

"I'm in love with Madi."

Oops.

At least it was out there, even if Oliver hadn't figured out how he was going to defend himself when they inevitably went after him. But their reactions were not what he'd expected. Cam paused halfway to taking a bite of pancake, Ben's eyebrows went high as he glanced at the other two, and Kit just froze, entirely emotionless. He looked like he'd errored out.

"Like, how deep are we talking?" Ben asked warily.

Oliver shook his head. He had to make sure they knew this was a real thing, not some way to pass the time or a misguided interpretation of something fake. But what could he say that they would believe?

He said it all: "Like, if I close my eyes, I'm imagining us painting walls in the nursery and cheering on our kid's soccer game and crying together when our youngest goes off to college and leaves us empty nesters. I want to be the guy who makes sure she's always happy and brings her flowers on random days and never has to say goodbye to her because we're a matching set. And I know we made a pact, but—"

"Dude," Cam said, and he laughed a little as he rose to his feet. "It took you long enough to realize it. It was so obvious."

"No kidding," Ben said. "Besides, Cam and I broke that pact years ago."

"You what?" Kit said, and he finally reacted, jumping to his feet so fast that his chair flew backward.

Oliver was right there with him. "Yeah, what? Are you telling me you've both been on dates with Madi?"

"Of course we have," Cam said with a wide grin.

"It wasn't meant to be," Ben added with a shrug. "You and Madi have always been a pair."

"I'm sorry," Kit said, and he held up a hand like he was struggling to keep up and wanted everything to pause. "They've been *what*?"

Cam grabbed Kit by the shoulder and led him to the couch, forcing him to sit down. "Don't strain yourself, Morgan," he said. "I'm off to work. Hamilton, make sure Kit doesn't have an aneurysm while I'm gone."

"I should go too," Ben added with a grin. "Got the Saturday afternoon shift to run. Good luck, Oliver. Thanks for breakfast." He patted Kit's head and followed Cam out.

Oliver felt like that had gone a lot better than he expected. Cam and Ben should have been angry with him and argued that they would have dated Madi if they thought it was an option. Someone should have at least thrown a punch, and yet the whole thing had been relatively painless. But it wasn't over yet. He still had to reconcile with Kit, and that could go very poorly, based on the way Kit hadn't moved since ending up on the couch.

Oliver grabbed a crutch and hobbled over to the couches, settling on the loveseat with some measure of hesitation. Kit was his best friend, but this was the sort of thing friendships ended over.

Kit let out a breath and crumpled a bit, dropping his elbows to his knees and pulling off his glasses so he could run his hand down his face. The leather bracelet he always wore shifted down his arm because it had come partially untied, though he didn't seem to notice. "How long?"

Oliver cringed. "What?"

"How long have you been in love with my sister?"

Oliver tried to think of a moment when it started, but he came up blank. He had known Madi for so long that it wasn't like a love at first sight thing. "I have no idea."

Kit's jaw went tight, making Oliver flinch, but he remained in his seat. For now. "Think really carefully about that question, Hamilton. We've known each other for more than twenty years, but don't think I won't hesitate to make your life a living nightmare if this is just some passing fancy and you're going to end up breaking Madi's heart."

"That's the thing," Oliver replied. "This isn't some passing fancy. It snuck up on me. Maybe for years. And you of all people should know there is no way I could do better than her."

"That's true."

Oliver sat forward, doing everything he could to make sure Kit knew he was entirely serious. There was only so much he *could* do without being given a chance to prove the depth of his feelings, but he would try. "I can't picture my life without her, Kit, and she is everything to me. She always has been. But you're my best friend, and if you don't think

I'm good enough for Madi, then I'll back off and let her find someone worthy of her."

Kit groaned. "You had to go and say that."

"What?"

"The thing is, there's no better man for Madi than you, and that's what kills me."

"I'm confused."

Sighing, Kit fell against the back of the couch and raised his gaze to the ceiling. He looked exhausted, and Oliver had no idea why. Maybe it was because Kit's life had always been perfect, and now that Oliver had thrown a wrench into it, he didn't know how to function.

"I always wondered if you two might end up..." Kit swallowed, shaking his head. "Do you ever wish things could stay the same forever?"

Oliver had never wished that in his life, but he knew Kit. He knew how long it took him to adjust to changes and stray from routine, and he knew how hard this whole thing was going to be for him. Oliver and Madi were one of the most constant parts of Kit's life; the three of them had always been together, and this kind of change was borderline catastrophic. He needed to tread carefully.

But the words that came out of Oliver's mouth surprised him. "No, and neither do you."

Kit glanced over but didn't argue, which was as surprising as what Oliver said. Instead, he let out another sigh. "You've always had things so great."

Oliver barely stopped himself from laughing. "Excuse me? Have you *seen* my life?"

"Yeah. I have. You have everything I could ever want. Looks, humor, money, free time, brains... You never had to study in school, and you are so easy-going that everyone wants to be your friend. And okay, fine, your parents are crap, but mine basically adopted you so you even have that. You never have to *try*, Oliver, and that drives me crazy.

"Do you know why I'm still teaching third grade?" He ran his hands through his brown hair, then dropped them at his sides. It was then that he noticed the loose bracelet, and he tugged it tight again as he spoke, shoving it back into its proper place like it had offended him. "Because I *started* teaching in third grade. And I'm too scared to try something new even though I'm bored out of my mind. I've been teaching the same thing for *six years*. And I'm not going to stop, no matter how much I want to, because that's terrifying.

"The one time I…" He grimaced. "I can't do it. But you? You started a business when you were twenty-one. You hadn't even graduated yet! Then you sold it for millions of dollars and gave yourself the kind of freedom I'll never have."

Oliver *wanted* to say something. He wanted to tell Kit exactly what his company had cost him. But telling Madi had been hard enough, and if Kit knew what Oliver had been through, he would try to help.

Oliver didn't need help. He needed to know his best friend was going to be okay with the future because there was no way he was going to be able to choose between them.

"It's not that I'm jealous," Kit said with a frown, clearly fine with one-sided conversation. "I'm not a spotlight kind of guy like you are, and after the crap your parents put you through, you deserve everything you've earned. But now you're telling me you're in love with my sister, and you're going to change one of the few good things in my life because I can't stop you. I can't stop you because you are the only person in the world who could make her as happy as she deserves to be."

He sighed again, and no matter how much Oliver wanted to argue against what he was saying, he couldn't. Kit was very much like his sister in that regard. When he made up his mind about something, it was nearly impossible to change it for him. He never made decisions lightly.

"Oliver," Kit said and finally looked over at him again. "I haven't seen my sister this happy in years. Since before we went off to college. I don't know what you did, but she doesn't seem as stressed as she usually is. She's smiling more. She's… She clearly needs you in her life as much as you need her." He sat up. "But if you mess this up, the Wonder Boys and I will kill you, and we'll hide your body in the ball pit at the fun center, and no one will find you for weeks."

Oliver winced. "That's horrifying."

"And probably accurate," Kit replied with a chuckle, relaxing for the first time since Oliver dropped the news. "Ben really needs to get a better job."

"We've been telling him that for years."

"Maybe he'll finally make something happen with this Grocery Girl and move on."

"Let's hope."

Letting out one last sigh, Kit reached for a game controller and tossed it over to Oliver. "I'm sorry."

Oliver furrowed his eyebrows. "For what?"

"For being a terrible friend the last few years."

Of all the things Kit might have said, Oliver never would have thought that would be one of them. Kit had always been the leader, the confidante, the one who noticed things no one else would notice. He'd singlehandedly saved the Wonder Boys from themselves, and he was the only one dedicated to keeping them together. In no universe would Oliver have *ever* called Kit Morgan a bad friend.

"I don't…" He couldn't even voice his argument because Kit's comment had caught him so off guard.

Kit raised an eyebrow as he booted up his game system. "You can pretend everything's been fine, but you know it hasn't. I'm trying to fix it, okay?"

"There's nothing to fix," Oliver said, still completely confused. "If anything, it's on me. I haven't been around."

"I haven't kept you around."

"Are we really about to start fighting over who's the worst friend?"

Kit laughed, shaking his head. "We probably shouldn't. Let's just…go back to normal?"

Normal had pretty much gone out the window when Oliver admitted his feelings for Madi, but he nodded anyway. It would probably take some time to get close to Kit again, but he had a great reason to put in the effort and avoid a repeat of their junior year falling-out.

He had no desire to have Madi look at him with disappointment ever again. He wanted her to be happy for the rest of her life.

Though Kit started loading a game, Oliver sat motionless in his seat, realizing his biggest obstacles—Kit and the Wonder Boys—were out of the way. There was nothing preventing him from telling Madi just how deep his feelings went. He had told her he loved her last night, but that didn't feel like enough. He wanted to make sure she never questioned his feelings.

He had to show her, not just tell her. But what could possibly be enough to encompass everything he felt?

"Hey, Kit," he said, though the thought that was in his head was probably a bad idea and would likely lead to him getting a broken nose. He hoped it would be worth it. *Go big or go home…* "Think you could help me with something?"

TWENTY-NINE

WEDDINGS HAD ALWAYS BEEN MADI'S favorite thing to shoot. She loved the venues, the colors, the flowers, and the way every bride and groom were different from the last. Each family presented different problems when it came to composition, and every wedding brought a new challenge that reminded Madi why she loved doing this.

Most of all, she had always loved the *love*.

So, the fact that she was miserable this time around had her worried.

Miserable was the wrong word. She had absolutely no reason to be miserable. She had an incredible job, a loving family, the Wonder Boys, and this outdoor wedding had nearly come to a close without a single hiccup, which was pretty much unheard of. The bride and groom were perfectly happy and had just rushed off to their honeymoon.

Maybe that was part of the problem. They were so *happy*. Danny had been right, and Madi wanted that kind of happiness. The kind where you had to throw a huge party for all your friends and family because there was so much of it to go around. She had gone so long without ever thinking she would find that kind of happiness, and now it was almost within reach.

Almost being the key word. It all depended on how Kit would react. Had Oliver talked to him yet?

"I stole you some cake. I figured it would be best not to give you a choice this time." Danny came up to her with a slice of double chocolate mousse cake in his hand, and he grinned when he caught sight of her overwhelmed expression.

Madi threw her arms around his shoulders, nearly knocking the cake out of his hand. "You are the best friend ever."

He laughed. "I didn't realize all it would take to get you to admit that was cake. I've been going about this all wrong."

With Danny around, it was a lot harder to be miserable, but she wished it was someone else here trying to cheer her up. *Surely* Oliver had talked to Kit by now. She'd been avoiding her phone in case it delivered bad news, but she was dying to know how her brother would react to such a giant change in his life.

One look at her empty phone—not a single notification—didn't make her feel any better. That had to mean bad news if Oliver hadn't told her anything yet.

She changed the subject before she started panicking. "How's Hannah?"

Danny grinned in a way Madi had never seen before. "Really great. How's Oliver?"

She didn't even know how to answer that question, so she pulled her camera strap over her head and sat at the closest table, wishing she had chosen to wear comfier shoes. But she'd felt like being pretty today, and now her feet were paying for her choice to wear wedges.

"You know how bad I am at making decisions, right?" she said.

Danny snorted. "Everyone knows that."

Though she wasn't even sure what she was trying to say, it felt like something important. Something she needed to voice out loud. "Is it a bad sign that I'm not even hesitating when it comes to Oliver?"

Though his eyebrows shot high, Danny smiled and shook his head. "If you know, you know…"

"I do know. I've never been so sure of anything in my life. I love him, Danny. And I'm going to love him forever."

"Do you mean that?"

Madi spun around to find Kit standing there, an expression on his face that was difficult to define. With his eyebrows pulled together, he seemed worried about her answer to his question, but the purse of his lips said he was hopeful as well. And terrified. There was definitely terror in his eyes.

Madi stood slowly, something in her gut telling her Kit hadn't just randomly shown up to the wedding for fun. "What are you doing here, Kit?"

He folded his arms. "Answer the question, Madi. Do you love Oliver?"

Did this mean Oliver had talked to him? But it was impossible to know how Kit felt about this change when he simultaneously looked sick and excited.

At least she knew the answer to his question. "Yeah. I love him."

Kit frowned. "Forever?"

Madi had only realized she was in love with Oliver yesterday, but that question was still easy to answer. "Forever. I've always loved him, Kit. I was just too blind to realize it."

Swallowing, Kit moved his hands to his pockets and seemed to speak with reluctance when he said, "Okay. Are you done with work?"

Madi glanced at Danny, who watched her with furrowed brow. He was probably going to have a lot of questions about the conversation he'd just witnessed. But for now, he nodded and gestured for her to go.

Kit jerked his head toward the parking lot. "We're going to go somewhere."

"Where?"

"Just trust me."

Madi followed him to his car, convinced they were about to have a heart-to-heart about Oliver until Kit reached into the backseat and held out a folded handkerchief, like a blindfold.

"Put this on," he said.

Madi stared at him. "Excuse me?"

He clicked his seatbelt on and then turned to her with one eyebrow raised. "I'm waiting."

"What is going on?"

"Don't ask me that."

"Kit."

"If I tell you I'm taking you to Oliver, will you put it on?"

Madi couldn't actually remember the last time Kit had been cryptic like this. He and Oliver used to get into all sorts of mischief, but Kit had been so grown up for so long that this more playful side was nice to see.

Besides, if he really was taking her to Oliver, she couldn't complain too much. "Does this mean you're okay with us?" she asked as she tied the handkerchief around her eyes.

Kit made a sound somewhere between a groan and a whine. "Maybe don't ask me that for a while. I'm still processing."

Well, at least he wasn't immediately against the idea. Madi would take it, though Kit would have to be okay with this change sooner or later. Like with everything, she had no intention of changing her mind.

The drive passed slowly with Madi unable to see anything, though she tried to make a guess based on the direction Kit initially headed. She was pretty sure at one point he took three right turns and started going a completely different direction, though, so she gave up on that idea pretty quickly and focused instead on the idea of Oliver being at the end of this drive.

It had been less than twenty-four hours since she saw him last, but that felt like twenty-four hours too long. Now that she knew her heart, she practically ached for Oliver.

When Kit finally pulled the car to a stop and stepped outside, he ordered her to keep the blindfold on and shut his door, leaving her in the silent car.

As tempted as she was to peek, Madi dutifully followed directions. This was all so strange and new, but she trusted her brother. Whatever this was, he would never let anything bad happen. Neither would Oliver. And something told her the rest of the Wonder Boys were probably involved somehow, so she really had nothing to fear.

The passenger door opened after a couple of agonizing minutes, bringing a breeze into the car that carried with it a familiar, delicious scent.

"Ollie," Madi breathed.

He chuckled, grabbing her hand. "Kit didn't cause any trouble, did he?"

His voice sounded close, which meant he'd crouched down. Madi reached out and grasped a...bow tie? "Kit forcibly kidnapped me from the wedding today," she said, frowning as she ran her hands down his chest and arms. Why would Oliver be wearing his tux?

"He did what?"

Madi laughed at the sharpness in his voice. "Kidding. He was the same Kit as always. Are you going to tell me what's going on?"

"In a minute. We need to go inside first." He grabbed both her hands, helping her out onto solid ground.

Madi immediately threw her arms around his neck and pulled him in for a kiss, though she missed the first time, getting more of his cheek before he corrected and met her mouth with his.

After several minutes, probably longer than he'd planned, Oliver laughed and pried her off of him. "I promise I'm not complaining," he said when she made a noise of protest. "But we probably shouldn't leave the guys waiting."

So they *were* here. Wherever *here* was.

"Fine," Madi grumbled, though she refused to let go of Oliver's hand for fear of all of this being some post-wedding fever dream. Had she passed out from cake overload? "Can I take the blindfold off yet?"

"Almost. Watch your step." Oliver stole his hand back but snaked an arm around her waist instead. Despite using a crutch on his other side, he was moving really well for a guy who had broken his foot only two days ago.

As they walked, Madi tried again to figure out where they were. The evening was cool around her, the air still laced with the fresh scent of yesterday's rain, and she caught traces of flowers somewhere nearby. A bird tweeted overhead, but aside from leaves blowing in a gentle breeze, she had no other clues.

"Why are you the one guiding me?" Madi asked when she nearly tripped, held upright by Oliver's strong arm. Not that she was complaining. It just seemed borderline dangerous—the kind of thing Kit would stress over.

Oliver chuckled and planted a kiss on the top of her head. "Because I didn't want to wait to see you, but I can't drive with the boot on my foot. And Kit wouldn't let me come with him because he thought we would just make out in the backseat the whole drive."

Madi snorted. "I'm not sure he's wrong."

"Hence me waiting here." He guided her to a stop, pulling her against his side where she snuggled right in. "I know you just worked a wedding and are probably tired, but I promise this will be worth it. There's cake."

"What kind of—"

"Red velvet. That's your favorite, right?"

Madi squeezed him tighter, wondering how she'd never considered this man before Danny's bet. "Have I ever told you you're perfect?" she said into his chest.

Oliver chuckled as his fingers stroked her hair, pulling it out of the braid she'd put it in halfway through the wedding and stroking it down her back. "I'm not," he said, "but I love that you think I am. It's because you make me better, Madi."

She shook her head. "You've always been exactly who you need to be. Who *I* need you to be."

His breath came in a shudder, his arms pulling her closer. "You have always been the brightest star in my sky," he said, the words thick with emotion. "How could I have gone my whole life without showing you how special you are?"

Madi hoped she could take the blindfold off soon, or it was going to be soaked through with tears. "Do you remember that time we—"

"Wait. Not yet."

"What does that—"

Suddenly the blindfold was gone, and Madi blinked in the sudden light as she took in her surroundings. "My parents' house?" she said in confusion, staring at the bright red door of her childhood home. She turned to Oliver to ask what they were doing there, but as soon as she saw the little plastic tiara sitting on his head, her jaw dropped.

He gave her a sheepish grin. "Do you remember the day we met?"

Madi shook her head. From her perspective, Oliver had always been a part of her life.

"I remember," he said, his gaze intense. "I snuck onto the bus with Kit because he made after school snacks sound like the greatest thing in the world. I'd been hanging out with him during recess for maybe a month at that point, and I was desperate to experience his life. Especially to meet his sister. You should have heard the way he talked about that girl…"

He reached past her for the doorknob and pushed it open, gesturing for her to go in first as he kept talking. "Lydia immediately called my parents as soon as we got off the bus," he said as Madi stepped into a front room filled to the brim with pink balloons and streamers. "Your mom said mine was probably worried sick, but when she called, Mom said she was busy at work and would pick me up after her shift ended at ten that night."

Madi sniffed, trying desperately to hold back her tears so she didn't miss anything. "Really?"

Oliver nodded as he took her by the arm again, pausing in the front hallway. "Lydia decided right then and there I should take the bus with Kit as often as possible. Knowing someone was looking out for me was worth driving me to my house after dinner every day." He focused on something over Madi's shoulder, his eyes rimmed with tears as he said, "I don't think I'll ever be able to thank you enough."

Madi turned, her heart picking up speed when she saw Mom and Dad standing on the bottom of the staircase with matching crowns. They were involved in this too?

"You have always been part of our family, Ollie," Mom said, her words reaffirmed by Dad nodding.

Oliver threaded his fingers with Madi's, leaning his crutch against the wall and limping at a snail's pace toward the kitchen as he talked. "Kit obviously thought me coming with him was the best thing ever and wouldn't shut up about all the things we were going to do after school."

It was okay that they were moving slowly, because the hallway was full of pictures. Pictures of Madi and Oliver together, from Oliver's kindergarten graduation photo to the day the Boys left for college. There was the time the two of them and Kit built a massive blanket fort (it collapsed in the middle of the movie they were watching inside), and Kit's first junior league basketball game (Madi and Oliver had spent the whole time playing tag under the bleachers), and Madi's first school dance where she took a picture with all the Wonder Boys because she hadn't had a date (Oliver was looking at her instead of the camera).

It didn't matter how many people were in the photos; Madi and Oliver were almost always right next to each other.

Oliver stopped at the end of the hall, where one picture sat apart from the others. "Then there was you."

Madi didn't remember this picture, but from the looks of things, she was about four when it was taken. She had two ponytails high on her head and little pink overalls, and she had the most obnoxious, full-toothed grin on her face.

She wasn't looking at the camera, though. No, she was looking at six-year-old Oliver as the two of them played with playdough.

And little Oliver grinned right back, though his expression was more of wonder than excitement.

Madi touched her finger to the old photo, wishing she could remember that day. They both looked so happy.

"When I found out Lydia was calling my mom that day," Oliver said quietly, reverently, "I was so afraid that my mom would never let me come back that I felt sick. I didn't want to play anymore. But then you marched up to me and said you wanted me to build a zoo with you. You took me by the hand and pulled me over to your little table, and then you showed me what to do until I forgot how scared I was."

Madi gave his hand a squeeze, not sure what to say. Her heart was full to bursting, and she knew he wasn't done yet.

Swallowing, Oliver continued forward into the kitchen, where the table was loaded with party food and princess decorations. Ben and Cam stood there, each with a shiny tiara on his head and a giant smile. Everything looked exactly like it had for her twelfth birthday party, down to the cupcakes waiting to be decorated.

"I remember so vividly the day you had your birthday party," Oliver said. "We were about to head to O'Reilly's to play some laser tag or something stupid, but then we found out that no one had been smart enough to realize they'd be missing out by not being your friend." He shook his head, his eyes distant as if he were imagining all of her absent classmates. "Kit went upstairs to find you, and I begged your dad to take me to my house so I could find you a present that would mean something."

Madi swallowed the emotion that sat thick in her throat, but she still could barely get the words out. "Why did you choose a camera?" He had said something back at the wedding about giving her a way to remember good times, but she had a feeling there was more to it.

He ducked his head, his smile small but warm. "Because it was the only thing on the planet that could capture even a part of your perfection. It felt corny back then, but it was the best I could come up with."

"It doesn't feel corny now."

His smile grew as he met her gaze again. "No," he agreed. "But a photo will never come close to encompassing everything you are." He nudged her toward the den, shifting so he was behind her.

She stepped into that final room with her heart racing, her tears making another push for freedom when she found Kit waiting for her with a tiara on his head and another in his hands. When Madi reached him, he gently set the tiara in her hair and wrapped her in a tight hug.

"Be good to him," he muttered, and then he headed for the door.

Madi turned to watch him go, wondering what that meant, and then she froze.

Oliver was right behind her. On one knee.

"I'm calling in that favor you owe me," he said with a single, breathless laugh. And then he held out a plastic daisy-shaped ring that had definitely come from the selection of cheap prizes from the fun center where Ben worked. "I'll get you a real one," he said, "but I wanted you to have something until you can pick out one you like."

Madi's knees wobbled, her heart threatening to pound out of her chest. Was this really happening? "I'm not good with decisions," she whispered, though that felt like the stupidest thing to say. "It might take me a long time to choose something." She could see her parents and the Wonder Boys crowded together trying to watch through the doorway, but she could only focus on the beautiful, wonderful man in front of her.

The man she was hopelessly in love with.

Oliver's smile was so soft and warm that Madi was sure it had to be real. She couldn't dream up something like that. "I know," he said. "And I love that about you. You never choose something unless you're absolutely certain." He swallowed, the Adam's apple in his throat bobbing. "It doesn't have to be anytime soon. Next year, the year after, I don't care. Heck, you could even say no, and I'll never stop loving you. But if you do say yes, I know you'll mean it. I know I do. Marry me, Madison Morgan?"

It didn't matter that they'd only been a real couple for a day; her whole life had been leading her to this moment. All of the years of growing together and learning together. The shared heartaches and laughter. Comforting one another and becoming better people for knowing one another. Like she told Danny back at the wedding, Madi didn't even hesitate. Even if Oliver had some terrible alliteration in his little proposal.

"Yeah," she said and gave him a wide grin despite her tears. "Yeah, I'll marry you."

Though he struggled to get back up to his feet, he grabbed her before he'd even caught his balance and wrapped her up in his arms. Though she'd expected a kiss, the hug was even better. Twenty-two years of building love wrapped up in one tight embrace. Madi shut her eyes and imagined being in this very spot for the rest of her life.

She was okay with it. More than okay. She was happy. The kind of happy that was going to need a party to celebrate.

"Hey Oliver?"

"Yeah?"

"Is this crazy?"

He chuckled. "Absolutely. But there is nothing in the world I have been more sure of than my love for you."

Madi's breath hitched in her lungs when his voice wavered, and she pulled herself deeper into his hold. "I can't believe you recreated my birthday party."

Oliver pressed a kiss to her temple. "That day changed my life, Mads. I think that was the day I realized you were the best person I knew and deserved the world, and I've been chasing a life that is worthy of you ever since."

Madi couldn't help but laugh a little. "And here I was thinking I could never measure up to you."

"Sounds like we both needed a good kick in the pants. Remind me to thank Danny next time I see him."

Madi winced, but she pushed away the guilt that rose when she thought about all the lies she had told Danny. The fact that she was now wearing a ring on her left hand *technically* meant she hadn't gone against the terms of the bet, but that didn't change the fact that she was still going to have to tell Danny the truth.

For now, though, she just wanted to enjoy the moment. To live.

Pulling away from Oliver's embrace, she bit her lip as she gazed up at him. "I know you said we don't have to get married this year, but you're really not going to make me wait that long, are you?"

Oliver's eyes lit up, a fire burning in them that quickly shifted into a smolder the longer he gazed at her. They were almost entirely green today, so she'd been right about the color being tied to his moods. Was that even possible? She liked to think so, and he certainly looked happy enough to add evidence to her theory.

"Six months?" he ventured.

She shook her head. "I have waited twenty-two years for you, Wonder Boy. Make it three, and you've got yourself a deal."

Someone groaned in the kitchen—probably Kit—but Madi didn't care. Oliver's wide-eyed grin had her melting on her feet, and she couldn't resist kissing those lips of his. Oh, if she had known kissing Oliver Hamilton would be like this, she would have done this years ago. "I love you, Ollie. Always and forever."

THIRTY

"YOU KNOW OLIVER IS LIKE a brother to me, but I'm not sure this will be worth the effort." Kit sat in the driver's seat of his car, staring at the closed gate in front of them like it might swallow them whole.

Madi rolled her eyes. "They know we're coming," she said. It wasn't like she thought she could just ring the doorbell and be welcomed inside. The only reason they'd even agreed to meet her was because she'd said she had important information about Oliver.

Kit swallowed. "The Hamiltons are terrifying, Madi."

"When was the last time you even talked to them?"

Shrugging, Kit pulled off his glasses and used the hem of his shirt to wipe them clean. What was he avoiding? "They're not going to come to the wedding, Mads. You know they're not."

"You think they would ignore an invitation from their own son?" She wished she had talked to Oliver more about his parents, but she hadn't wanted to break the spell that had been the last few months. Everything had been so perfect since the day Oliver got down on one knee.

But their wedding was only a few days away, and Madi knew Oliver was still tending to some deep wounds when it came to his family. If her plan could help him in any way, she had to follow through. She owed him so much for the things he'd done for her, both in the past and in recent months.

Kit let out a deep sigh that seemed to leave him partially deflated, like he could no longer sit up straight. He didn't often let things bother him, but this seemed to come from too far inside him to be anything but a years-old pain. "I don't know if they'll listen to me," he said weakly. "The last time I talked to them, I sort of…Well, I blew up. I was so angry, and I didn't…" He sighed again. "This one will have to be you, Madi."

Madi had planned on that. Really, the only reason Kit was here was because he wouldn't tell her the address of the Hamilton home. He seemed to think this conversation would legitimately be dangerous and had only let her come if he was with her.

Maybe that sense of danger was why Madi was okay with stalling a bit longer. She couldn't delay forever, but… "Why were you angry?" she asked.

Kit glanced at her, but only for a second. He kept his eyes on the dash in front of him like it might have the words he needed. "It was when he sold his company," he admitted. "Oliver refused to tell me why he did it, and I thought maybe it was because his parents made him sell."

Madi swallowed. She didn't think Oliver had told him about getting sick yet, and that definitely wasn't something for her to share. She hoped Oliver would be brave enough soon so she wouldn't have to sit on that secret much longer. If Kit knew how much Oliver had been through, he would probably be marching into that house regardless of how afraid of the Hamiltons he might be.

Kit dropped his hands from the steering wheel, rubbing his thighs instead. "They laughed when I confronted them.

They said they'd lost control of their disappointment for a son the day he met me. And I exploded. Basically let out twenty years of frustration all at once because I was too full of…other things to hold it in."

Madi sat up straighter. "What other things?"

But he shook his head, a frown pulling at his lips. Kit was always the one helping everyone else with their problems; did he have anyone helping him with his? Madi was only two years younger than him, but he had always played the protective big brother role. Maybe it was time the roles were reversed.

"Are you happy, Kit?" Madi asked slowly.

Kit looked over, his eyebrows pulled close together. "Of course I'm happy…for you and Oliver."

If he hoped Madi missed that hesitation, he was out of luck. "That isn't what I asked."

"I'm ha…" But he couldn't finish, and his frown turned into a scowl. "I'm working on it," he said instead.

"You told Mom and Dad you were fine being single."

This time he flinched. "It wasn't a lie," he mumbled. "For now."

But that didn't make any sense. For as long as Madi could remember, Kit had been the one who planned out his life, complete with a big house and a giant family and a wife he adored more than anything. He had several different honeymoon plans drawn up and baby names picked out, and sometimes Madi wondered if he went into teaching because it was a way to be around kids until he had his own.

There was no way Kit Morgan was perfectly content being on his own. Sure, marriage would be a big change, but could he really be that terrified?

"Kit?"

His hands shifted back to the steering wheel, gripping tightly. "I'm sorry."

"For what?"

"I know I haven't been great about this whole wedding thing."

Really, Madi had been so busy with wedding shoots all summer that she'd barely had a chance to see her brother. She hadn't noticed him being difficult, but maybe Oliver had. "I know this is a big change," she said, reaching over and putting her hand over his. "But we're not going anywhere, Kit. You're still going to be my Wonder Boys, and the five of us will keep being terrible at bowling and awesome at laser tag."

That brought a smile out of him, though it didn't last long. "I know. I just… I always thought there couldn't be anyone good enough for you. Not unless Oliver opened his eyes for once. I'd given up hope of that happening, but I think he's been in love with you our entire lives but was too stupid to realize it. So I'm glad he wised up. I'm still wrapping my head around it all."

It had been three months since the day Oliver proposed, and Kit still hadn't reconciled this change in his life? There had to be something more at play, some reason Kit was having a hard time letting go of the past to make way for this great future.

"We should probably go inside," Kit muttered to change the subject, pulling up to the gate and rolling his window down to speak to the security guard. *Security guard, really?* "Kit and Madi Morgan," he told the man in the booth. "We're expected."

The guard studied them for a moment as if trying to decide if he should believe them. But then he nodded once and hit a button, and the intricate metal gate silently swung open to a long and winding driveway.

As Kit slowly inched his way up the drive, Madi leaned forward to take in the view of the literal mansion in front of her. Three stories high, the size of her childhood home three times over, with perfectly manicured landscaping... It was so much more than she'd ever imagined.

"How in the world did you and Oliver end up in the same kindergarten class?" she asked breathlessly. Had Ollie really grown up in this place? No wonder he'd spent all his time with Kit.

Kit laughed a little. "Honestly, I have no idea. Every year I waited to see if they would finally put him in a private school, but they never did."

"What about that first semester of junior high?"

Immediately turning bright red, Kit pulled into what looked like a miniature cobblestone parking lot, only big enough for two or three cars. "Oh," he said, fumbling with his leather bracelet. "Right. I forgot about that."

Kit forgot about nothing. Madi might have pointed that out if a plain door hadn't opened to their left. A middle-aged woman in a simple black dress stepped out, smiling at them—definitely not Oliver's mom.

Kit relaxed, unbuckling his seatbelt and climbing out of the car. "Grace!"

"Mr. Kit," she replied, her smile growing. "I haven't seen you in a long time. Who have you brought with you?"

"This is my sister, Madi. Madi, this is Grace. She's the housekeeper."

As Madi approached with some caution, having not expected to meet anyone but Oliver's parents, Grace's eyes went wide. "You're Madi?" she whispered, almost reverently. "Oh, but you've grown up so beautifully."

Madi's face burned, and she wished she could hide behind Kit until she figured out how to respond to that comment. But she was trying to be brave, and she didn't want to show any weakness. Even to the housekeeper. "Um, thank you. I didn't think you would know about me."

"Grace knows about all of us," Kit explained. "She helped Oliver and me out of plenty of scrapes over the years, and she helped me convince the Hamiltons to let Oliver do that campout on the trampoline. Remember that?"

Madi couldn't help but laugh. "That night is basically the reason Oliver and I are getting married next week."

"Married?" Grace shrieked. "Ollie's getting married? Why didn't you tell me?" She whacked Kit on the arm.

"That's why I'm here," Madi said. "I have to try to convince Dr. and, uh, Dr. Hamilton to come to the wedding. Oliver doesn't think they'll come."

Grace sobered, her excitement fading as she considered that. "Oliver might be right," she admitted. "Kent and Faith are proud people, but..." Reaching out, she cupped her hand over Madi's cheek. "If anyone can convince them, I believe you could. Ollie always did say you had more influence than anyone he knew, and I never heard him talk with more admiration than when he talked about you."

"Hey," Kit complained.

Grace didn't even look at him. "You know it's true, Kit. I'll take you to the doctors, Madi, and I wish you all the luck in the world."

As Grace opened the door to let them in, Madi rushed back to the car to grab the only thing she could think of that might be a peace offering: her very first camera. As much as it hurt to give it up when it had been part of the day that changed her life, she was willing to do anything to make Oliver happy.

No matter what it took.

"Ready?" Kit asked, holding out his arm.

She was glad he had come with her. Whatever happened, Kit had her back. And whether or not Oliver's parents chose to accept their son back into their lives, everything was going to work out.

As long as the Wonder Boys all stuck together, they could get through anything.

THIRTY-ONE

"WOULD YOU RELAX?" KIT PUT his hand on Oliver's shoulder and gripped it tight, preventing him from bouncing up and down. "You're making *me* nervous."

Oliver couldn't relax, so there was no point in trying. He was lucky he was standing there at all, and he hoped his foot would last the whole night. Assuming time didn't come to a complete halt, like he suspected it was doing, he needed his foot to be functional if he was going to have a proper first dance with his bride. It was the only reason he hadn't started pacing.

The last twelve weeks had been the longest of his life. Whoever said all good things came to those who waited, well, they hadn't known the agony of waiting for someone like Madi Morgan.

Kit had made it his personal mission to keep Oliver occupied over the last few months, partly to keep him from losing his mind but also—Oliver suspected—to keep him from grabbing Madi and eloping. Once school had ended for the summer at the beginning of June, Kit had had plenty of time to devote to Oliver, and it had actually been pretty great for their friendship. Things felt like old times again, and Oliver was closer than ever to the Wonder Boys.

Though Oliver had hoped wedding plans would keep him busy, all of Madi's wedding vendor friends had stepped in at a word from Danny, so even that part had been simple and easy. Anything that did need doing had been taken over by the Wonder Boys, leaving Oliver with absolutely nothing to do outside of beating Kit in *God of Battle* over and over until it wasn't even fun anymore.

"What if she got cold feet?" Oliver muttered. Not the smartest thing to say while he was literally standing in front of a hundred wedding guests, but he couldn't help but wonder. Madi had told him daily that she loved him and couldn't wait to be married to him, but maybe she'd changed her mind.

"Kit," Cam said, standing at the end of the row with Ben in between him and Kit. The three of them had opted not to do the whole procession up the aisle, possibly because they worried Oliver would freak out like this. "Could you please smack him for me? I'm too far to reach."

Kit actually did it, whacking Oliver in the back of his head. "Stop being an idiot," he said.

"Madi was more excited than I've ever seen her," Ben added.

Oliver's heart ticked a little faster. "So you've seen her? She's definitely here?" Whose idea was it to say it was bad luck for the groom to see the bride before the wedding? Oliver wanted to punch him in the face. The Boys hadn't even let him see Madi last night, choosing to take him on one last adventure as four single men.

Their idea of "adventure" was to play video games and eat pizza until they wanted to puke. Oliver had loved every minute, minus the fact that Madi wasn't there. They had at least given him access to his phone long enough for him to call her last night.

"Still love me?" he'd asked.

"That's a stupid question," she'd replied.

Neither of them had brought up the wedding—apparently they were both strangely superstitious when it came to these things—and they'd spent an hour talking about inconsequential things like how dumb it was that cheese-stuffed crust wasn't a universal feature on pizza.

When Ben had come into the room to steal Oliver's phone back, Oliver had told Madi how tomorrow couldn't come soon enough.

"I love you," she'd said.

Now it was sixteen hours later, and Oliver was losing his mind.

As the Boys all chuckled, Kit put his arm around Oliver's shoulders. "My sister has never made a decision she didn't follow through with, even if she knew she'd made the wrong one," he said.

Oliver's nervous energy doubled. "You think she made the wrong decision?"

Kit groaned. "Would you guys help me out here?"

"Madi Morgan has never made a bad decision in her life," Ben said, rolling his eyes. "Do you really think she would start now?"

"But if you mess this up, you'll have us to deal with," Cam added.

Oliver scowled at him. At least Ben had said something useful. But why was it taking so long? Oliver had been standing here for at least twenty minutes, and all of their friends were in their seats and ready to go, and the priest was right behind Oliver with his Bible in hand, and—

The music started up, stopping Oliver's heart in the process, and everyone in the rows of chairs stood and turned to the back.

There she was. The most perfect sight Oliver had ever seen. Madi smiled at him in a short white dress that billowed at her knees, with a sort of sheer, lacy fabric over her shoulders where the sleeves should go. The bouquet in her hands contained every color of the rainbow, and she'd put her hair up in the same style she had at the art gallery with a braided crown.

She was beautiful, and Oliver had never been happier in his life.

It felt like hours before she finally reached the front and accepted a kiss on the cheek from her father, who winked at Oliver before sitting next to his teary wife. Then, when Madi took Oliver's hand, all anxiety disappeared at her touch. This was real.

"Are you ready for this?" she whispered.

Oliver had never been more ready for anything in his life, but all words failed him, so he nodded. She was here. Here to be married to *him*.

Taking her other hand as well, Oliver guided her to the spot in front of the priest. He couldn't bring himself to look away from her face, so he hardly heard what the priest said until Madi spoke the words, "I do." When the priest asked if Oliver would take Madi as his wife, it took everything in him not to shout his own answer.

"You may now kiss the bride," was the last thing he heard before he lost himself in a kiss as the crowd cheered.

It seemed like mere seconds before someone coughed loudly behind him. Based on Madi's laugh and the pained look on Kit's face, Oliver had gotten a little ahead of himself. They still had a celebration to enjoy, though Oliver was asking himself why a reception was necessary to begin with. People really only came for the free food.

"We'll make it through," Madi whispered in his ear, though Oliver wasn't so sure.

He lost track of how many people congratulated them. He'd had a good deal of buddies in college, many of whom had come to celebrate with him, but it was Madi who seemed to know everyone in Diamond Springs. Person after person stole her from his arms to give her a hug, and for a girl who had never been good at making friends, she certainly had a lot of them.

When it was Danny's turn to offer up his congratulations, Oliver pulled the man into an embrace. "You may not know it," he murmured, "but I have you to thank for this."

Danny turned red as he stepped back to Hannah's side. "I don't know about that. You would have gotten here eventually, right?"

Oliver glanced at Madi, who winced. "I don't think so," he said, which was a horrifying thought. If they hadn't done the pretend dating because of Danny's bet, Oliver likely would have remained on the outskirts of the Wonder Boys and never reconnected with Madi like he did. They would have seen each other, of course, but nothing would have pushed them together.

"I'm still sorry for lying to you," Madi said quietly.

Danny waved her apology away. They had told him the truth the same week Oliver proposed since getting engaged after only a few weeks of knowing each other would have been insane. He had been hurt, Oliver knew, but Danny was a decent guy. It didn't take long before he invited Madi and Oliver on another double date.

"You did what you had to do," Danny said with a shrug. "Besides, I can't complain too much. I have some awesome new photos on my website that I only had to pay half price for, and an amazing girlfriend." He lifted Hannah's hand and pressed it to his lips, and Hannah turned so red that Oliver wondered if Danny wouldn't be too far behind them on the whole marriage thing.

"Congratulations," Hannah said with a grin, and then she and Danny went to find their seats for dinner.

There was a whole line of people waiting to greet Oliver and Madi, but when he glanced over at her, her eyes were following the caterers who had started setting out salads. He knew she would never say anything, and his attempts to convince her to sit down would be for nothing, so Oliver took matters into his own hands.

Madi shrieked when he lifted her into his arms, and though his foot complained about the extra weight, he carried her over to their table and set her down by her seat.

"I am not letting you starve," he said, then pulled her chair out for her.

When he sat next to her, Madi leaned over and stole his breath with a kiss. "I love you."

He grinned, though a little dazed. "I certainly hope you do, because now you're stuck with me."

A wonderful caterer set two plates down in front of them, and Oliver considered giving the man a massive tip for recognizing neither of them would want salad today. They probably had very little time to eat before they were accosted by guests again, so they needed to get right to the good stuff.

Madi was already shifting the pineapple from her pizza slice onto his with a fork, and he grabbed half his ham for her. Kit had nearly had a heart attack when they said they wanted to serve pizza at their wedding — "That's not how weddings work!" — but as Oliver took his first bite of melted cheese and sweet pineapple, he didn't at all regret their decision.

This was *their* day, after all, and his wife—Oliver would never get tired of that word—beamed with happiness as she practically inhaled her pizza and looked out over all her loved ones.

Oliver would do anything to keep that smile on her face for the rest of her life.

The rest of the wedding seemed to go by in a haze. Dancing with Madi, a bouquet toss, cutting the red velvet cake—and subsequently forcing Madi to sit down and eat a slice while she had a chance—and the evening sky steadily grew darker as time dragged by. Oliver eventually had to sit and give his foot a rest, and he watched Madi as she danced with all three of her brothers in turn.

How had his life come to this moment? He had no idea, but he wasn't complaining. Everything about his life was completely perfect.

"Son?"

Oliver stiffened. He had invited his parents, of course, but he honestly hadn't expected them to show up. So when he stood and found himself face to face with both of them, he wasn't sure how to react.

His father held out his hand. "It seems congratulations are in order."

Oliver reluctantly took his hand, but his eyes were on his mother, who watched Madi with an intense look. "Thank you," he said, his voice wavering.

"I hear you've created a new photo editing software," Dad continued.

Oliver's eyebrows pulled low. "Where did you hear that?" Madi was the only one who had the program, until he could work out all the bugs and get it copyrighted. He planned to sell it, but a part of him was tempted to keep it as a gift solely for Madi.

"Your wife told us."

Oliver suddenly felt dizzy, because it was his *mother* who had said that. His mother, who hadn't spoken to him in literal years, and who now looked up at him with something akin to pride in her eyes. It forced Oliver back down into his chair as he tried to understand what was happening.

The always proud Dr. Faith Hamilton *smiled*. A real smile. "That Madi of yours is quite the spitfire when she is passionate about something," she said, though she seemed to be feeling the tension as much as Oliver as she leaned into her husband. "And she is certainly passionate about you. She wouldn't leave our house until she knew we would be here for the ceremony, even though we thought you wouldn't want us here. I'm so glad she did that, or I would have regretted missing this for the rest of my life. You've chosen well for yourself, Oliver, and I hope you can forgive us."

Was all of this a dream?

Dad put a hand on Oliver's shoulder. "We have always been proud of you, son. Even if we didn't know how to show it."

"We only want what's best for you," Mom added.

"I'm sorry we pushed you so hard. We never meant to push you away."

His mother sniffled a little. Oliver had never seen her cry before, and it sprouted tears in his own eyes as he stared at her while she spoke. "That darling girl reminded us—me—how important family is," she said. "I don't want to lose you, Oliver. Please give us another chance."

Lost for words, Oliver nodded, and he watched them wander back to their own table, though he could hardly see through his tears. He had never in his wildest imaginings thought he would begin to reconcile with his parents.

Then again, he had never thrown Madi into the equation.

"Ollie? I saw your parents. Are you—"

Oliver jumped to his feet and wrapped Madi in a hug so tight that it squeezed the air out of her lungs. "I love you," he said shakily.

She laughed weakly, breathing deep when he gave her a chance. "I thought you should have them in your life. I didn't tell them about when you got sick, but—"

"How did I get so lucky to have you in my life?" he whispered, and he cupped her jaw with his hand. "I don't deserve you."

Her eyes sparkled in the string lights overhead as she gazed at him. "You have that backwards," she said after a long moment. "I'm the lucky one." She touched a finger to his lips, sending a shudder through him, and he wondered how much longer they would need to hang around. There was still at least another hour of the reception, but Oliver wasn't sure he could last that long.

"Now's your chance," a voice said to Oliver's left. Cam stood there, his eyes locked on something on the dance floor. "Kit is busy dancing with his mother."

"Your car's all ready to go," Ben added as he appeared on Cam's other side and tossed a set of keys to Oliver. "You should go before Kit realizes you're leaving early and tries to stop you."

Madi laughed as she slipped her hand into Oliver's. "He does know he can't prevent me from loving my hus-band, right?"

Why were they still talking? Oliver gripped her hand a little tighter and searched for the quickest route to the car.

"That won't stop him from trying," Cam said with a chuckle. "You know Kit; the schedule is everything. If I were you, I would take the chance, Hamilton."

Oliver had never liked Cam more than he did at that moment. He knew Kit only wanted their wedding day to go smoothly—they had talked enough over the last few weeks that Oliver knew he really was happy for them—but it was high time Oliver stopped letting Kit think he was in charge of anyone but himself.

"What do you say, Mads?" he asked, though he was tempted not to give her a choice. He had waited long enough.

But Madi slipped out of his hold and rushed over to kiss Cam and Ben on the cheeks. "You are the best brothers in the world," she told them.

As Ben blushed bright red, Cam grinned and said, "We know."

Oliver grabbed hold of Madi's hand and was tempted to pick her up again. He figured they would be able to move faster with Madi on her own two feet, though, so he gave her a tug. Thankfully, she seemed as eager as him. They reached his car without incident, but before Madi climbed inside, she grabbed his collar and pulled him down for a kiss that sent his heart racing.

"I love you," she whispered. "And you are so important to me."

For a moment, Oliver forgot what he was doing, and he stood there in awe of this woman who made his life better than he could have dreamed. But then his heart caught up to his head, and he coughed and held the door open for her.

They had a honeymoon to get to.

And then the rest of their lives.

The End

Special sneak peek of Book 2 in the Wonder Boy Series,

Love in Writing

EXCERPT FROM *LOVE IN WRITING*

BY THE TIME BEN GOT to the grocery store, he was definitely running late. His shower had turned into a full-blown conversation with himself, going over the pros and cons of finally making a move after all this time. He didn't know the girl's name or if she was even single, but somehow he had managed to talk himself into finally showing up.

He just hoped he wasn't *too* late and had already missed her.

She usually came in the mornings, before she went into work, he guessed. He didn't even know what she did for work, though he imagined it was in an office somewhere. While not strictly professional, her clothing was usually business casual at the very least with a hint of personal flair. Usually in her shoes.

She had awesome shoes.

"Don't talk about her shoes," Ben told himself.

He had a whole list of things he probably shouldn't mention to her, like how he had noticed once that she was on a baking streak because she kept buying flour and sugar, or the fact that she liked to match her Converse to her outfits and had several pairs of varying colors. And he probably shouldn't tell her about how he had started requesting Tuesdays off back in June so he could shop at the same time she did.

Ben shuddered. It was *October*. At what point did a person cross into stalker status? He had probably reached that point weeks ago.

He did his usual route across the grocery store anyway, grabbing things at random as he kept an eye out for anyone who looked familiar. Normally, he never let himself get fixated on anything—being the fourth of seven kids had taught him the impermanence of personal things—but something about this girl had caught his attention last spring, and she had been in his head ever since.

Normal people didn't shop at the exact same time every week, so Ben felt like that gave them something in common. She was always on her own, too, which was promising. Plus, she generally bought the kind of food Ben wished he had the energy and time to cook, so he figured they would get along in the food department. It was something. However small.

Had she already come and gone? Ben was halfway across the store when he started to panic. He probably wouldn't be brave again—he wasn't sure he was even brave enough today—so he would be stuck watching her from a distance forever. Or, until she stopped being so predictable or showed up with a partner.

By the time he reached the final aisle, where the ice cream was, Ben leaned over the handle of his cart and let all his breath out at once. She wasn't here. Of course she wasn't. Because why would anything go right in his life? Being the friend of three successful men had never been easy, but Ben had always been at least a little hopeful that their good luck would rub off on him.

He should have known better.

Glancing at the utter nonsense in his cart—peanut butter cups, a whole pineapple, and a jar of pickles among other things—Ben sighed and pushed forward to work his way back through the store and put everything back except the peanut butter cups.

That was when he saw her.

His breath catching, he tried to figure out how he hadn't seen her earlier. She was at the other end of the aisle, her eyes fixed on the glass case in front of her. He had no idea what color her eyes were—he'd never gotten close enough—but he imagined they were beautiful.

Like the rest of her.

So he hadn't been too late. For once, Ben's plan had actually come together, and all he had to do was walk up to her and start up a conversation. Channel his inner Oliver Hamilton, if such a thing even existed. They'd been friends for eighteen years, so surely Ben knew him well enough to act like him.

"Just walk forward and say hi," he told himself. "Easy."

Then he turned and walked in the other direction, veering off into the next aisle over.

What was he thinking? He couldn't just walk up to her! He could barely have a conversation with his friends, who had known him for years, so what made him think he could talk to someone he had never met? He was being ridiculous, and he should just go home and enjoy his rare day off before he had to get back to his terrible job.

His phone buzzed at the end of the aisle, and Ben paused before he did something stupid, like leave his cart and run for the doors. The staff would probably think he was shoplifting and tackle him in the parking lot, and he would get arrested, and he'd lose his job and have to move back home or join the circus or turn into a hermit in the woods who survived on crickets and leaves.

A shudder ran through him, and he grabbed his phone before his imagination ran away from him. *Too late.*

It was a text from Madi, Kit's sister and Oliver's wife. She was basically a sister to Ben, too, even though he already had plenty of those.

Madi: Any updates with Grocery Girl?

It was like she *knew*. He glanced around, just to make sure she wasn't somehow watching him, then let out the breath he was holding. She hadn't technically said anything about his cowardice, but Madi knew exactly how long Ben had been avoiding this girl. Maybe she was going to give up on him like the others had, and that hurt worse than anything. Disappointing Madi would kill him. Metaphorically.

Groaning, Ben took hold of his cart and headed back to the ice cream aisle before he gave himself time to overthink what he was doing. He could do this!

He could also nearly run her over, apparently.

He had mistaken how far down the aisle she was, so as he turned the corner at top speed, his cart collided with hers with a crash.

"Sorry!" he said, eyes wide as she jumped back. "I wasn't looking where…"

Her eyes were blue. Dark, like denim. And they took him in so quickly that he felt exposed. He almost didn't care.

"It's fine," she muttered, turning back to the ice cream in her hands with a frown. A pint in each.

Say something.

Ben cleared his throat. "Rough week?"

When she turned back to him, her expression was wary. Like she was trying to decide if she needed to call the store's security guard over. She swept another look over him that sent his knees shaking. "Pardon?"

What was he doing? He had no idea. He had just said the first thing that came to mind. "You know." He pointed to the pints of ice cream she held. "Girls and ice cream."

Ben, you idiot.

His eyes went wide. "No, sorry, I didn't mean… That was terrible." How had he managed to dig himself a hole so deep so quickly? "That was really terrible. You don't need me judging your decision to buy ice cream. Not that I was judging. Ice cream is great. Pretend I didn't say anything. Have a nice day." He bowed—*What?*—then tripped over his cart in his attempt to grab it and run away.

He had made it to the end of the aisle by the time she spoke, halting his steps. "I got passed over for a promotion."

Had she just said…? Spinning back around, Ben did his best to act like a normal human. *So much for acting like Oliver.* He would be lucky if she didn't think he was missing a few crucial things from his brain.

"I'm sorry," he said, leaving it at that.

Though she shrugged, her expression conveyed all her disappointment as she pursed her lips. "The guy who got it is qualified, but he has the voice of a sixty-year-old man."

He had no idea what she was talking about and no clue how to respond, but he did his best. Something told him she needed to talk, and seeing as he was the only person around… "Is…is he a sixty-year-old man?"

She actually smiled, and Ben was pretty sure his internal organs shut down for a second. In all the months he'd gone down aisles a second time to get a glimpse of her, he'd never seen her smile. Grocery shopping wasn't exactly entertaining work.

"Yes," she said. "He is. But that's not the point."

"What is the point?"

"The point is I work for a company that writes children's books."

Now it was starting to make sense, and Ben's heart pattered back to a normal rhythm, even though he knew this conversation was probably a one-time thing. Now that he'd made first contact, the rest of it wasn't so bad. He could do this.

Offering up a little smile that *hopefully* didn't make him look constipated, he folded his arms so his hands didn't shake. "I'm guessing he writes for sixty-year-old men too."

Her smile grew, meaning Ben's shaking did too. He'd thought she was cute the moment he first saw her, but up close… "Exactly. I'm Allie." She shuffled the pints she held to one hand and held out the other.

Red alert! System failure! Danger!

"Ben." He might have said that. He didn't know. All he knew was when his fingers touched her cold ones, some-thing shattered in his brain and left him a pile of mush. Could he get more pathetic? Probably. He didn't want an actual answer to that question.

Allie wrinkled up her nose a little as she looked him over yet again, and then she turned back to her ice cream. "I've been standing here for ten minutes, and I can't decide which one I want more."

"So get both." *You can't tell her what to do, Ben. She doesn't even know you! You might not have even told her your name.*

But Allie's eyes lit up—holy Toledo, she was absolutely beautiful—and she tossed both pints into her full cart before taking hold of the handle and heading for the checkout. "I like the way you think, Ben." She paused, though, and looked back. "Thanks, by the way. For talking to me. I feel a bit better now. See you around?"

Ben hoped he nodded; there certainly wasn't any sound that came out of his mouth. And as soon as she was out of sight, he collapsed against the ice cream case and pressed his burning forehead against the cold glass. He'd done it. He'd talked to her. After months of psyching himself out, he had finally made a move.

And even crazier?

It had gone well.

Dana LeCheminant has been telling stories since she was old enough to know what stories were. After spending most of her childhood reading everything she could get her hands on, she eventually realized she could write her own books too, and since then she always has plots brewing and characters clamoring to be next to have their stories told. A lover of all things outdoors, she finds inspiration while hiking the remote Utah backcountry and cruising down rivers. Until her endless imagination runs dry, she will always have another story to tell.